Women on the Edge

WOMEN on the EDGE

WRITING FROM LOS ANGELES

EDITED BY

Samantha Dunn
and Julianne Ortale

FOREWORD BY

Janet Fitch

The Toby Press

First Edition 2005

The Toby Press LLC

POB 8531, New Milford, CT 06776-8531, USA
& POB 2455, London W1A 5WY, England

www.tobypress.com

ISBN 1 59264 125 3 *paperback*

A CIP catalogue record for this title is

available from the British Library

Typeset in Garamond by Jerusalem Typesetting

Printed and bound in the United States by
Thomson-Shore Inc., Michigan

Contents

Foreword

"Out here on the perimeter, there are no stars.
Out here we is stoned, immaculate."
The Doors, from *L.A. Woman*

The paradox of the perimeter, the edge, is that it is both the disregarded margin and yet the place where all growth occurs, the region of interaction with the unknown. It's the surface of a cell, the border between countries, the periphery of consciousness. Thus the edge keeps the center alive, from cellular life to the culture of a nation. The bulk of culture always exists at the center—that which has already been established, been explored. The edge is what is still forming. As Kandinsky noted in *Point, Line, Plane*, the edge is the place of maximum tension, the anteroom of a breakthrough, a realization, and release. When we say "on edge", it means irritation, anxiety, the place where we're not supported. Where you find yourself on the edge of a cliff, you wait to jump, fall or be pushed.

Traditionally, women in particular have lived at the edge, the margins of culture, as outlanders. Central was "male culture," "real culture," while women were left the borderlands, badlands from which to glean their strange harvests. While out on the perimeter, women discovered the freedom of the badlands. They were curiously free to invent, without having to liberate themselves from the forms and rewards of the cultural norm.

The restless pushing of the line between silence and speech, of what can be spoken, what can be known, can be seen in the stories in this collection, their freshness, their unexpectedness, their danger—the playful surrealism of Julianne Ortale's "Milk." The sandpapered fingertips of Karen Horn's "Levinium 241." The power byplay within a marriage in Michelle Latiolais' "Boys." The edge in the work of the women is sharp, and fine, and cuts close.

The short story itself, at the millennium, lives on an edge. It no longer commands the novel's readership; indeed, even the novel's popularity is giving way to that of non-fiction. Now the story is truly left to do what it does best, not to please mass audiences, but to explore the moments that comprise consciousness, to handle the unstable elements which reveal themselves in a flash of illumination, to map out new terrain, take new territory. These short stories make surgical openings into contemporary experience with the audacity of physiologists after the Dark Ages, opening the physical body and taking a look inside.

Finally, the stories in this collection achieve the ultimate outland status in the point of their creation, the edge of the continent—Los Angeles. The edge of the great water, the last stop before tomorrow. For Los Angeles writers, the boundariness is taken to the furthest extent—for what could be more peripheral than serious short stories written in a town known predominantly for its big screens and action figures and silicon-enhanced plasticine femmes?

Women writers specifically, examining the sharp edges of the human condition in the very mouth of unquestioning archetypical/industrial production, are the ultimate outsiders, and it is the great freedom of the outsider which is celebrated in this compendium. Women working without applause, without the hope of points and percentages, without big advances or recognition or great audiences, in freedom to pursue an idea without any hindrance or allegiances to recognizable cultural iconographies, reaping their strange harvest. Out here, we is stoned, immaculate.

—Janet Fitch
Los Angeles, *July 2004*

Notes

When the editors of *The* Toby Press asked if we would
be interested in putting together a collection representing Los Angeles women writers, we instantly said yes. After all, we're two women
writers who, throughout the past fifteen years, have been publishing
and attending readings and teaching and showing up at workshops
throughout this city. We've done our homework, we know the lay of
the land, we are up to the task, etc., etc....

But that turned out to be exactly the problem. Because we
have an intimate acquaintance with this world, we were immediately
struck by the futility of attempting to create a definitive statement of
truth about it, something that would corral all the disparate points
of view, the cultural traditions, the bountiful literary legacy, the academic illustriousness and—lest we forget—the laméd glamour held
within this megalopolis.

That said, it did seem to us that there exists a certain beat common to stories we were reading and trading between us and among
the writers we know—many of whom are girlfriends of the meet-
for-coffee, housesit-and-water-the-plants, shoulder-to-cry-on variety.
What we heard was a rhythm created from women not afraid to say

the hard things, the dark things; women who know there's always more going on underneath the surface. It's the condition shared by all here who try to build lives on a fault line. When you can't even take for granted the stability of the ground beneath your feet, possibility becomes illimitable. Each day holds the chance that everything can be transformed. It's just a matter of time.

So consider what you hold in your hands to be not a definitive profile of the fabled L.A. woman, but a Polaroid of the moment. These are the stories we loved and passed among each other, over email and in book stores, sometimes in diners with big coffee rings warping the pages, sometimes read over the phone on insomniac nights. They came to us and they created their own gravity. This is, in many ways, a personal collection; the picture we are seeing from this shaky ground—blurred, colorful, heart-pounding, heartbreaking, inventive.

Above all, we want to give thanks to Janet Fitch for her fierce support of something different, for all the writers who were game enough to go with this experiment, and to *The* Toby Press for its commitment to putting into the world writing for readers who will stand on the edge and aren't afraid to look down.

Samantha Dunn and Julianne Ortale
Writing at Swingers Diner, Santa Monica CA
July 2004

Karen Horn
Levinium 241

T he feet of Abraham Levin are lifted into the wheel well of the car by his daughter, Leslie. Two leather popovers filled with cement; they used to be his but they aren't anymore. Things on the exterior perimeter seem to be going first: his feet, the knuckles at the ends of his arms so crinkled with arthritis. Useless now. Draw a line around his ankles, a dotted line, like the perforations in the telephone bill, detach here. Leslie will need to remember to cancel the phone, afterward. Abe sits still until he recovers from the effort of moving from the wheelchair to the car.

The glove compartment in front of him holds a secret. Does Leslie still carry the tire gauge he so carefully trained her to use, every single time she stops at a service station? Or has she tossed it out along with the rest of the advice he gave her: major in electrical engineering or, after she dropped out of college, go to nursing school. Moving to Benares to weave shawls on a loom was not the way to make a contribution. He'd be damned if it didn't have something to do with all that LSD she took in college.

Maps, maps, the glove compartment's stuffed with maps of Los Angeles, of Oxnard, of Disneyland. You can't get lost if you carry a map, but if you don't it's easy to find yourself at the dead end of a one-way street, out of gas, dangerous men gathering. Abe digs out the tire gauge from under the rubber dinosaurs and packets of sugar. Good girl.

"Do you want me to check the tires?" Leslie asks.

No time, can't be late. Seat belt, pull it up, but the catch doesn't work. Seat belts are not really necessary; he drove for years before they were invented.

"Let's just go."

After today's treatment, Breevort's going to assess his progress. See if he has any possible moves left. Abe knows he's been in check for years. They can't cure it, only slow it down, Breevort told him in the most gentlemanly way possible.

"No need to whimper, you're doing well. I lost a patient last week—a fall, an infection, gone in a week. Pneumonia. That's why they call it the old man's friend, it's quick and relatively painless." Not like cancer, he meant, only he didn't say that.

The beach comes as a surprise, always, out of the darkness from under the trees of the canyon, suddenly it all opens up and the light, the sun, it's all before you, dazzling. Is this why people wear sunglasses? The horizon pulls the breath out of you, confuses with its distant islands appearing so close, then beyond, the visible curve of the earth. Measuring from here to a point on the horizon, that point is a dot in a matrix. Draw a line from there to the top of the avocado tree in the backyard. He hasn't been back there in nearly a year but it's probably still there, they do seem to go on without tending, and at its tip, hovering weightless, is another of the points in the Levin grid.

The car turns inland toward the hospital. Abraham Levin. His name is on the books, under his mailbox in the math department office, on the mastheads, in the catalogues, decorating the journal covers. They call now to sell Professor Levin life insurance, time-sensitive stock tips, satellite TV for every room, they want to give Dr. Levin a free trip to Las Vegas to inspect an available acre that has core samples of pure borax, they want to give him a lifetime free safety deposit box, lifetime membership in the Marine Mammal Friendship Society, lifetime color credit, unlimited lifetime money-back guarantee, and does he want to sell his house? They can handle that for him too, no problem. What's in it for them? Do they know something Breevort doesn't know?

No more papers, no more books. That was the first thing he did after Breevort gave him the bad news, came home and sorted through his papers, throwing out all the calculations that led nowhere but that he knew would be solved someday. No need to give anyone else a head start. His reputation was made and it would either grow or wither, based on factors totally outside his control. He had contributed something valuable, everyone who understood his work knew that. It went without saying, but they said it anyway. They gave him a medal after the war, attached to a somber ribbon. He never wore it, that sort of behavior was for show-offs. Come to think of it, he hadn't seen the thing in years. Maybe threw it out, just as well. No reason to burden Leslie with it.

It had been a good life, working at the university. The earnest faces of the students who came to him asking for advice, every year a birthday cake in the faculty lounge, family picnics on Labor Day. Leslie with everyone else's kids in a sandbox and Clara, before she left him in 1968 to marry a motorcycle mechanic, putting her bowl of coconut fruit salad next to the deviled eggs on the picnic table. The faculty softball game, the day he actually hit the ball, sailing it over the pool and beyond the hedge. The crack of the bat applied to the ball. That was another point on his four-dimensional grid.

He's been holed up in the house for years, except for trips to see Breevort or pick up provisions. A sitting duck for every C student who has time to kill. Even the boy who sweeps avocado leaves out of the gutters would engage him in conversation, usually about extraterrestrial abduction. He's nearly finished assembling his set of videotapes of the complete oeuvre of Laurel and Hardy, carefully taped off late-night television, and the concordant logs of dates and subject categories that index them. They will join the others in Leslie's bedroom, now full of shelving from floor to ceiling and over the windows, and more shelves in the middle arranged into aisles, thousands of videotapes, the fruit of his retirement.

Between the programs he taped was always the business of the world, the news. It had been bad ever since Eisenhower was elected. The disgrace of politics, the shame of the unfortunates who live in conditions unfit for animals. Lately he had been keeping his ear open for word of an asteroid as big as New York on a trajectory to rendezvous with planet Earth. Abe was convinced that's how the world would end. Human beings would either escape in rockets or slowly turn to sludge, replacing with their bodies the petroleum they used up in their cars.

"Are you OK? You were groaning in your sleep." Leslie is going on about her daughter Amelia and where to send her for high school.

"She wants to be in a string quintet but all they offer is full orchestra."

Abe opens his eyes to see the football field and tennis courts in back of the school go by through the window. It's so lavish it could be a country club. Amelia will have to learn to land on her own two feet.

"If she's going to play the cello, she'll play, no matter where you send her," he says.

A sports car shoots in front of them and Leslie slows down. Abe feels a moment of vertiginous anger. Leslie has absolutely no instinct for the classless jousting of the road.

"You never came to see me in my recitals, plays or swim meets, did you? And I so much wanted you to be proud of me," she says.

As usual she's distracted, letting a convertible get the better of her, opening herself up to losing all her pieces.

Abe sighs. So he should have sat in the bleachers instead of going to work? Leslie seems to enjoy displaying her wounds. It's no surprise she can turn him into one of her tormentors. But to be fair, she does have a point. Leslie grew up somewhere else, in her room, at the beach, in the backyard. Abe didn't witness it personally so he couldn't comment. She'd said *Leave me alone*, and he had given her plenty of breathing room. A mistake, in retrospect.

"I didn't have a father of my own, so I never knew what fathers were supposed to do." Abe's father, mowed down in the prime of his life, by…who could say? Abe's relatives had always been vague on that point. It might have been spores from the flu of 1918 reappearing in 1922, or smallpox, insanity, food poisoning. Nobody seemed to remember much about it. People crashed to the ground all the time in those days; he had even seen a man trampled by a horse on Delancy Street.

If you don't expect much, you're never disappointed. When his father died and shortly after that his mother followed, dying while giving birth to his sister, that was when Abe first felt the presence of companions around him. They were not beings exactly but facts, constants, unaltering entities, real as people but more like stars. He learned later to call them numbers. Not numerals, but what the numerals stand for—the numbers themselves. Five, two, three thousand, six. They spoke to him in colors.

Today Abe is waiting for a miracle, like the one that happened to him in 1923. In the darkness of his exile to the orphanage run by the Department of Child Protective Services on Essex Street, the sight of his grandmother threading her way up the block was truly miraculous. Abe leaned out the third floor window and called to her and, wonder of wonders, his grandmother called back, *Don't move, I'm going to bring you home,* and he was rescued. Abe always believed if he hadn't called down to her, she would never have known where to find him. Only after that did Abe begin to leave footprints in the world. And every footstep created a point in the very personal matrix of his life.

"There is one other thing I want to say." Leslie takes her eyes off the road and turns to him. It doesn't matter; traffic is static. Stopped on an overpass, the San Diego Freeway coursing beneath them, he tries to remember the last time he drove its perfectly banked curves. Too long ago to remember. "I forgive you," Leslie continues. "For working on the bomb."

Bomb? What bomb? He's been doing pure research for the last fifty years.

"For being on the Manhattan Project. At all."

It was a lark, an adventure. What's to forgive? Has she been waiting a lifetime to say this? To send her poor father to his death with no hard feelings? It's sweet that she cares, I'm sure she means well, but Christ Almighty!

"We just did the math." Abe spent the entire war in California, one of the boys in Room 467, desks in rows facing front, a mimeographed problem to solve face down on each one. It was like graduate school except there was a view all the way to San Francisco outside the window and as soon as he solved an equation, instead of giving him a grade, they would take it away without comment and give him another.

"I mean you must have felt guilty afterward, when you saw what happened in Japan."

Afterward? What about before?

"There was a war on, you don't seem to remember that. Just as many people would have been killed in a land war, and they wouldn't have all been Japanese."

He sat in the room in the Berkeley Radiation Lab with the view of the Bay through all of it, through the Nazi boot to the Warsaw ghetto, the Battle of the Bulge, Tarawa.

One day a knock on the door of Room 467 summoned them into the hallway. Ernest Lawrence was there with an announcement. Someone carried out a chair and helped the great man up so he could tell them all what had happened that morning in Hiroshima and Nagasaki. *This means the end of war,* he said. A bottle of champagne was passed from hand to hand, everyone laughing as it spilled down their shirts. Of course it didn't turn out to be the end of all war, the politicians saw to that, but it was the end of Abe's war.

"If we hadn't figured it out first, Hitler would have gotten it." Unthinkable. Then Leslie wouldn't even have been born.

"I know you think there's nothing to forgive. But I forgive you anyway. For my own sake," Leslie says.

"What's done is done," Abe answers. "Forgiveness in and of itself is trivial."

Abe switches on the radio. *Diplomatic moves afoot to free American pilots held in China after yesterday's spy plane crash.* More bad news. He turns it off in favor of listening to the occasional Doppler effect from the horns of passing cars.

Plane crashes. Somehow, they were rare. It's too bad frequent flier miles aren't transferable. Leslie would get a nice vacation after he died.

The avocado tree, the horizon's center, his desk in Room 467, Abe's footprints stopped just west of the surf break in Santa Monica Bay, but far across were two other points, the cities in Japan, threatening to tear the matrix with their leverage.

There were balance points along the tracks of the Southern Pacific. Abe thought when he started graduate school at Berkeley he would be traveling away from the war in Europe but as it turned out he was on a Möbius strip, still staring down a group of men across an ocean that stared back with knives in their mouths. He sat up all night in the observation car going across Missouri and Oklahoma, looking at the stars and trying to fathom their star-ness. During the day he slept, preferring not to witness the vast emptiness of the west populated only by the occasional cowboy armed to the hilt, tough customers every one.

He brought only his calculus textbook and the writings of Omar Khayyam. He thought California in 1939 would be like Persia, an oriental rug spread out in a forest of nightingales, the ancient texts, girls in silk with only their eyes showing, *Thou beside me singing in the wilderness.* After the harvest, more girls, this time dressed in flowers, log dancing down Wilshire Boulevard on wine vats, past swimming pools filled with burgundy. How did that turn into empty bottles rolling down hillsides at dawn, DUI's, liquefaction?

Abe was prepared to die. Just in time, as the morphine didn't work anymore.

The lights are going out all across Europe, and Leslie is worried about forgiveness? Just the variety of thought that he's spent a lifetime avoiding. Coastal fog warping the brain. Let her be. She too will have to find her own way without him.

Abe told Grandma when he figured it out. It was a winter afternoon in Brooklyn and he had sat through *Platinum Blonde* three times in a row. Grandma was huddled over the eternal pot of barley soup. The dazzlement of sunlight on Jean Harlow's hair had emboldened him to speak that which before he had been afraid to say. *There is no evidence that God exists. So I must believe he does not.* She held the corner of her apron to her eyes. *Why does God give me such a grandson? Even Meyer Lansky goes to synagogue.* Abe added the corollaries: *Every man is master of his own destiny. There is no such thing as morality or forgiveness. We can come and go without explanation.* She turned to the snow swimming by the windowpane, not wanting him to see her cry. *No offense, Grandma, but it's a free county.* Fool. He'd been a stupid, stupid fool.

The waiting room. Coffee, powdered milk, and cellophane packets of soda crackers, on the house. Wheelchairs pulled up around the couches and magazine tables, like circled wagons, with their backs to the door the doctors come from. A young man wearing a necklace of small stones looks up from the couch as Leslie locks Abe's wheels. Just because you have all your hair and aren't in a wheelchair doesn't mean you're not dying. Healthy people don't get radiation treatments.

"What are you in for?" Abe asks.

"I already lost half my stomach and all of my prostate. Now they want to zap my lungs." He closes his book and Abe deciphers the title. *The Tibetan Book of the Dead.* "Could be bad luck, could be that I grew up in the desert, due west of Yucca Flats. When they tested the bombs, the wind usually blew to the east. Usually, but not always."

In the summer of 1945 Abe cleaned out his desk in Room 467, pausing one last time to take in the view of the light over San Francisco Bay. This was the same air that the physicists decided to risk in the first nuclear test, hoping they were wrong that the atmosphere might ignite and be completely consumed.

"Nothing is for always," Abe says.

"Amen," says the man. "It was caused by radiation and they're using radiation to cure it. What a time we live in."

"Cracker?" Abe asks, opening a packet.

The man reaches for one and says, "Shall I include you in my prayers?"

"Can't hurt," says Abe, surprising himself. That's what happens when you ask for a miracle—you're on par with everyone else.

Leslie comes back from the bandits who sold her a two-dollar cup of coffee.

Abe feels the floor shift under him and the familiar pain in his spine beating inside him. To be rescued is the last miracle that Abraham Levin will ever ask for. For the radiation to get rid of it. Take as much of me as you want, just get rid of it.

Ricky comes up behind him and squeezes Abe's shoulder as he unlocks his wheels and turns his chair.

"Ready, Professor?"

Leslie waves to Abe and lets her head rest against the wall behind her.

This is the purpose of Abe's life now, to visit the linear accelerator. The ritual of setting the riser below the table. The square of light in the machine, aligned with the four inked dots that mark the map to his prostate. The minor adjustments. Ricky's dash for cover and then it is just Abe and the isotope.

He has always been alone like he is now, stretched out under a sheet, a white offering to the blue sun above. He feels the sun grow hotter as it takes control of the machine. He moves to enter the zero.

That hum is the klystron power passing into the wave guide. Now the electrons are injected, they ride the wave, reach the velocity of light, bend and hit the target: cells that are in him but not of him, using him as food.

He tries to feel the growing absence of tissue but his nerves don't run through that foreign territory. Suddenly he realizes there is a mistake. The blue heat is seeping beyond the DNA of his tumor and the flesh around it, into the marrow of his bones, boiling away those vital blood cell factories, the matrix deep in his long bones. It is too hot, but Ricky has disappeared and there is no one to turn it off. He struggles with the straps holding him to the table but he can't find the release button. It must be an accident; the accelerator has gone critical.

Abe's heart races and the bile in his stomach rises and falls. Grandma's voice calls his name, *Avrom, Avrom,* from the kitchen, calls him to wake up. She wants him to come and drink his boiled milk. But when he kicks open the kitchen door, she isn't there. Abe's sister says, *Grandma's sick.* They leave a cup of tea and some bread next to her bed. In the morning the undertaker carries her away. *She just stopped breathing,* says his grandfather. *Like that.* He snaps his fingers, and leaves for the *schul.*

Abe sits on the floor in front of the radiator, holding his knees. It seems wrong to use the furniture. The cold of the wood floor, the square of sunlight moving across it, touching his feet then moving on, out of the room. He wishes he had never told her he didn't believe. Fool. He is a fool.

Abe feels his bones, heating with electron activity, mutate into something entirely new. Solid bars of Levinium 241. He snaps the restraints on his wrists and hips, opens the door of the treatment room, starts down the hall, away from the heat of the reactor. No one else is there and he begins to run, his sheet flying behind him and slipping to the floor. Breevort stares dumfounded as Abe runs naked through the glass doors of the lobby and into the street.

The Brooklyn sun shines bright on Alabama Avenue. The men, behind the soda fountain in the candy store, in the print shop setting type, on the Boardwalk at Coney Island, are always talking. Their jackets held by a thumb over one shoulder, ties loosened, Abe watches them laughing, gesturing, stamping out cigarettes as they fall from their lips. They hold their own in roomfuls of women, these men, take the best cut of meat, close the door and smile as they listen to the family shushing each other, *Be quiet. Papa's sleeping.* These are the men Abe loves above all others.

They didn't see him then, watching them at work and their family tables, but Abe was learning their ways, taking on their mannerisms and rough way of speaking, trying to be noticed, and if noticed, to be beloved among them. All he got for his efforts was a job as a printer's devil for *The Sport of Kings,* a racing form, and a reputation for finishing his deliveries after the races had taken place.

They don't see Abe now, don't notice the naked man among them, but that is just as well. Abe hates saying goodbye. In fact, he'll stay here in safety, surrounded by the fathers. He won't go back. In this place, the disappointments of his life haven't happened yet. No accidents, no blue sun like a thousand suns, no Leslie crying alone in her room with the door closed, it never existed, none of it.

All that is left are the rainbow vision that is 16,921, emerging from an infinite line of prime numbers arrayed on a ladder of light. Accompanying the colors he hears counting, like the beating of a heart. Then 1,753. They come to him fully formed, never to grow, never to age. Sweet eleven is next. These primes have been his only true companions. The silver seven, beating out the space of a breath. They are all still here. The aqua three. Pause. Three beats. Then one. Then nothing.

Julianne Ortale
Milk

Mrs. Poovey woke feeling achy and a little unwell, oddly, in her belly and breasts. But the dog was on her bed, strad-, dling her, barking loud in her face, and was not going to let her sleep in. Her son Carl had given her the dog because she'd been depressed; lackluster, he'd said, not getting out enough. And she did feel something missing in her life, a certain emptiness she couldn't quite name. But even if the collie did make her get out of the house, he hadn't helped.

Laddie was a bad dog. Despite her son's instruction, *you're the big dog mother! Show him who's boss!,* despite obedience school, Laddie still threatened passersby, biting at their coats or pant-legs if he could get close enough. She didn't much care until Cox on Rodeo came out of his house with the camcorder to tell her he'd caught her letting Laddie crap in his marigold beds and she hadn't cleaned it up, and when he came close to her, smiling and mad, with that camera in her face, Laddie snapped at his ankle and tore his new forty dollar pants. He said, look what you've done. She said, Sue me. So he did. Now she carries a baggie and newspaper and has Laddie on a choke-chain.

The rain makes her face feel fresh. Laddie keeps trying to run, but the choke-chain stops him. They lurch along Prentice Drive, Rose Avenue, Valentine Place, past the Circle K and the DQ and the church. They're wet but she's a Kansas girl and isn't afraid of what passes for bad weather in California, and her tan slicker glistens with drops and Laddie's gold-and-white coat gives off that good wet-dog smell she remembers from her farm days.

When a young woman comes their way with a shitzu on a long leash, Mrs. Poovey tries to hold Laddie back. She tells him: *Sit boy!* but he's not going to sit. He's not growling either, just standing still watching that shitzu scuttle his way. Mrs. Poovey doesn't much care for the woman's skirt, too short for decency, never mind the weather. She has her newspaper rolled and ready and keeps her hand right down near his collar. When that little bitch starts yapping at Laddie, he turns his head and nips Mrs. Poovey's arm hard enough to break the skin.

"Damn you," she says, whapping Laddie with the paper.

The woman scoops up her dog and stands clear, asking, "Are you all right?"

"Damn you," she says to the woman whose face goes red, taken aback.

At home, she listens to the morning news while she looks up the number for the pound. Laddie curls up on her TV chair by the kitchen fireplace, sulking at her as she dials, standing with the heavy black receiver held out in the slanted morning light.

"You're going, buddy," she tells Laddie. He barks, two short sharp notes that sound to her like *up yours*. The newscaster reports a series of abandonments at St. Mary's, two newborns, one boy and one girl. Teenage mothers are suspected. This, followed by the weather report, heavy rains on the way, and the reservoirs that had been threatened by last year's drought are now remarkably flush, and spring promises to flood the riverbanks at the south end of town. The phone rings and rings and finally a woman answers and tells Mrs. Poovey that she'll have to make an appointment, wait ten days, to make sure this is what she really wants to do. The woman's voice is soft and righteous.

"Look missy, I'm seventy-three years old. I know what I want," Mrs. Poovey says, "He's a mean, miserable dog."

Laddie huffs off the chair. His nails click on the linoleum as he walks toward her, his mouth slightly open, panting. His pink tongue gleams in the light, and he seems to be smiling. For a moment she feels just a bit guilty, and she's not feeling so well today, that odd achiness, maybe the flu, a certain tenderness in her soft places, and his eyes, she thinks, are not unkind.

"We can send someone to pick him up," the woman says, "we'll keep him for the ten days while you think about it."

His white throat fur looks majestic in the slanted light. As he lowers his haunches and shivers, all the time looking up at her with his tongue out and his eyes gleaming, he does a number right there on the floor and the stink rises immediately on the over-heated kitchen air.

"Get him out of here," she says "or, believe me—I'm a farm girl—I'll do him in myself."

Alone in the house, she lies on her bed on top of the bedspread in the dark, drifting. It's evening and she doesn't have to take the dog out, or feed him. Nobody barks at her, and she can listen to the rain falling against the windowpane without interruption. The morning chilled her, and after the man came to take Laddie, she didn't feel guilty at all. But she did feel weak and peckish, and her hunger was peculiar. She couldn't quite place it. She'd taken a spoon and dipped into the cottage cheese, the small glass jar of cling peaches, a mouthful of peanut butter, a prune, and then she found the taste she craved: pickles, and she jammed her fingers in the cold briny water and pulled out one fat dill.

In her bed, her hands and her feet are cold, but her chest and belly and head grow sticky with fever. She thinks to call her son, but then she'd have to tell him about the dog, and she's had enough of his meddling for now. So she rises, and as she does, a slight wooziness seizes her. But she rights herself, pulls her two sweaters and t-shirt over her head. Walks in the dark to her closet with her hands in front of her, testing for the doorknob. She switches on the light.

In the mirrored door, she catches a glimpse of herself, her pale slack skin laying along the bone, narrow shoulders, wider bottom in smart brown pull-up pants that never rumple. Her white belly smoothes like risen dough, a paunch she's grown accustomed to over the years. She places her hands on it because it feels strange and tender like it did when she was a young woman. She runs her hands over it, up to her bosom harnessed in sturdy white cotton. And notices the bra cups, wet.

Dropping a strap, she lets the cup fall away. Her breast, heavy and sore—she hadn't noticed just how sore—spreads and settles against her belly in a way that is familiar and unfamiliar. Hanging low and fuller now, blue veins running trails under the bluing skin, and her aureole, wide as a fist, three shades of rose, puckers, slightly crusted, leaking.

She unhooks her bra, lets it fall to the floor. With shivery fingers, she touches the wet. Tastes it. Sweet. *Milk.* In the closet light, her breasts appear waxen, the skin so taught, they seem to be lit from within. She cups them in her hands, and she has a sudden memory of her husband standing behind her before this mirror, cupping her breasts as she does now, squeezing them when they were sore and full to make the milk flow, and how it had been a marvel to them. They were as close as they'd ever be, that night. She tries to remember the last time she thought of him in this way, dead so long now, or noticed her body beyond the annoyance of creak and ache. Her breasts, their shape, different now than when she was a young woman, and yet not so different, fill her hands, overflow them, so she makes a cradle with her arms and holds them this way.

In the morning, her nightgown's bodice is wet and sticky with milk. She thinks to call the doctor, or her son. She turns on the radio for the morning news. Rain all day. Mrs. Poovey takes her lipstick from the vanity, gazes at her face that has changed somehow during the night, and draws herself a new red mouth.

It's not the second Wednesday of the month, but she backs her Buick out of the garage, carefully navigating the passage, and drives to Rosenberg's Department Store. When Rosella Rosenberg greets her in Women's Wear, her face registers the odd day. Rosella's voice has always grated on her nerves, as has her too showy orange fingernail polish and diamonds, but Mrs. Poovey always trades locally. She's never been one to gossip or chit-chat, play Bingo or Uno or Bridge. She goes to church, will make up a Jell-O salad for a church feed or bazaar, but won't hang around, and when they got pushy trying to get her on the prayer chain, she'd said, *Hell no!*

"I need a nursing bra," she says.

Rosella looks at her, and Mrs. Poovey looks hard right back. Rosella drops her gaze to the floor, adopts that humoring voice people get when they think a person's lost their marbles. "Okay, Mrs. Poovey. What size?"

"I've been shopping here for forty-four years, Rosella. You know I'm a 38D," she says, her face flushed, wet with rain. "But you'd better measure me. I'm growing."

"Okay," Rosella says, takes her slicker for her. "Alright."

In the pink curtained dressing room, Rosella can hardly speak. "My goodness, Mrs. Poovey. My gosh. My goodness." She runs the measuring tape under Mrs. Poovey's bare breasts, then around their fullness, then above them. Rosella's fingers chill her spine. Looking up at Mrs. Poovey, regarding her in the mirror, Rosella takes a deep breath and says, "Double D."

Mrs. Poovey nods, sharp, brief. Her red mouth is fuller too, and she cannot help smiling.

"What could it mean?" Rosella says.

Mrs. Poovey looks at the marbled linoleum floor tiles. Then back up Rosella's own curvy figure.

"Maybe it's some kind of miracle," Rosella says. "You know, like when somebody starts crying blood tears or sweet oil weeps from their hands, or the Virgin starts appearing over their head?"

"Aren't you a Jew?"

"Yeah. No. I mean, I saw a show about it."

Rosella hands her a nursing bra, new and white and pretty

with eyelet trim. She gives her round flannel pads backed with plastic, says, "Know how to use these? Tuck them in the bra. Soak up the leakage."

Rosella helps her into it, demonstrates the flap, tucks in a pad, hitches it back up. She leans her head in close as she works the elastic around the button that keeps the flap in place. Mrs. Poovey blushes at the sudden pleasure she feels from Rosella's breath against her bare skin. "Thank you. That's fine," she says, and does the other side herself.

Rosella puts her hand to her mouth, as though she wants to say something, but also wants to stop herself. Mrs. Poovey's face opens up like a question.

"Have you been to the doctor?" Rosella asks.

"No," she says, shaking her head, looking askance, "No. I feel right as rain."

"Of course," Rosella says, swallowing, "You know, you might need to pump them. They won't hurt so much. It'll keep them from getting infected."

Mrs. Poovey hadn't thought about that, hadn't thought about why this might happen to her, and hadn't thought about the milk backing up or what she should do about it. It has been a long time and she had forgotten many things. Rosella reaches out both hands, shaky but sure, holds them in front of Mrs. Poovey's breasts, not touching them, but as though she might, tracing their shape in the air with her orange nails that seem less showy now, and Rosella smiles, and Mrs. Poovey cannot help returning it. And though why this is happening to her is mysterious, she knows, suddenly, unequivocally, what she must do.

She's thinking about those babies on TV, the abandoned newborns at St. Mary's, how it hadn't quite registered, but now it did. They had no one, and she had milk. Unlike Rosella, she's not inclined to believe in miracles or any sort of hocus pocus, but this did seem like providence. Or fate. She despised the hospital. Especially *that* hospital where Dwight spent his last days doped up on morphine, smoking imaginary cigarettes and calling her Lucia, a name she'd never heard him use before, and her name was not Lucy or Lulu or anything of the sort that might make him call her Lucia. He called her Lucia and talked the Italian he must have picked up when he was in the war.

She hasn't been to St. Mary's since he died, and the doors, automatic now, swoosh open and the wet heat as she enters hits her in the face. Everything is orderly but slightly overdone. A flower stand and a Catholic memorabilia shop flank the lobby. A Methodist herself, Mrs. Poovey has always been suspicious of shops like these, but today she slows as she passes its window. The virgins are lined up like beauty queens. She stops a moment to look. She never understood the fascination with the Virgin Mary. Idolatry aside, the figurines' slack faces always looked stunned or sullen or drugged. She was raised a Methodist, to pray only to Jesus. Saints and even the mother of Jesus were just people and not to be magnified. And the bloody Jesus on the cross always struck her as fundamentally wrong. How was that uplifting? She preferred a clean simple cross. Or Jesus preaching to the children, or the lion and the lamb, or a cross-stitch sampler of the Lord's Prayer, or a pair of praying hands. Though she does like the Catholic rendition of the Sacred Heart Jesus. In that picture, his face fairly glows, and he looks young and healthy and his heart is not bloody, and it's crowned with fire. This is something she understands. She likes this Jesus who looked like He had some spunk to him. The Catholics are big on miracles, so she figures if she's going to use what God has given her (a gift, isn't it? And aren't gifts from God supposed to be used?), then this must be the right place to be. She feels the virgins' gazes pressed up against the glass, and this time it doesn't feel prickly or blasphemous, and their faces do not seem so sullen. Instead they seem knowing to her. Maybe miracles do that to a person, and she feels kind of knowing too. She stares at a blue robed virgin straight ahead of her and sees her own face also reflected in the glass. She touches her red lips and fancies that they are color of the virgin's own mouth. She's struck by the thought that miracles hit hard and sudden and wipe the face clean, and what might look sullen or drugged or bonked over the head might just be the aftermath of the mysterioso, the unexplained act of God that leaves a person empty of what was known, and filled with mystery.

And yet, in the glass glare, Mrs. Poovey doesn't find her own face sullen, or stupefied. She does look wiped clean, smooth, full. She doesn't look so much like she has a secret than like she has something she means to do. Purposeful, whereas the virgin just stands there with her empty hands out.

The Catholics have painted the walls a pale pink, and the blue lines and red lines and yellow lines running along the corridors make good sense to her. She walks toward the nursery following the yellow trail.

"I'm here to feed those babies," she says. The skinny nurse has a face like a nun, but wears a locket instead of a rosary, so Mrs. Poovey figures she can't be a nun.

"You from the parish? We could use help with the bottles."

"Methodist. And I'm here with these," she says, taking firm hold of her bosom. She unbuttons her slicker and hands it to the nurse who gives her a look like Rosella did, but even more skeptical and kind of scared because her pinched face has never seen Mrs. Poovey before. But she takes Mrs. Poovey's slicker from her and lays it over a raspberry colored chair.

Mrs. Poovey presses her hands against the glass, staring into the soundproof room filled with cribs. Babies are cooing or crying or sleeping. There are six, but she knows exactly which are the abandoned ones. She doesn't know how she knows, she just does, and her heart beats hard in her chest, and her bosom feels heavy and right.

"Who are you?" the nurse asks, not rude, but soft and curious.

"Mrs. Dwight Poovey. But you can call me Mrs. Poovey," she says turning to face the skittish woman. She unbuttons her sweater and her shirt, revealing her white stomach. She slips the elastic from the button holding the flap of her nursing bra. Pulls away the flannel pad now soaked with milk. Mrs. Poovey holds her breast in her hand while the woman, astonished, keeps looking at her face and down again at her breast.

"That's unusual," she says.

"You a Catholic?" Mrs. Poovey asks.

"I'm a nun."

"You don't look like nun. Where's your get-up?"

The woman's mouth turns wry. "You don't look like you should be nursing."

"It's a miracle. By trade, you ought to recognize one when you see one. What's your name?"

"Sister Agnes."

"Listen Agnes, I know it's a shock. It's a shock to me too. But I'm here and I've got real mother's milk." Mrs. Poovey tilts her head toward the nun, conspiratorially. She points to the two far cribs side by side. "Now why don't you open the door, and I'll feed those two babies right now."

"I'll call for some help," Agnes says, raising a hand as if to say wait right here. She turns, scuttles down the hall in her squeaky shoes, her starched shift swishing. Mrs. Poovey figures that bird's calling a shrink, or maybe the cops. She sees a key with a big red tag hanging in a hook behind the station desk.

Mrs. Poovey sits in the rocking chair in the nursery. She'd unbuttoned both flaps, picked up the babies one in each arm. First the girl with the tag that says Girl Baby. Then the boy called Boy Baby because no one must have known if they already had names. They're swaddled in blankets, and when Agnes walks in with a priest, Mrs. Poovey asks her to loosen the blankets so the babies can hold onto her while they nurse, one at each breast. Inside the soundproof room, there are lots of sounds, monitors beeping, heater vents humming, Agnes and the priest's shoes, but the sound Mrs. Poovey hears is two small mouths sucking, noses breathing hard, pushed against her white flesh. Tiny nails knead her blue-veined skin. The suckling hurts, but it's a good kind of hurt. She doesn't wince at all like she did when she'd nursed her son. He was greedy, her Carl.

The priest moves in close, wrings his hands. He's old, but not as old as she is. He wrinkles his nose that's mashed like a boxer's. His hair is a sooty color and he smells of soggy ash. His fingernails are soaked in nicotine.

"You a nervous man?" she asks.

"Mrs. Poovey?" he says, tapping the tips of his fingers together.

"Because if you're nervous, you should leave. You'll ruin their meal."

"No, no. I'm just…I've never…I didn't…"

"You smell nervous. How many packs you smoke a day?"

"Two." He leans in closer. "When did this start?" He kneels down, his hot breath in her face. Her husband smelled like this.

"You should get a new addiction, mister."

"Sorry, should have introduced myself," he says, "I'm Father Joe." He looks up into her face. He has dandruff and an emphysema look. The stink of it leaks from him and reminds her of Dwight, and Carl puffing away in the car with the windows rolled up in the rainy season, how she'd breathe through her hand but they never did think to notice it bothered her. But they needed it. They both needed a lot and she let them have it because that was her job. "How about you give us some room, Joe?" She holds Girl Baby and Bob Baby so their faces smush harder against her.

"How did you get in here?" Agnes says. Her voice has that soft righteous note like the dog pound girl, but it quavers as she holds the priest's shoulder. Mrs. Poovey regards her and despite the tone in her voice, the nerve of it, she is somehow moved by the way Agnes touches him, gentle but firm, protective, proprietary, the way she'd hold Dwight's shoulder when she felt threatened.

"God showed me the way," Mrs. Poovey says, nodding at the key on the changing table. Agnes' doesn't smile, but Mrs. Poovey can tell from her glance that Agnes has a thick skin and can appreciate a good-natured dig.

"So when did it start?" Father Joe asks again. He steeples his forefingers, touches them to his mouth as if to quiet some urge to wrap them around her neck, or shout hallelujah, but she's not sure which.

"Late yesterday. I was taking a nap."

"Did you dream? Did anything unusual happen when you woke?"

Boy Baby nuzzles deep, opens his mouth then bites down again.

"His nails are sharp, Agnes. You should cut them or he'll scratch himself," Mrs. Poovey says, then looks at Father Joe, "I took my dog to the pound. He's a bad dog. He bites. He shits the floor on purpose."

"I see," he says. Taps his lips with his steeple hands. "Anything else? Did you see anything odd?"

"Listen, Joe," Mrs. Poovey says softly, making her voice low and soothing for the babies. "You want me to tell you I was pruning my plum tree and the virgin's face materialized right where I whacked off a branch. You want me to say God told me this or that. But I'm an honest woman, Joe. I took my dog to the pound and I didn't care. My son gave me the damn dog and I hadn't wanted him in the first place. I was relieved to be rid of him. I'm not proud of that, but that's what happened. I took a nap. I woke up full of milk."

"Does your son know?"

"About what? The dog? The milk? No."

"Maybe you should tell him," Father Joe says in a way that seems practiced.

"I'm not Catholic. I don't need to confess."

"No, of course not. I just thought he probably meant well. I mean with the dog."

"Means well—means well for him. He was just feeling guilty. He bought Laddie for himself, for his wife and kids. But then nobody liked the dog. Carl brought him to me. It was a selfish gift. But what can I expect? I spoiled him.

"Can't wait to get me out of my house, booked into some sort of Love Boat for old farts, a ship that never sails, final ports those places. He's not fooling me, those places are just waiting rooms. He just wants to cash in on my house." She gives the priest a long hard look. The babies' breath moistens her skin and her face feels hot and worked.

"Maybe it's not as bad as all that," he says. "I'm sure he loves you. You must have been a good mother. Look what God has given you," he says, nods at the babies, their kneading hands. "He chose you. He gave this to you." Agnes looks at the priest's head, then down at her feet. She looks like she'd been waiting all her life for something and it just passed her by. Mrs. Poovey feels bad for complaining.

"Well, I sure didn't ask for it," she says, her face flushed, "But I suppose it is a gift, and it does mean something."

When Girl Baby clamps down hard, Mrs. Poovey thinks of the farm, of kittens, and how barn cats were always hungry. Her mother always scolding, *Don't feed them or they won't catch the mice!* She recalls their soft fur against her, their rough tongues as she held the babies up under her shirt. This makes her think of Laddie's white neck, his good smell. She imagines him at the pound, shivering in some last stop room. Her arms are bowed and full with Girl Baby and Boy Baby, who opens his eyes and blinks up at her. His head is covered with fine black hair and his hand never stops moving against her and he makes soft sounds in his throat. Was she a good mother? She tries not to question too much; with children there are no guarantees. They'll shut their doors against you. Accuse you of not having given enough. Give you gifts you didn't want but you accept them because they need you to have these things. They'll call you a burden. They'll leave. Maybe.

Still, she cannot help wondering who could have left these children after having given birth to them and held them and listened to their breath. Circumstances can make a good person do terrible things.

Boy Baby blinks up at her, his mouth loosening around her nipple. He digs his fingers into her breast, squeezing it hard and smiling up at her with her nipple caught loosely in his gummy mouth.

Outside in the late afternoon light, rain pastes her blouse to her arms and shoulders and outlines her breasts like two pears under the polyester. Running down her bosom's slope, the water chills her. She forgot her coat at the hospital. Her blouse is buttoned but her nipples hurt too much to hitch up her bra. She makes her way around the cinderblock building, out back where they keep the bigger dogs.

Laddie's in a big cage with a tin roof and sides and a wire fence in front. Water pings loudly against the metal, sounds like timpani. Mrs. Poovey chews her lips, rakes the last of her lipstick, peels bits of loosened skin with her teeth. He barks at her, three sharp notes, *how could you?* She puts two fingers through the cyclone fence. Wiggles them, she says, "Come on." He huddles in a far corner. Rain trails her face, the space between her breasts as she kneels, sits her fanny down on the wet cement.

A woman's voice, the one from the telephone, "You taking him home?"

She's young, fat in brown gas-station clothes.

Mrs. Poovey can't help feeling like a fool. Her eyes are hot and wet. She rubs them with her thumb, the other hand still wiggling for Laddie. She's all welled up and she's ashamed. "I haven't been myself lately," she says.

The girl leans down reaching, fingers outstretched. Mrs. Poovey takes the girl's hand. It's soft and cold. Her bosom aches as the girl pulls her up, loose breasts swinging as she rises and this makes them hurt more; but its not the ache of the morning, not the ache of fullness. "I want my dog," Mrs. Poovey says.

Rain Thursday. She'd let Laddie sleep on the bed all night. She hadn't slept at all. She goes to the hospital to feed the babies. She walks down the corridors to the nursery, proud and tired, but she feels God's eye on her and she's making herself useful and that makes the exhaustion giddy and sweet. People gather at the window to watch. Nurses and patients and some women in sweatpants and children with sweaty faces smudge the glass. The babies are so hungry; they have that heady baby smell and she takes it home on her skin, and realizes the smell is her milk.

That night she gives Laddie a meat dinner. She sleeps and he sleeps and he doesn't bark at all. She dreams of the farm, of the deep irrigation ditches surrounding the fields. She is sliding down muddy slopes on her butt. The sun is bright and hot, the sky spreads white and empty. She stands in mud to her knees.

Friday morning, the babies are sucking really hard and looking up at her, and grunting a little. Boy Baby pulls and pulls on her right but he doesn't get much before it's gone dry. There's a big crowd at the glass. People are smiling and pointing and crossing themselves. Sometime during the night, someone placed red votives with pictures of saints on the windowsill. Our Lady of Guadeloupe. El Nino. Lilies fill the nursery, and roses too. Despite Agnes' disapproval, some bring cameras. And some, their babies too, asking if Mrs. Poovey will suckle their child. They hold their infants up to the glass, small arms and legs swimming in air, faces scrunched like pink and brown blooms. Boy Baby and Girl Baby suck fast and deep, beating their small fists against her. She shakes her head at the spectators: *Not enough, nothing, nada.* Father Joe comes by to check on her, smiling until he sees Boy Baby turn his head from her, fixing to wail.

"You'd better get him a bottle," Mrs. Poovey says. Her voice is thick in her throat. The priest's face darkens. Girl Baby works hard in her sleep, kneads and sucks and finds what she can. The hands of gawkers press and press the glass. Mrs. Poovey thinks of the Mary who'd been given a gift and how it filled her and used her and then went sliding from her. Figurines stare from the window-ledge. Their disturbing faces. Empty hands beseeching God. Agnes holds out a white flannel blanket, comes around back of Mrs. Poovey in the rocking chair, drapes the cloth over her and the babies at her naked breasts.

Mrs. Poovey knocks Agnes' arm with her chin because her hands are full. She bites the edge of the blanket up around her neck and spits it out. "Get an eyeful!" she calls toward the window, startling Girl Baby from her feeding so her eyes snap open and she makes a shrill dragging cry.

At home, her bathroom's steamy, smelling of rose salts in the tub water. The rain stopped and left a deeper chill. Her skin reddens where the water touches. It's good to get heat back into her bones. Laddie noses through the door. He'd been wagging his tail when she got home. He'd licked her hands and face. The pound girl had sent plenty of wet food along, and Mrs. Poovey fed it to him, and he'd eaten, greedily.

His nails click on the tiles but she doesn't look up. She's holding her breasts in her hands, squeezing them. They feel emptied and shriven and her cheeks are hot but her thin lips are cold. Laddie stands next to the tub, his white paw at its edge, scratching. He paws her hand as she squeezes harder. Nothing comes. Red marks from his nails score her hand. He barks loud in her face.

"What?" she says. She looks up at the white ceiling, at the bare bright light. "What?"

He barks and his meaty dog breath disgusts her. The red marks burn. Her chafed nipples throb and sting. She drops her hands, her face. Her breasts lay slack against her belly. He barks high and loud and sharp. "Why are you doing this to me? What do you want?" She sees her face reflected in the water, sullen and angry and stupefied. Laddie's red tongue, white teeth, hot breath, barking.

Erin Julia McGuire
Crowfeathers

R

eal estate wasn't a job anyone was good at, then. There was plenty of room for every family that wanted to live in this part of the county, bringing along their kids and wives, their jutting station wagons to garrison on concrete driveways, birdbaths to break in new backyards. You couldn't be good at real estate because there was no challenge to it. Lots went fast, they just did, no matter what man was behind them. Even a dirty, no-paint job like the house my father sold to Mrs. Crowfeather.

My mother actually got mad, that he did it. "What a trap," she said. "What a place for that woman to raise a son, in swampland."

"It *was* swampland," my father corrected, "and it will make the boy industrious."

He believed what Eisenhower believed: good roads made good lives. At a stretch of six miles, Highway 62 was a good road, and a house adjacent to Highway 62 might radically alter the lives of its occupants. My father saw himself as a savior to both the divorced Mrs. Crowfeather and this lonely farmhouse, whose acres were parceled and sold ages ago. In reality, however, the house leaned dangerously to the left. A creamy layer of stucco was slathered over the back half. The front was an addition of faded white planks, distended, beseeching arms. A porch clung to it. Cats came from nowhere.

"It would be the best thing for her," my mother declared, "if this place burned to the ground. At least she'd have the money from the insurance company."

My father was digging out his sign from the front yard. Dead branches and old railroad ties, smelling heavily of oil and tar, were everywhere. "Stucco insulates. They'll be warm." His voice scratched over her.

"Does the school bus even come out here?" I wanted to know. I was picking up cigarette butts. My mother gave me a *look*. She meant I shouldn't join in.

On my street was a house like that, ashamed and shy, out at the end where the cement slab sat preventing through-traffic. It belonged to a lady from my school, who worked on a floor I didn't know, in an office I was never called upon to see. Her name was Miss Epperly. She was shaped like a camping lantern: her small and stout body, sometimes topped with a wide, cheap straw hat, betrayed no curve. Her flat feet were swaddled in dark cotton slippers that hissed as she walked down to the mailbox at the edge of her yard. Her face was hard like glass. Her eyes flickered sometimes, as if lit by kerosene. She even gave off a smell a little like sulfur, but you had to get close to catch it. We didn't get close, not often. She was an old lady to us, but not like the others we knew, our grandmas and church teachers. Her hair was grey only in sweeps. Her skin didn't crimp in that delicious way, like peaches in the sun. No, she was old to us only because we felt how alone she was, how separated from our lives spent watching television and fighting over bottle rockets and gum. Her kerosene eyes watched us go into our houses and the cats come out of them. Until we moved from the neighborhood when I was fourteen, I held a tricky, secret wish: to run onto Miss Epperly's porch on Vernon Street and by some provocation turn her to "high," to see what brightness she could have had, how many rooms she could have lit up.

Miss Epperly's sole function, as far as we ever saw, was to bring new children to our classroom, to walk them through the door and say their names slowly and spell them. She did this with a look of flagging faithfulness, as if she had been promised the classroom would not tear the new student limb from limb, but now she doubted everyone's good intentions. Unlike the other teachers, Miss Epperly never looked into our faces. She usually scrutinized the windows when she spoke to us: "This is David" (birds flying by); "This is Richard" (a dark thunderhead cloud); "This is Christopher" (sailing baseball from first recess). When she introduced us to Fond du Lac Crowfeather, however, she did something she didn't do with anyone else. She gave his shoulder a pat, and pushed him out to us, but she forgot to let go of his elbow. His body turned in a small, funny way, like a lawn ornament in wind. Fond du Lac quickly looked back at her, as if he misunderstood a direction, but she was gazing away. In a second she eased her grip, allowing him to take a seat at the empty desk next to me. Then she exhaled, glanced over at Fond du Lac, and left the classroom.

She didn't stay to see: we *didn't* tear at him. He was interesting to his classmates. His skin was stretched and soft like new suede, dark and different. I, too, decided he was of use. I had questions. Which room in that house did he pick out as his, if boys were likely to do that? Was the house cold at night, drafty; was there a bone to pick—I loved that expression, then—with my father? After sums I'd lean over and ask, pulling my desk with me, stretching my neck owl-like, launching little beads of saliva over his jagged, pearly fingernails. *Got a bone to pick?* I would feel goopy and delirious with the power of blame. *We're all picking bones, here.*

At recess, I had a chance. As a girl, I was inexplicable company for the toughest boys in the class, but somehow they accepted my ponytail and hard mouth. Today we stood with our new find. "So what's your dad? Is he a black?" Gary was a card; he riled us all up. The joke, from a popular classmate, proved our ownership of Fond du Lac. He was ours to keep if Gary thought so; he was ours to torture and tease, to love if we wanted and keep about anyway if we didn't.

"He's a Sioux, by half. By my grampa," said Fond du Lac, tall in his shoes. Soon I would measure myself by the shoes he wore on any day. I loved best his thick-soled canvas sneakers, the Converse All-Stars he said made him a basketball hero. I liked to feel small next to his body.

"Was your grampa the chief?" That's how we were; we didn't know anything.

"Yep," said Fond du Lac.

"No way, no way," Joey protested, making too much of it, and his words coming out a whine. So Gary laughed at him, and so did I. Pretty soon, so did Fond du Lac.

"Miss Epperly—she likes you, huh?" Gary said.

"Does she?" Fond du Lac considered us with caution.

"She's fatter than a Mississippi barge." I said stupidly. Like it was an answer.

Just then Joey found a nail in his shoe, going all the way through. Gary wanted in on a nearby fight. Fond du Lac turned his green eyes on me when we were alone. "Do you know what I think?"

"What?"

"That Miss Epperly is *lovely*." His word stopped me. I never would have thought of saying a word like that, about anyone. It was a grown-up word, a smart word, so elegant and *polite*. I blinked a few times like I had some dirt in my eye. "Miss Epperly could be my mother," said Fond du Lac. "I wouldn't mind."

Fond du Lac Crowfeather got burned just before third grade was done. Excused for the rest of the year, he was in the hospital and didn't come back home until just before July. It wasn't the house that caught on fire, my folks told me. That was the first thing I had thought of. No, he passed out in the sun one day, and six hours later Mrs. Crowfeather found him behind the garage. Besides blood on his teeth, he had second-degree sunburns across his face and a broken arm. He had fallen off the roof of the garage.

I didn't like to visit him when he was in the hospital, or at his house when he came back. He was so ugly to look at, I couldn't bear it. Both of his arms were peeling from the bad sunburn he got, and so was his nose, below the bandages. He smelled like the outhouse at my grandparents' in Rochester. The worst part of it was, his eyes were always runny-looking. Like they would leak right out of his head onto the floor. I joked, "Did they hit you in the face, Fond du Lac?" That just made him look the other way from me. I felt bad.

But I also thought about going over there all the time. I made like I was checking on his progress, like I knew all about how his body would heal itself up, because my mother was a nurse. I don't know if he believed that or not, but he never kicked me out or made me feel useless.

At dusk, after I'd visited, Joey and I would play beside placid houses of pale, uniform stucco. I watched as they became illuminated by streetlights. Set against the deepening sky, they looked like a row of white moths, pinned to a page: beautiful and dead, serene and ugly. The grass beneath our feet was brown from the soil up, the blades soft and small, curled like small hairs—grass turned bad from dogs who chose the same place to urinate on every walk.

"Do you think Fond du Lac looks like an Indian?" I'd catch Joey's awesome curveball.

"He looks like a maggot now," said Joey.

"But when he's not all burned? Do you think he looks like an Indian, or more like Mrs. Crowfeather?" We had seen her once, during mid-session Open House, where she glided from room to room on tall, pink shoes. The seat of her dress curved out, side to side. Her mouth was open in a loosely pinched "oh," like she was not getting her way. When she spoke to the teachers, her voice was rocky caverns and dry, dusty corners.

Joey thought about this for a while before he said, "Mrs. Crowfeather is French."

"So?"

"I mean, she has dark hair, too. So who knows what Fond du Lac looks more like."

We seemed to be in agreement. I said, "His dad's only half-Indian, anyway."

"I think Fond du Lac looks French," Joey nodded.

On the Fourth of July I stopped by on our way to my half-sister's house in Winona. My dad and mom waited in the car with the motor and the brand-new A/C running, but they didn't remind me to hurry up, which was a nice touch. I had a half-dozen sparklers I thought I'd bring Fond du Lac, to make him feel festive and like we weren't all forgetting him just because we had to spend the day with our families.

Fond du Lac must not've heard the car idling in the drive, and he must not've known I was standing on the porch. I waited for Mrs. Crowfeather to come to the door and let me in with her familiar sigh. The whitewashed planks had already soaked up three or four hours of direct sun, and they sent an ache right into the bones of my feet.

I turned my face towards the roof of their old place, ready to shout up to Fond du Lac's bedroom window, and I heard something that clattered my senses together: Mrs. Crowfeather and Fond du Lac, their voices simultaneous and lifted, foamy and bright, singing a song I'd never heard.

> *Insufficient Sweetie,*
> *You haven't got the kind of love for me*
> *Insufficient Sweetie*
> *You're just as insufficient as can be.*

I remembered what he said: "lovely." I heard it drawn out in his pleasant slice of a voice: love-ly. Love-leeee. *Lovely*. Miss Epperly might be fat but he hadn't thought about that. Mrs. Crowfeather could pout at the teachers, and Fond du Lac wouldn't care. He'd sing. He'd look back for more directions. He thought they were lovely.

Dropping the sparklers in a corner of the porch, I went back to the car.

My sister wasn't married; that was going to be a problem. They talked about it over rivers of creamed corn. I just waited; I was told to be "seen but not heard."

"People know my name," my father said, and I bit my bread.

"It's not like that anymore." If she found a way to keep up his

yelling, my mother would use it—she thought of arguments as necessary. They were a suffering she'd been born to, that she kept track of,
held up to God as prayer. ("Offer it up," she told me when I cried
later, over broken dates or breasts that were too heavy. "Offer it up."
It seemed ridiculous, insulting to all involved. My breasts were not
God's business and He knew it.)

"Not like that?" my father cried. "All your friends ever talk
about is who shouldn't be at Mass on Sundays and why. They notice
when a man is working late hours, then talk about it over canasta." His
tongue slid over the last word, making it slithery and mean. He had a
thick baritone voice, and when he wanted he could hurl it out, worse
than dishes breaking on the walls. He was staring at my mother.

"This won't reflect on you, Frank."

"Let me tell you one thing about real estate"—his favorite
words—"it's a business of reputation. It's a good business, too. Let's
not forget how good to us it has been."

Rae, my sister, was red. She stood out against the blue-corn-
flower painted walls. Like me, she didn't talk. I met her glance. She
smiled at me, a little, and gave a half-roll of her eyes. She seemed
more sorry for me than for herself. Rae didn't really need us, anyway.
Her foster parents were rich and reliable. It was only a matter of time
before she cleared us away from her table, dropped the dishes from
which we'd eaten into a sink of hot cloudy water, and leaned back
against the refrigerator door to think about what we actually were
to her. We weren't much; the three of us made a racket wherever we
went; even divorced Mrs. Crowfeather, whom everyone said had
married a drunk, made an effort at harmony. But I wanted Rae, to
see her again sometime. Her baby would probably be like her, hanks
of brown hair, pale eyes, with a liking for the kind of humor Mom
called "ribald" and that easy way of walking over the drive to wave
you goodbye.

I'm asked about it. Even now. In my version of the story, I tell what
happened. I tell what happened in Fond du Lac's head, why he acted
like he did, why the cat was inside when they looked around. I tell
why Fond du Lac slipped up. I tell why Mrs. Crowfeather came into

the kitchen, with a look of sunshine on her face, a sweet smile she could not have possessed before. I give a thousand reasons. I don't worry about who listens. I know where I was that day—nowhere near them, sitting at a dinner table in Winona, in my half-sister's blue kitchen.

I see Mr. Crowfeather, on his way east to get his son. He took off his brown cotton glove, jutted out a thumb, and rode toward the only place he ever made an easy time of it. His cigarette dangled, movie-star-like, from his large, wide mouth. His face was peaceful. He rode for five days with a former cattle driver who now took to trucking. They rode side-by-side in the cabin of the rig, and didn't say five words in a row to each other, but it was a good time. The scenery filled him with satisfaction. That was how Mr. Crowfeather convinced himself what he was doing was the best that could be done. How he dictated from a thousand miles away the course of his son's life, measuring it out for him, opening him up to a host of sweet, terrible feeling. How mean things became beautiful.

A day away, he called Mrs. Crowfeather from a Happy Chef payphone. He hung up when she said "hello" in her way: a gemstone, facets shining, glorious reflection.

Fond du Lac and his mother planned to celebrate the holiday with ice cream and raspberries. Mrs. Crowfeather had a bowl of them, fresh from the wreck of bushes out near the garage. An unopened quart box of vanilla was in the freezer. Fond du Lac had found the sparklers when they came downstairs, and he put them on the counter, far away from the sink so they wouldn't be ruined.

"I'm having someone over tonight," she said to him. "Fred Gillman."

Mr. Gillman worked for the only dairy company that still delivered milk to people's doors. Everyone knew him. He smiled at you and waved when your car passed his on the street. Fond du Lac said he had the reddest hair anyone could have been given by God. "Why's he coming?"

"I just thought it would be fun. To have some company," she said. "Don't you like him?"

"I like him alright," Fond du Lac answered. It wasn't a lie, either. You couldn't dislike Mr. Gillman. He played the clarinet in a pub band and made jokes about himself.

"I'm going to put on something decent," Mrs. Crowfeather said after a while. "Then we'll change your dressing." And she went into her bedroom with the bright pink door, and Fond du Lac sat at the kitchen table with a million thoughts in his head.

Often, from his room, he could hear his mother downstairs at the kitchen table, on the telephone to her sister that Fond du Lac had never met. The things she whispered or shouted or cried into the telephone, from where she was, so many miles away from her family, from those who understood her. "I'm crazy here." Fond du Lac was ashamed of listening to her, ashamed of himself and his curiosity. And it came upon him like a bruising heavyweight, like walking out of water. The assembling feeling of swimming in sickness, as he listened to his lonely mother after those calls, her trembling voice, crying after she put down the phone. Hugging her elbows into her breasts, staring at the linoleum or at the free calendar from the hardware store. Or as he listened to her now, through the thin wall, singing "Paper Moon" in wavering low notes.

He wished he could correctly identify what life she had given him, what she alone had done and led him through. He felt shame for that, too. His father appeared at the screen door and he felt sick. Heron-still, he felt fear and relief at the same time. His father did not open the door, though. He tapped on the frame with a finger, or partly on the frame and partly on the door itself, and the door banged but only a centimeter if that, it just waved and banged slightly, but the noise frightened Fond du Lac.

He could have thought it was a wind, or one of their cats. His mother kept plenty of cats. He looked up and saw the mouth first; his father's reedy mouth hung open as he breathed and whistled through it. Mr. Crowfeather's eyes tightened and squeezed, and stayed shut longer than people's usually did. They were bruised and red. His neck was short and also thick and meaty, a fish's. His skin was dark which might have been a tan, but was his part-Sioux heritage. Fond du Lac's skin was not so dark. Was not dark at all, in fact, if you compared. Of his father, he received black hair. None of his features. Fond du Lac's legs were long, his neck thin, his eyes green. Like swimming, he went to the door and flipped the latch, opening it to his father.

Mr. Crowfeather came in without stopping. His feet tracked in dust and grass; a cat slipped in also. His eyes took everything in like an ocean. Fond du Lac was unsure of himself: he seemed able only to breathe out, had difficulty inhaling. He heard his mother's slight steps, echoing with inquisition, grow louder; he heard her call, "Who's at the door, sweetie? Is Mr. Gillman here already?" And like a pile of salt in warm, still water, Fond du Lac felt he was dissolving. Reeds bent back. Sticks snapped. Birds' wings flapped high, then higher, beating twists into mud. His father, though large, was quick: Mrs. Crowfeather's neck was broken before the cat could run out of the room, twitching its tail, suffering the indignity.

It was Mr. Gillman, of course, who found her. No one could say about Fond du Lac. Probably he was kidnapped, maybe killed, who knew what that man could have done? A picture of the boy was put in the paper. Miss Epperly set up a private telephone number for information. The truck driver was interviewed. "He seemed, you know, normal. Like a buddy. Dint talk much. I kinda knew he was an Indian, but you couldn't tell, necessarily." Everything was useless. Some Indian, his boy. They wouldn't look for either of them after winter.

What do children want, when one of their own goes missing? When I heard, I placed myself near the scene of the crime, chronologically, and felt proud.

Later, we lived in a bit of housing on the edge of a chopped-off part of Minneapolis, split away by the river from the rest of the city. North of business. East of affluence. Matchbooks in the grass, skinny streets pimpled with potholes, and running through the backyards a railroad junction of seven tracks and dirt piles no one was coming back for. By this time I was in high school, studying trigonometry. Both my parents worked late hours—my father gave up real estate and, still in love with Eisenhower, took a job with the city, administering elections. My mother sold cosmetics in a pink Olds.

I was at the kitchen table, listening to a Rolling Stones album, looking out the window at the sloping, rusty tracks. I saw three kids I recognized from the neighborhood, little boys with flattened pennies in their dirty hands. One of them was my friend Rita's brother, who stuttered. We sometimes worried whether others made fun of him. The three were playing with a dead dog. Its eyes were moved out, its fur oily and clumped. They poked the dog, curious, with sticks. It was stiff. They straightened their small backs, stared, wiped their foreheads. Their white t-shirts fluttered in the twilight.

I watched them. I thought, brutally, they must have wanted an audience for their discovery. A show-and-tell. A place to bring the dog, or some ceremony of recognition.

Or perhaps they didn't want anything, but things began to happen to them, a scarlet feeling, a distant danger coming closer. One of them said "let's go in" and another said "dinner anyway" and all three of them said they were cold. But they stood on a couple of railroad ties and looked out and around them. The stars were chrome. They breathed in the scent of the black trees. Oil. Tar. Motion.

Aimee Bender
Debbieland

Debbie wore the skirt all the girls had been wearing, but she wore it two months too late. By then the skirt had lost its magic and was just a piece of cloth with some tassels at the bottom. It resembled nothing more than a shred of curtain—something all the mothers had said at the beginning—but for a few months, the skirt had held inside its weave the very shimmer of rightness. If you wore it you were queen of them all, and both girls and boys followed you like strays. But you had to take the risk to wear it even though it was strange, and as soon as enough people caught on, well then. Done with. Back to curtain status. Debbie wore the skirt because she'd seen enough people wear it to know it was okay. She wore the scary skirt safely. For that, we despise Debbie.

We find Debbie in the lunchroom. She is trying, always, to lose weight. We are repulsed by Debbie's cottage cheese and her small Styrofoam bowl of pineapple slices. One of us has worn all her rings, in preparation for the harming of Debbie; Debbie, wearing that skirt, eating her pineapple slices by carefully cutting them with the side of her white plastic fork. Soft yellow droplets clinging to her napkin as she wipes her mouth. It is so easy to lure Debbie out. All we have to do is put out some bait, bait in the form of a beautiful magnet that everyone knows, one who sits down out of the blue like a daydream and asks for a slice of pineapple, please. She shares Debbie's fork. She tells Debbie some casual praise. Perhaps, for the final net, she compliments Debbie on the skirt. Debbie blushes. All day long, she has been in love with her legs swishing underneath the skirt, with how the tassels tickle her ankles. In the corner, our bile multiplies. We feel it passing among us like disease.

The girl who is bait asks Debbie if she will go with her to her car as she has something she picked out for Debbie. Something Debbie might like. It's that easy. The girl who is bait, is today totally focused on Debbie, and Debbie cannot resist this, could never have resisted it; even when she thinks about it later, there is no twenty-twenty hindsight. It is the stopping of her heart. A dream come true. She has no interest in the boys, or if she does, it is only in how they will make her look to us. And today! The girl has something for her! Something for Debbie! At last it will be true, at last we will have seen Debbie, at last we will have noticed the way she has been improving her walk and clothing choices, and that beauty her one aunt always compliments on the Fourth of July barbecue will finally be a truth in the company at large.

We follow the bait and the fish, hooked. We follow the fate and the wish. Cooked. Silent on our toes. Walk soft, like whispers.

We don't wait long. Naturally, there's nothing in the car and only so long that the bait can pretend to rummage around in the back seat. After a minute, we pounce. Two of us hold Debbie down against the passenger door. Two others grab her feet so she can't run or kick. The one with rings strikes Debbie several times—a few times hard in the stomach and one fist in the face so it will show, tomorrow. So she will have to explain. Debbie is screaming and crying. We rip the skirt off with our bare hands and her underwear is almost too much to bear, with that pattern that is the rip-off of the expensive one, and a giant maxi pad weighing down the middle. We rip the skirt into pieces, which is what all the mothers have wanted to do, because it is rags anyway, it is a rag skirt, made of rags. The one with the rings slides her hands down Debbie's arms and the rings she bought at the street fair cut lines into Debbie's skin, where drizzles of blood rise freely to the surface. The bait sits in her car, smoking a cigarette and listening to the radio. It's a giveaway; the tenth caller gets tickets to go to New York City.

We release Debbie once she's bleeding, and she slinks off, sobbing. Trying to pull her shirt down over the whiteness of her ass. Shoulders hunched, hair askew. She will never tell on us. She will never be the rat. She has a tiny part of her, the tiniest part, that still hopes this is part of some cruel initiation or test, and that if she passes it, she will still be included.

We think we could not despise Debbie more. But when we realize this, the loathing is bottomless. Possibly we could bait and hook her every day for a year, preying on that tiny hope until all of Debbie's clothes are in a rag pile and her face is a disaster. If it was not so boring, maybe we would.

We do not speak to our mothers. Long ago we gave up on our mothers. All of us, even though some of us don't even have mothers at all. Our mothers died, or our mothers left. Our mothers changed form into toads. Our mothers became presidents of companies or jumped off of buildings. Our mothers gave up everything for us. One of us has a father who beats the mother. We cheer him on. We like to hold the belt in our spare time and slap it against our palm like we are in a movie, with a cigar, and a damsel in silver tinsel that is ours waits privately on the couch. We go home after the Debbie beating, thrumming from some kind of adrenaline high, and somewhere close by, Debbie checks herself in the mirror. We can sense this. We begin to be concerned she might slightly admire her bruise, so we are hoping the bruise is in an unflattering spot. Since Debbie is not particularly good-looking, the odds are high in our favor. In general, we feel terrific about it all, maybe we even call each other up on the phone to talk, but generally the phone is for people like Debbie. We have better things to do. We realize life is not just a dress rehearsal and if you realize it, you don't need a bumper sticker to remind you. We take off our rings, one by one, and in the sink we wash them clear of any blood left from Debbie's arm. Her arm hairs were a little too black, frankly. We remember this as we stay up late, watching wrestling on TV because it's so funny. We don't mind being tired in the morning; often, we prefer it.

Many years later, we make a mistake. We make a grand error. It begins with the girl who comes to ask for directions on our college campus because we look like we always know where we are. In our features, we resemble, somehow, a compass on a neck. We see the girl approach us, with that walk of hers, very quick-paced, and her eyebrows look funny. We have to look twice. Her eyebrows are straight and black and fierce but underneath the arch we see a garden of tiny weak brown hairs growing out from under the black. She is, apparently, in between eyebrow maintenance. She is one of those girls. We, ourselves, have never once given a shit about our eyebrows which are fine and pros-perous on their own. Still, she asks nicely, so we give her directions, and then we follow her, because there's nothing else to do today and our classes are over. At her location we find we are waiting outside. Strangers float past, in particular that embarrassing person with her cell phone talking so loud. If our cronies were here, we would nudge her into a dark corner, but our cronies have gone off to different set-tings by now and are extremely poor at writing letters.

Where did Debbie go? Who cares. As soon as Debbie was removed from her skirt, we washed her from our viewpoint. She of course will remember us forever. Such is the deal we make with memory.

After about an hour or so, the one with the eyebrows exits her building, which seems like it might hold within it doctor's appoint-ments. We follow her. Eventually, she looks behind her. We ask her her name. She recognizes us and makes a witty comment. Because it is college, we seem less like a stalker than we will later in life. We are not sure what is going to happen as we are only one today, and therefore less certain, but there is something in those eyebrows that makes us take her hand unexpectedly near the lower parking lot. We end up kissing her by the fountain that is straight shoots of timed water. She is not as surprised as we might expect. She seems to be used to this. We end up kissing her for an hour, and her lips are so soft they are almost like a joke.

It lasts almost a year. It is our longest relationship. She has nightmares all the time, and huddles into our armpit in the darkness, but during the daytime she walks like she's a cartoon hero. We actually catch some of her tears in a vial and hold it in our pocket and finger it when she's at events working the crowd with all her teeth doing all that business. We grip the vial of tears knowing at any moment we could expose her and the crowd might turn and tear her to pieces. We want to take care of her every minute. We want to make sure her eyebrows are safe; every time she shows up with those weak brown hairs growing in like poor weeds, like murmurs from a third world country, we are filled with a desire to strangle her while we whisper her name for the rest of our lives. We are worried all the time because she seems like the type to walk into danger without realizing it; after all, she let us kiss her by the fountain in broad daylight. She, however, is not worried about herself, or about us. We are very rarely the receptacles of worry, what with that compass we hold upon our neck.

On month eleven, she leaves us. She finds the tear vial creepy, and she's annoyed with the constant worrying and questionings. After waxing her eyebrows until they are invincible, she goes somewhere else, to ask someone new for directions. She has taken on a new map; us, we have lost our sense of order. We find ourselves heading over to sit by the same wall where we met her. We go there every day. We go there too often. We cannot stop going. We end up Debbie.

Many years later from that, we meet Debbie again. It is not at the reunion because we don't attend reunions. We have lost touch with each other anyway, and why else would we go? The rest of the people in high school were an uninteresting blur. We do not know who Debbie is, but she knows who we are, as we sit outside at Bob's Coffee Shop on Wilshire Boulevard pulling change from deep inside our pockets. She has a couple of kids that she is lugging along, and she stops to say hello. Remember? she says. You used to beat me up?

We squint. She is not recognizable; this woman is a middle-aged woman, with her hair cut short for practicality. Do I know you?

She describes the whole incident, and when she mentions the skirt it clicks into place. Oh, we say. Yes. Oh, we are sorry, we say, because at this age it is appropriate to say, even though we do not know if we are sorry. We do not know if we would do it again, if we had the chance, if we were surrounded by our friends and hula-hooping with pineapple rings.

She sits down. The baby on her lap is blue-eyed and has light hairs on its arms, unlike Debbie, with that black hair we still dislike intensely. The older child, also a girl, lolls behind her, looking at the stand-up menu. She is wearing all expensive clothes and something about her mouth is very ungrateful.

Why did you do that? Debbie asks simply.

The waiter comes and retrieves our change, annoyed by all the linty pennies. Anything else? he asks dryly. The baby burbles.

We stare at Debbie's baby, who looks like it is from another person's body. Boy? we ask. Girl, she says.

It's Debbie, right? we ask.

No, she says, wincing. My name is Anne.

Oh.

We can't think why we have always been sure she is Debbie. Did she change her name?

I don't know, we say. I don't know why we did it. Sorry? we say again.

She shifts the baby like a sack of flour.

Everyone I tell the story to says you must have been feeling pretty awful about yourself to do such a thing, she says to us, gripping the top of our chair with her hand.

We listen and nod. We realize now that it has been a good story to tell people. She must get a lot of sympathy, and she has always enjoyed sympathy. Suddenly we feel she must owe us a thank you for giving what would be a fairly dull life otherwise a little bit of texture. She stands and holds the baby close, and the baby starts to cry.

It was a good time, we say. We do not mean it in the shocking way. We just mean it was a good time, then, high school. We appreciated that time.

Debbie leaves. She doesn't say goodbye. She has more fodder for her insulted self; she has a new way to tell her old story. We give up our table which is being eyed by new customers. Cars toil at the stoplight. We glimpsed sympathy for Debbie, yes, when we stood at the wall after our lover left us. We found ourselves hungry and desperate in the pit of the stomach, revolting to ourselves. Then we got over it. We don't go by that wall anymore. Sure, we think of our old gal sometimes but unlike Debbie, we know what should be kept to ourselves, not available for public consumption. Sure, we still keep the tear vial in our car, even though we understand how it could be perceived as creepy. Most of it has evaporated anyway. If we ever happen to see her again, though, we like to think we could prove to her that she cried in our arms, just in case she is pretending to have forgotten. We hear, through college acquaintances, that she married some man. Of course. She always was predictable. We hear she is possibly pregnant. All we know is that her nightmares were intense and we were very comforting then, and we said smart things, and when she was crying in the middle of the night we were paramount, and that sort of connection does not evaporate. We own her, we think, as we walk west down Wilshire, toward the tar. The sky is an easy breezy blue. Perhaps, in a way, we own Debbie too. Perhaps, in a way, if anyone cries on us, we then own them, a piece of them, forever. Perhaps the vial is redundant. It seems nice, to think this. We begin the long walk home feeling refreshed. We look for who we can see crying, because after all, crying is not an endangered action. There are endless tears to hunt down and possess. To provoke or extract or soothe. We are delighted with this new world, this world full of possibility.

Samantha Dunn
Going Green

Chile Queen has decided which day she will leave.

It will not be Thursday. Thursday the General Electric guys will be through town on their way to the Carlsbad Caverns. They pretend their mission is secret but Chile Queen doesn't need a Geiger counter to sense their radiation. Of course they're digging salt caves in the desert. Of course they plan to seal nuclear waste there in steel drums, in barrels that can also hold diesel oil. As if she cannot smell the salt crystals dusting the thinning hair on their fat heads, as if she cannot tell the difference in the sulfurous burning of their blue eyes.

Still, they always tip equal the tab. She has considered the odds—their money could be contaminated with that indelible print of radiation—but she takes the risk. It'll be worth it. After they finish their lunch, they tell her they'll see her next week (as if they believe she regulates her calendar by them). Chile Queen then evaluates the vinyl on the chairs they rub their bodies into, and the spoons they use to shovel in *caldo* and *chalupas*. Inevitably she senses an inappropriate luminescence in these items.

On Thursday the one called Mike will say to her, "Hi ya, Rosarita. Change your mind about going out yet?"

He will again remind her of why he calls her Rosarita; he will explain that she looks like the Mexican señorita on the plastic label of the tortillas he buys at Safeway. Chile Queen will not smile but he will laugh anyway, as if he had just invented something new and invigorating. She will look straight at the point on the bridge of his nose, and she will recognize him as the face of an otherwise nameless plague. He will believe she is staring into his eyes. He will say to the other men once they get back in the truck, "See the way she looks at me? She wants it."

After they leave, she will tell Amadee to watch the tables. Amadee thinks Chile Queen takes a break to grab a cup of coffee and get off her feet for a minute. This makes Chile Queen smile. They have no clue, she says to herself. None of them. She takes the *Doña Ana County Courier* article out of her apron pocket, laying her fingers over the words as if the tips can absorb the ink. She doesn't need to read what she now can recite:

WORLD WAR II MEMORIAL:
Alamogordo Man One of
First Inside Hiroshima

Forty years after the bomb dropped on Japan, one of the world's first "atomic veterans" remembered the experience for an audience of Memorial Day observers.

She skips the nuts and bolts information, repeating the sections she believes hold the codes:

"I saw Japanese people in the doors, the houses were leaning all different ways," recounted Franken, 67. "Then, at the next step, there was nothing. We were right close to ground zero. We didn't even see a rat."

Franken said the gray-black ruins of the metropolis were a sight neither he or anyone else in his division could truly grasp: "We said, 'One bomb did all this?' We'd bombed cities before, but they took months to destroy."

No smell pervaded the destruction, he remembers, because the intense heat had burned everything away. Only the shells of larger building stood, and inside lay the corpses of victims "that collapsed like cigarette ashes if you stepped on them," he said.

Chile Queen doesn't read the part where Franken says he's not bitter about his health problems because "it all was so new, no one knew anything." That is the part which doesn't mean much, like words spoken by the General Electric guys. But the other words, when she first read them those months ago, it was as if she had finally received the special visor allowing her to view the world in 3-D.

She doesn't know why this gift came to her in the *Doña Ana County Courier*, she was the girl in high school who had no class photo in the year book, she has straight black hair no one can pick out of a crowd. This knowledge was so uninvited, so inconceivable among the other gray columns of news—a spray for squash bugs, livestock judging finals for the 4-H contest, another zoning ordinance. She has listened for a sign that people like Amadee received it too, but all she can pick up from their voices is static.

She has collected other evidence from the *Courier* that she keeps in a plaid-patterned box under her bed. One report about a "deadly, unexplained illness" infecting Navajo children. She underlined the important sections: "All the victims have in common a recent visit to a New Mexico town, the name of which health officials won't release pending further study." At the end of the story, on another page next to the classified section, she found: "There is a hole in the sky we have caused by rockets, jet planes and wars," said Earl Three Friend, 78, a Navajo tribe leader. "Bad things are pouring through it."

And this appeared the next month:

STRANGE HUM REPORTED IN TAOS

Residents in the north are complaining of a humming sound that seems to surround them and keeps dogs barking. A team of scientists from the state's universities is now investigating. Last week Sen. Pete Domenici asked Pentagon officials to state for the record whether anything in its arsenal could produce such a sound. Officials there quickly denied any possibility of that.

"It could be movement in tectonic plates," one official observed.

Chile Queen used to wake up and look out her bedroom window across the west mesa, see the talcum-faced flowers of the daisy fleabane and the ocotillo twisting its thorny spines upward, and she would be thankful the wind makes the mornings cool. But now she can't see anything in the landscape that doesn't make her imagine hidden toxins or mute explosions making hairline fractures in the ground, or wonder what mutations occur in plants and water too slow to be perceived. Once, at one of her tables, she heard two students from the university saying the Manzano Mountains up in Albuquerque had been hollowed out and were supported with titanium warheads. Now when she sees the local mountains cutting the skyline ragged, she thinks those peaks could be like some impossible firecrackers.

She has been thinking about last year. She had a boyfriend named Neto who joined the army because he got laid off from Stahman's pecan farm. She took four days off from the restaurant and went to see him at the end of basic training in Biloxi, Mississippi. Chile Queen had never before seen a vista painted in so many series of green, where everything has leaves, where rain could be accommodated. She wonders what it would be like to live in a place with so much oxygen. She couldn't imagine someone looking into the tender plane of that horizon and saying, "Now here's a place to build a bomb."

She remembers telling that to Neto.

"Danita you say some fucked-up shit sometimes," he answered, his voice snapping out syllables the same way melting fat hits coals on a grill. They were lying in a $17 motel bed; his arms around her were thick, hairless and rubbery, strong like steel-belted radials. Neto had the words "Jesus, mi vida" tattooed over his heart in large script, and although he was only 23, the lines had already bled and faded to a certain shade of algae.

"Maybe we could move some place like this?" she told him, trying to make her words small enough to fit through his ear canals. "Some place more east…. Like where the president lives. Nothing happens in Washington. They all live there and make decisions and everything."

"Yeah?"

"Yeah, I read about it. Not about it exactly, but that's what it all meant."

"Shut up already about that shit. You're getting weird." He dropped his arms and turned his body away from her as if she were something broken, no longer serviceable. He pretended to sleep but finally moved his foot to touch her leg and said, "I'm coming back home, ok? And you been at that restaurant so long you're like the chile queen or something."

She accepted this coronation silently, pleased, believing it suited her. She knows the shades and textures of these fruits, intuits the heat of a pepper just by its length and by counting the folds in its skin. She knows the alchemy of them, how the glands on the plants' placentas hold the capsaicin, how this chemical floods the brain with endorphins just the same as a roller coaster ride at the New Mexico State Fair. And like some *curandera* she knows what to serve customers with colds, the flu or a hangover: *posole* with red chile and stewed pork. For ulcers, one plain *relleño*. Rapid cell multiplication, she believes, is the only thing you can't eat yourself out of.

The possibility of Neto wanting to stay in Doña Ana County

made her stop reading the *Courier* for some months, filled her with the need to walk the Home Accessory aisle at Wal-Mart considering marigold cotton curtains. But she quit going there in May. The letter read:

> *Dear Danita,*
> *Hi how are you. Im good. Its hot hear. This is a bitch but I dont think Ill see you anymores. I am signing on for Germany I hear its cool over there. You are fucked up bad in the head even my home boyz are saying you are crazy over raydeashun every body knows it. To bad cuz I liked you.*
> *Keep rockin, peace, Neto.*

She keeps the letter in the plaid-patterned box because it fits with the other evidence. Chile Queen thinks they must have gotten to him. Neto could not protect himself from dividing molecules; he didn't know they have a geometry. Maybe they pumped artificial compounds through the air conditioning in his bunkhouse. They intercepted the mail, read the newspaper clippings she sent him, and they used their science to break him like mud through a rotary tiller.

Without Neto she has no reason to stay. The roads and houses and stores and faces have all become brittle, wasted to beige. She had been keeping a list of the places with the highest yearly rainfall from the weather page on the back of the *Courier*. She had $589, a new timing belt on her truck, four canisters of trail mix, and the belief that if you're going to alter destiny you better do it on a Monday.

And then, last week, Amadee's uncle didn't have a chile crop to sell. He told her an entire hectare had to be plowed under. "Weevils," he had said. "Never seen anything like it. Everything infested. The snout-nosed weevil bastards must have come in from Mexico."

But she knows better. Here is the real proof; it is no longer coming through in code.

Lindsay Fitzgerald
Hunger

See this edge of road named for Saint Germaine. It is lined with trees that have self-amputated, discarded limbs on crumbling pavement. The houses are pale under the sun. The roofs are black and speckled with wrens. You can't see them, but bees nest in hives beneath the shingles. Once or twice a year they surge in a pack, screeching furiously, swarm around a child's head and send him to the hospital swollen and toxic. No one knows why the bees do this. No one prepares. It is simply the way of things, as unquestioned as the heat of July.

See the smallest of the houses, the one at the end, mint green with a rusted pick-up truck in front. The orange cat sleeping on the porch railing is called Pup, and Pup will fall in a moment, topple into the garden below. There are no flowers to catch him. Poking from the dirt are weeds with poor posture, chewed popsicle sticks. The head of a baby doll is jammed on one of the sticks. It stares out at the neighborhood with blue glass eyes that have forgotten how to blink.

In front of the porch steps, a boy quivers, thrashes on the grass. His stringy yellow hair flaps in his eyes, his limbs twist, his face contorts and colors red. Can't breathe, he says. Can't, can't. Spittle comes from between his lips, runs down his chin. The boys around him step back.

Old Bat from next door opens her window, yells, What are you doing! Help that child! She disappears from the window and opens the door. She lurches forward on her walker, laboring across the porch. She is wearing slippers and a sleeveless housecoat. One of her breasts, flat at the top and full at the bottom, like a half-drained water balloon, comes through an arm hole. She stops at the top of the steps. She has not made it down them without help in some years.

The children ignore Old Bat as the boy shakes harder, his limbs flailing wildly. They are impressed.

The front door of the mint green house opens, and a teenage girl shouts, Hey!

The children look up at her, mouths open. She is the no-tits older sister who paints pictures all over the dirty house, on cabinets and mirrors and walls; she is the one who busted Dumptruck Harry's nose nearly right off his face because he swung her cat by the tail, wound it in the air over his head and let go. The children scatter, yell, C'mon! They run toward the road, toward houses on other roads.

The boy stops shaking, sits up and wipes the spit from his face. I win! He yells at the children's backs. You hear, motherfuckers, I win!

The children are not his friends, they pass by occasionally and fight with him, rouse him from his solitude. He is sad to see them go.

The sister taps a foot, crosses arms over her midriff hiding beneath the concert T- shirt of a Christian rock band.

The boy ignores her. He glances at Old Bat at the top of her porch steps, looking stricken and confused, wobbling.

What's happened? Old Bat asks. Her scalp from beneath sparse puffs of hair is coated with sweat. Her mouth hangs open, trying to suck in oxygen, but the air is sluggish with wet heat.

I'm okay, the boy says. He makes a thumbs up and stands, brushes the grass from his shirt and backside. We was just playin' a game and I won. You think I did a good job at that seizure?

Old Bat nods vaguely.

Those turds owe me a buck now, says the boy. I told 'em I could be an epileptic retard and I was.

Old Bat stares.

You better get back inside, he says. It's awful hot out here.

The sister from the mint green doorway says that *he* better get inside before she comes out there. Her foot has stopped tapping. She means business.

The boy turns his back on her and looks at Old Bat. See ya, he says, one corner of his mouth creeping upward into a sunburned cheek. It is a rare expression on him, this hint of a genuine smile, different from the violent grin he makes at his sister and neighborhood children, at teachers who bark orders. He invented the grotesquery as a smaller boy, found it the afternoon he ran down the driveway and stomped on a nail. Blood rained onto the dirt and spread into a muddy crimson pool. He tried to pry the nail from his heel but it wouldn't come. He vomited. Daylight darkened to dusk and finally from a distance a neighbor child noticed him lying in the driveway, flat on his back watching clouds disappear. The neighbor asked if he was some kind of queer, mooning over the sky like that. The boy grinned, his only protection, grinned until the neighbor left him alone with his nail.

Now he lifts his hand in a wave. Old Bat's hands are braced on the walker and she mumbles something nonsensical.

The boy nods as if he's understood and picks up the rocks, pocket knife and rubber salamander that fell from his pockets while he humped the lawn. He trudges up the porch steps.

The sister grunts. You were makin' a *racket*. A *racket*. I'm tryin' to get things done in here.

The boy slumps toward her, mutters, I won the game.

Whippee for you.

She ushers him toward the door, painted with the face of Jesus. It was her spring project for youth group, her manner of witnessing. A write-up appeared in the paper. The headline read, LOCAL TEEN BRINGS JESUS CHRIST TO LIFE. Photos showed her slouching with hands stuffed in blue jean cut-offs, posing startled by the mournful, empathic face of Jesus—nearly as long as her body.

The boy scoots past her and mock punches Jesus' jaw.

The girl makes a hissing sound and the door closes.

Still sprawled on the railing, Pup's tail twitches. He starts at something in his dreams and tips into weeds. He scampers out and looks around, shakes his head, licks his back end. Old Bat has forgotten to go inside. She stands on her porch, hands shaking around the bars of the walker, her face and arms frying under the sun. Her housecoat is soaked with sweat, plastered against drooping skin. Through the neighbor's open window she hears the boy say to the girl, We gonna have grilled cheese for lunch? and the girl say, We're outta bread. Have Fruit Loops.

Old Bat tries to remember what just happened, why she's out on the porch listening to the children, but the memory has left her. She slowly turns and makes her lurching journey back inside toward dusty, whirring fans, plastic plants with candy wrappers hidden in the soil, framed photos of faces she sometimes remembers having touched.

Saint Germaine is quiet now but for the burblings of a lone television a few houses down, talking at an empty living room.

Inside the mint green house, the boy stands with his hands on his hips. I'm sick of Fruit Loops, he says, but no one hears him.

Look now at the sun blisters rising over dirty freckled cheeks. Watch the eyes narrowed, searching, then flat. See him staring at a blank strip of wall, standing motionless in the center of the hot, hot kitchen. Hear his breathing, quiet like the fleeing of small winged things. Feel the air around him grow wetter, heavier, slow to a halt.

Do you recognize him?

He is you. It is the hottest weekend of July, it is your eleventh year.

You want to go to the Little River. Your sister shoots a look and continues to write on the special paper sprayed with perfume. Everyone knows that boys who swim at the Little River alone go missing but you like to suggest it anyway, one or twice a week to see if you can rattle her. You lean against the counter and watch her compose a letter to her boyfriend, Lloyd F. Sherman, whom she has never met. She found him while flipping through Cousin Princess's yearbook. There he was, sharp cheekbones, sad eyes, long brown hair, like her Jesus on the door, but prone to acne. According to the yearbook, he is part of the woodworking and archery teams. She has been writing to him since spring, just after your father left, and he has not written back. If asked, she tells the kids at school that her boyfriend goes to school two towns north, he is seventeen and tall. She carries the yearbook with her, in case anyone wants proof, but no one has taken her up on it except Fanny Robinson, and no one cares what Fanny thinks.

At first you wanted to taunt her, make her feel pathetic. Then you realized she already feels pathetic.

She tells you to quit spying and quit crushing Fruit Loops under your hand because once they're all gone, that's it, no whining. Quit! Or else.

Or else what, you say. Or else she'll cover your body with honey while you're sleeping and dump ants in the bed. You remember the last time she did this, so you quit.

You go outside and stand on the lawn, look to see if Old Bat has left her windows open, if she's forgotten to put underwear and pants over her private part that looks like a fuzzy fish mouth.

Later, your sister says it is time to go food shopping, and you get to go with her because she can't carry everything in the basket on her bike. You don't cause a fuss because occasionally she lets you buy something, sparklers or novelty worms you light with a match and watch grow. And you're hungry, very hungry for something that isn't Fruit Loops.

You pedal past Old Bat's house. You lag behind because her front door is open. She is hunched over her walker and looking at a hanging bird feeder. I told you no, she says. I told you NO. You leave those little buggers alone. They're HUNGRY. A crow gazes back at her, holding her gaze for a defiant moment, then turns and pecks at the hummingbirds' juice. Stop, I said. Mongrel. Stop.

The bird ignores her and she glares at it, trembles. You look away because watching her frustration hurts, as much as a nail in the heel.

You pedal faster to catch up. It is an uphill ride, two miles, and you push against heavy pedals and heat, but the ride back will be smooth.

Three trucks and a lone car are parked in front of the convenience store. Your sister leans her bike against the building and pauses before going inside, counting the money in her change purse. The roll of bills your father left in his sock drawer is getting smaller. You don't talk about it. You have caught her at night sitting on the edge of the bed, counting, counting. She looks old then, slumped and grim-lipped.

C'mon, high tail it, she says, and you follow her inside the store. There is a country western song on the radio, a woman singing through static. Canned soda, beer, potato chips rise in towers around you. A group of men sits at the only booth, drinking coffee. Two of them smoke and talk and one of them flips through a newspaper, muttering, Can you *believe* this bullshit?

An eight-by-ten color photograph of a smiling blonde girl rests on the counter, in between lighters and Beef Jerky. The edges of the photo are yellow and curling; there is ink smudged on the girl's cheek. You read the sign, though it's been there for three years and the girl is probably dead by now, or cured. In round forceful letters, the sign implores: SAVE BETH ANNE. HELP HER GET A BONE MARROW TRANSPLANT. You eye the change in the container under Beth Anne's photo but the cashier is watching you from behind the register, biting into a meaty sandwich. Your stomach growls.

Hey, you say, following her, watching her gather the week's food in her arms. Can we have hot dogs?

No.

The men glance up from their conversation as your sister walks past them. The man with the newspaper continues to point angrily at a headline and the man across from him nods, while another sucks a cigarette with thin yellowed lips and looks at her, in a way you have not noticed anyone looking at her before.

You look to see what has stopped the man with the yellow lips from talking, what he sees as his eyes skim down her hair, brown with a silvery dullness like the ashes from his cigarette. You follow the cross hanging around her neck, falling between sweat-damp breasts small and round like the yolks of fried eggs, the shorts skimming her thighs that seem nervous in their sweaty smallness.

The man nods to her, says, Hotter'n hell, huh?

Sure is, she says, walking past him, her arms full.

The store has gone quiet except for the singer on the radio, who worries about whose bed her lover's boots have been under.

So, the man says, looking at the backs of her calves and scratching his neck. Your pop come back yet?

Everyone in town knows that your father has been gone since spring.

You watch her in profile, watch her stiffen. He's coming soon, she says finally, in a low voice.

Well, he says. You just let me know if I can help you kids with anything till he gets back. I'm just up the road.

She says okay but she does not look in his direction. She puts her things on the counter and hands money to the cashier. Her back is straight and her head held level, but her eyes are cast down, focusing too intently on cans of fish bait beneath the glass counter top. The cashier tells her she's a dollar fifty short. She starts and fumbles in her change purse and you can see that it holds only nickels and a few pennies. She says she's sorry and she doesn't want the package of sliced ham after all. The cashier sighs and the man from the booth is beside her, dropping two dollars on the counter. You watch the man's eyes, certain of their right not to blink or look away from her. He smiles, a small upward lifting of lips into moustache. There is something wet about it. You be good, he says.

She is still for a long moment, not turning in any direction, not moving her eyes. You can see the pulse point at the base of her neck twitch. Finally she nods and picks up the paper bag.

When you get to the bikes you say you're starving, you've got to eat something to get you home. You grab the bag from her and pull out the ham. But you hesitate.

She reaches for it, says quietly, Gimme that.

She throws it into a dumpster around which flies swarm and you are filled with a kind of lust, a shaking need to stick your arms inside, hunt for it and rip open the package, stuff the pink meat in your mouth. You swallow the need, get on the bike and follow her.

You ride in the middle of the pavement as a caravan of two, and only one car passes you, honks for you to get out of the way. She lifts her feet from the pedals and coasts down hills. Her hair flaps behind her, like dark birds flying at your head. You think you hear her laugh. You laugh too, and you don't know why.

She has gone to church, an all-day affair with two services and choir practice and youth group in between. You hate church, church people. They are all liars, fake smilers, they talk about you and your house and your dad, you can tell. They think you're going to hell and even though she thinks they have accepted her, maybe even like her and her Jesus on the door, you know they judge her too, wait for her to date a man with beer breath and a big loud truck, wait for her to show up to church with a black eye and a baby-swollen belly. You know there are only two good things about church. Communion, because the blood of Christ grape juice is served in tiny cups that look like shot glasses, and the body of Christ bread is fresh baked—you can grab a hunk of it and no one will complain. Offering, because everyone's heads are bowed, and if you are careful while the plate passes from hand to hand, you can drop in some change, and pull out a five or ten dollar bill. Once you pulled out a twenty but the deacon caught you and shot you a look of such fury you slipped down in the pew and hid.

Your Sunday will be spent trying to keep cool. You suck a sugar cube and stand in the driveway, digging a hole in the dirt with your foot. You get on your knees and dig deeper until you are satisfied, then pull Old Bat's hose across the lawn and fill the hole. You sit in it. The water isn't cold but it feels good against your skin. It has turned to mud but you don't care. Pup slinks next to you and drinks, dips his paws in and licks them. You pick burrs out of his tail.

The Devlin sisters are in the distance, on their bicycles, Legs in back and the Hunchback in front. They are fourteen and fifteen. Legs is older, she is in your sister's class but they are not friends. Legs rides like she's about to lift into the sky. You watch her pedal and her red hair float, and you would be bored if you didn't remember you were supposed to be excited, like the older boys. The older boys say they get wood when they see her, and you've tried to make wood yourself, but it doesn't work. Supposedly all you need to do is look hard at a girl like Legs and wood happens. You worry that something is wrong with you because down there you are always soft.

You expect them to ride past you and on down the road, but the Hunchback is speeding toward you like a rocket. She is grinning a mean grin and her eyebrows slant up. You don't move and you squint to let her know *you're* not going to be scared by a hunchback on a rusty banana seat bike. She comes closer and Pup bolts into the bushes. She is almost upon you. You roll and flop just out of her tire's reach.

Pussy, she says, riding into the puddle, and grins so her big teeth take up her face.

Legs floats to a stop beside her. She looks around then glances toward you, says hello. Her voice sounds pink, pinker than cotton candy. She makes a vague smile at you and you try to look down casually to see if there's any wood there, but nothing.

The Hunchback drops her foot off the pedal and into the puddle, splashing you both. You'd like to say something mean but your words have run away so you stand up muddy and look her up and down. Don't you look at me, she says. Did I fucking give you permission? She yanks her shirt down hard over her belly, bottom. You often watch girls do this, watch them pull sweatshirt sleeves down over their hands, watch them push hair over their eyes, watch them suck in stomachs and hunch in shoulders or push them back depending on the size of the breasts they do or don't have. You like to pretend these gestures are ridiculous, but a tiny hidden part of you, no bigger than your tiniest toe, and so hidden it is secret even from you, recognizes these are their versions of your grotesque grin.

The Hunchback wants to know what kind of jackass sits in a puddle of mud with a cat named after a dog.

You say a smart jackass and where are they going.

They're just riding around, there's nothing else to do, maybe they'll go get a soda, and what's it to you anyway.

If they give you a buck they can have two cans of your orange soda.

The Hunchback snorts. Legs says she likes orange soda.

You get them two sodas, risking that they might not pay up. They want to know where your sister is, and what's up with the Jesus on the door anyway, they've never stood this close to it.

You tell them it's complicated. Legs sits down on the steps and crosses one long long leg over the other and drops her chin into her palm. She looks at the sky as if waiting for something to happen there. She asks if you have cigarettes. The Hunchback says that's enough bitching about the goddamn cigarettes.

You say you don't have cigarettes.

Well, can she take that truck and go get some?

The truck doesn't work and is missing a tire. You point to where it's jacked up. Does she even know how to drive?

She could figure it out if she had a truck that worked. Can't be that complicated.

She stands up and says she's going to go get cigarettes. The Hunchback says she doesn't want to ride that far. She's staying here.

You're not staying *here*, you say.

She asks what you're so afraid of, do you think she's going to rape you or something?

Yeah *right*, you say, forcing out a loud strange laugh. Picture that.

Legs says she's going to ride to the corner store, she'll be back.

You watch her straddle the bike and ride down the driveway, and remember something one of the older boys said about her tasting good but you have a hard time imagining a person tasting good.

The Hunchback sits down where her sister just was. You got anything to do? she asks.

Like what?

She shrugs, asks if you're always *this exciting.*

You ask if she wants to see something.

She sniffs. As long as it's not your dick.

You manage to grumble, You *wish.*

You open the front door. She watches you. What, you ask, you waitin' for an engraved invitation?

She squints, flares her nostrils, and you imagine fire rumbling deep inside them.

Inside, you start up the stairs. You look back at her, say, I don't got all day, you know.

At the top of the stairs you stop and face a wall that was once a cracked white and is now painted with scenery. There wasn't money for more of your sister's art paper so she began to court walls and tables. You expect that she will start on the kitchen tiles next, eventually working her way around the entire outside of the house. And when she is done with that, you will find house paint, maybe you will steal it from the houseware store, and you will help her paint the house clean so she can start over again.

The Hunchback is standing closely, following the detail. The mural is of your neighborhood, each of the houses in a row. The life-size yellow haired boy standing in front of the green house looks at you both. His eyes stare from beneath long limp bangs. His lips curl in a monstrous grin. There is something vastly sad about it. You have gotten into the habit of avoiding it when nearing the top of the stairs, of turning your head. Standing face to face with it fills you with a kind of quiet terror, one you will never admit but which prevents you some nights from leaving your room to go down the hall to the bathroom.

The Hunchback doesn't say anything, just examines the wall, and you regret showing it to her, wonder what made you do that. With a pang you think that she might be considering the best way to insult it. If she does, you will slug her.

You better go, you say, I don't got all day to lollygag with you.

It's somethin', she says.

Somethin'? You make fists.

Yeah. Somethin'.

You know, not everybody can paint like that. Bet *you* can't.

I said it's *somethin'*.

She pokes you in the ribs, hard, turns her finger as if drilling a hole.

That your room?

She walks toward the door and opens it.

You say hey, that's none of her business. She looks around, steps over crumpled underwear and a science fiction magazine that claims on its cover, *The truth is out there and we have found it.*

She says, You wanna see somethin?

Depends.

She turns, facing away from you, lifts her shirt and releases the snap of her bra. You are stunned by this and stare at her back— rounded and spindly, with vertebrae like door knobs. It is not as terrible as you had imagined, and this is disappointing.

She says, You wanna touch it?

No. Well, maybe.

Then hurry it up. I don't got all day to lollygag with *you.*

You place your hand at the top, near the base of her neck, and slide it down in an arching slope. You expect to be kicked in the palm by a raging vertebrae. The horror of it is softened by something warm that licks up your sides.

She shifts, asks, You done?

She pulls down her shirt and sits on the bed. She opens the drawers of the night stand, picking up a flashlight and shaking it, aiming the light at the wall and turning it on and off, opening a pack of gum and putting a piece in her mouth. You like to think that before you would have socked her one, but now you feel oddly permissive. You're not sure why.

You sit down, far away from her at the end of the bed.

So, she says, trying to blow a bubble. You like my sister?

Not really.

That's good because she's fifteen and can have anybody she wants. When she turns sixteen she's getting a car and moving to Florida.

Why?

Disney. She's going to be Sleeping Beauty or Cinderella. They dress you up in some queer ball gown and you ride around in a pumpkin carriage. Once in a while you get out and talk to little kids. It's pretty good money.

You gonna go with her?

Nah.

A fly buzzes.

She half turns toward you, says, I won't kiss but if you want to fuck we can.

She stands up.

You imagine you feel a rash spread over you, but when you look down it is just plain sunburned skin. You say, Have you done it before?

Sort of.

How much?

Just trust me.

You stand, facing her. She is taller than you by half a head.

You don't know what to do. You have seen dogs do this, you have heard neighbors late at night and in the morning, you have seen pictures. Once, when you sneaked to the Little River through the woods, you saw two men: a teenager and an older man. The teenager was lying on his belly and the man was behind him. You watched for a minute, thrilled and disoriented, but ran away before they caught you.

She clears her throat because you are doing nothing but gawking and pulling on your ear. You think you should apologize, then you feel angry at her for making you feel that way.

Get undressed, she says. She kicks off flip flops and pulls down her shorts and underwear, shirt and bra, in that order. You feel you should turn away but she doesn't tell you to. She crosses her arms, then uncrosses them and looks toward the center of your head, like a blind person, or someone bored with your conversation, trying to pay attention but thinking of better things. She nods her head at a poster on the wall, asks, You like the Beatles?

I dunno, you say, your voice squeaking. I never heard 'em. I just like the poster.

She keeps her head turned, and you take this as her granting of permission for you to look her over. You do, and since this is the first live naked girl you've seen—other than Old Bat, who doesn't entirely count—you think you should start from her toes and work your way up, but you can't seem to move your eyes from her breasts. They are spaced far apart, almost beneath her armpits, and something about them looks confused. It is hard to tell where her nipples begin because the skin is so pale. You feel a delicious alarm and continue to examine her as carefully as you would a fish or frog cut open on a rock. The top of her stomach is small and the bottom is wide, bulbous. There is something comforting about it, and you are startled by the feeling of comfort. You take a breath before looking at the outside of her genitals, partially hidden beneath curling red hair that seems like it wants to be yelling.

She senses that you have had a long enough look, and turns her head back toward you.

You know you have to take off your shorts. You grip the waistband and pull down. They are stiff with dried mud. She itches her elbow so long and hard you think she will scratch it raw. She takes her time, considering all of you, the birthmark across your ribs, the pale hairs down your legs, the cut on your knee, the mud crusted on your toes.

She looks at your penis. It hangs quietly.

You feel filthy. You like this feeling, it is a different kind of filth than you are used to.

She continues to examine you, and you have never felt so breakable. It is as if she could kill you just by looking. You reach down to cover yourself, but she sends you a sharp cutting of eyes, says to knock it off.

She steps toward you and takes your penis in her hand, her

fingers firm but her face dubious, as if it is a tiny eel or squid that might wiggle out of her fist.

You are the only one who has ever touched it, and when you do, not a lot happens. You have rubbed and pulled and it has grown a little, hardened slightly as it does sometimes in the mornings on its own, but you haven't known what to think of specifically, and your mind tosses around and calls up images you don't know what to do with. You don't know why, but you often picture Old Bat and that kid Gummer who beat you up last fall, and you try to redirect to think of Legs, or that woman who turns the letters on the Wheel of Fortune, or the neighbor with the red lipstick who winks at you. But nothing. It always goes away, shrinks and folds up as if it's going to burrow inside of you and hide forever.

In her hand it isn't so stubborn. She doesn't rub or pull, but skims it with the tips of her fingers. She frowns in concentration and you look down to watch, stunned, as it grows and stands up entirely.

Okay, hurry, she says, before it goes away.

She flops back on the bed and opens her legs.

You stare at her, then slink to the bed and climb over her, lie down beside her, watch her face.

She says to do it before it's too late. She explains that her mother says you've got to move quickly on these things.

You lie on her. It feels good, even if you are much smaller than she is and about this you feel awkward, as if she is a mighty raft upon which you are sprawled and clutching, panting and seasick. You lie like that, motionless, her far apart breasts hugging the edges of your ribs, and you sweat. You stare down at the moon white skin of her face, startling in its perfect pale color. You wonder, from far away, how you can notice something beautiful at a time like this. She wiggles, taps your shoulder and nudges you to move down lower. You lean back a little and she wrinkles her mouth, says, Honestly. She frowns down at your penis and takes it in her hand, says Help me out here, huh?

You aim tentatively toward the growth of hair, hoping you will launch it in just the right place. It occurs to you that there is more than one avenue and you are scared of putting it in the wrong one. She tries to help you line it up but you are overcome with something—like a fist full of tears at the back of your throat—and you feel yourself shrinking in her hand, trying to fold up and away from her. She watches this happen and your entire body pulses hot then cold with instant shame.

You roll onto your back and cover your eyes with an arm. You steel yourself for her insults, wait for them to jab at you.

After long minutes, you peek. She appears to be studying the ceiling. You're not sure if you should cover her up with a blanket or smother her with it, if you should fan her, if you should tell her to go home and never talk to you again.

She turns her head toward your face, still hiding beneath an arm, says briskly, I still won't kiss you. But if you want I'll hold your hand.

You can't answer so she takes your fingers in hers. Both of your palms are slick with sweat but she manages to keep them entwined.

She says, Did you know that during the Depression they used to throw babies on the train tracks right next to this house? They couldn't afford to feed them all. That's why sometimes at night you can hear wailing babies all along the road and even near the Little River. Did you know that?

You peel your arm away from your eyes, swallow. No.

Well. She looks at you earnestly. It's true.

You sit on the porch steps in the dark, looking out at the road. It is sweltering even after dusk. Evening church will be done soon and your sister will be dropped off by one of the families, wearing a look of guilt for sins she did not realize she committed until reminded again tonight of the importance of shame, of starving.

You hope she will not be able to sense what happened with the Hunchback. She will likely glance around quickly to make sure you haven't burned anything, burned yourself, broken anything. She will zoom past you with her Bible, kicking off pumps and peeling nylons down her legs. She will huddle with paper and pen and write to Lloyd, and you will sense that she feels the most guilt about this; as if the habit of craving him, of lusting after the notion, is one she should give up.

You watch Pup snap his mouth open and closed to catch darting mosquitoes, but they elude him.

You try not to think about the Hunchback. It occurs to you that after this evening you should think of her by her real name but you're not sure you can bring yourself to it—naming her feels like a concession. When she left, in a clumsy hurry because Legs would be back soon, she said, See ya. You had the urge to shake her hand, be a man, but she was gone too quickly.

You snap at Pup, Quit tryin to eat them bugs! and he gazes at you with round eyes, startled by the attack. From the blackness, you notice Old Bat's porch light go on and off, on and off. It is probably nothing, but it feels like an SOS, a desperate call into the night. Like a moth you are called across the lawn to her porch.

The front door is open and you press your nose to the screen door, trying to see inside, but it is too dark. The place smells of wet trapped towels and overripe bananas.

You tap the door, say, Hello?

You listen for rustling, for labored breathing.

There is silence.

You knock again, ferociously this time. Hello?

You try to open the screen door but it is locked. You run down the porch steps and around to the living room window. It is open partway but too high. You drag a large ceramic lawn ornament, a leftover Santa Claus from Christmas, step on it. You grip the window ledge and the Santa gives way beneath you, cracking down the center. You fall and get up, run up the porch steps with a rock. You make a hole in the screen by jabbing at a tiny tear and reach in, unlock it and step inside. You say Hello, anyone here? Are you okay? and grope the wall for a light switch. Light fills the room and you sweep your eyes from left to right over dusty stained furniture, knowing you will find her crumpled on the floor, bones broken, heart stopped, her walker fallen beside her. Sickness swells in your stomach and you look for death. You can smell it, you can feel its fingers toy with the hairs at the back of your neck. You run toward a bedroom, knowing now you will find her flat on her back, eyes open, breath gone.

Then you hear it, a noise from the bathroom, the splashing of water. You open the door.

She is trying to stand, holds on to the handle bar outside the shower door, gripping it with all her might. She is naked but for the underwear tangled around her ankles. Her walker is against the wall. She stares at the faucet longingly.

At the sound of you she turns her head. Honey? she says, looking you in the eyes. Frank, help me.

This is not your name. You don't know anyone named Frank.

It's so hot, she says. I need to cool off. But my legs are tired. Tired.

She wobbles.

You reach for her, wrap skinny arms around her stomach from behind. She is clammy against you, and the skin of her stomach is so loose you think your arms will be swallowed by it. Her long breasts droop over your forearms and she smells at once decomposing and sweet. She sinks against you gratefully, heavy in your arms. You think your knees will buckle under the weight and send you both crashing.

You tell her to keep holding on to the shower. You reach for her walker, touch it with the tips of your fingers. You close your eyes, willing the thing to leap into your hand. It doesn't. You stretch until you think your arm will come out of its socket and pull the walker toward you. She reaches for the bars and you hold her tightly.

I've got it, she says, and you are doubtful but slowly let go.

She starts to labor forward and you tell her to wait a moment. You unwind the underwear bunched around her ankles. You walk behind her, ready to catch her. In the center of the living room, she pauses, says, Why hasn't it rained?

You tell her you don't know.

You nudge her to keep moving forward into her chair. She wheezes, eases back into it.

It's just so hot, she says. I'm baking up inside.

She picks up a piece of rope from the side table and worries it between her fingers. Naked, sucking her lower lip, she reminds you of a newborn, with skin too tender to be in open air.

You look around for something to cover her with, pick up a throw. You drape it across the front of her and she shoves you with a strength you would not have expected, says, I told you it's too hot. Don't put that on me.

You stumble from the shove and right yourself.

She stares out the window, at air so heavy, impenetrable, it could be a wall.

You sit down in the chair facing her and look at that same air.

There are car lights pulling into your driveway. Your sister steps out and you hear her say: Thank you so much, see you next week.

She goes inside.

Old Bat is pulling at the frayed seam of her rope. She stares down at it, her chin resting on her chest.

You stand and she looks up at you. Time to go? she says.

I'll be back.

She looks at you with eyes suddenly sharp. You have the feeling other people have said this to her, have smiled as they lied and left.

You run down the porch steps, across the lawn and into your house.

I need help, you say. She is kicking off her pumps, putting away her Bible. She opens her mouth to object but you say, Please.

You grab one of the kitchen chairs and move quickly. She follows and as you put it in the center of the lawn, stick the legs into the grass, she asks what the devil you're up to but you say again, Please.

Old Bat is sitting where you left her. C'mon, you say. Where are we going? she asks, but is startled out of resisting your hands under her armpits, pulling her up.

Your sister is suspicious, wants to know where you're taking her, and you look at her, at a loss to explain. Something is exchanged in your silence and for once she seems to be really looking at you, she doesn't put up a fight. She helps you and between the two of you, you manage to get Old Bat onto the porch and down the steps, across the lawn.

When you get to the chair stuck in the grass you ease her into it. By the porch light's glow you see her stare up at you. She asks, Are you going to hurt me?

No.

You get the hose and turn it on, close your fingers around its mouth so you can control the release of water.

You hold it in the air and a fine spray arcs. Old Bat raises her face, startled, watches the drops hang above her in the moonlight before falling onto her forehead. They descend upon her gently, course down her naked body.

Yes, she says in a small voice. She opens her lips, hesitantly, allows the water to slip into her mouth.

You stay like this for many minutes. Your sister is quiet beside you, making no attempt to stop you. She stands on wet grass in stockings and her Sunday best.

When you finally move the hose away, Old Bat says, No, more.

It is then you notice a group of neighborhood children gathered like ghouls at the edge of the lawn, staring with open mouths.

But they say nothing, and when you are finally done, they have vanished into the night, and Old Bat is saying, Thank you, Frank.

Dylan Landis
Rose

My grandmother washed and dried her dinner plates, stacked them in the oven and set it on broil. She hid her pearls in the toilet tank, where they coiled under a rubber flap and created a perpetual flush.

"Nine is green," my grandmother said. "Four is red. Mint tastes like flashes of light."

My parents decided it was time. They said I could stay with any friend I wanted. Oleander, I said. They were so busy gabbing on the phone to the social worker in Massachusetts and the Hertz people on 77th Street and my grandmother's bank, they didn't say no.

"I don't see why you have to put her away," I said, watching my mother fold tissue paper into her clothes—a winter-white sweater, because fall came early to Massachusetts, and a herringbone silk scarf. My mother hated wind in her hair.

"Leah, this is tough for me too," my father said. He was talking from the hall, where he was tethered to the phone. "She sees sounds; she hears shapes," he said. "How can she communicate her needs? Her mind is deteriorating."

Grandma Rose's mind, I decided, looked like her bedroom. I

loved her bedroom. Hair pins napped in the rumpled bed. Dark hairs from her wiglet drifted into the cold cream. Tubes of Bain du Soleil lost their caps and slid into open drawers, releasing the oily fragrance of summer into white nylon bloomers. Nor did my grandmother seem to register, when I was allowed to stay with her, that I smoked in the basement, riffled through her pocketbook and skimmed every paperback with a passionate couple on its cover.

"Why do they mix up the colors?" my grandmother said, peering over my shoulder at a title. "O isn't red." The word was "romance." Red like a heart, I said. "Listen, *shayna maydelah*," my grandmother said gently. "O is as white as an onion."

"She'll burn the house down if she keeps baking the plates," my father said.

"Maybe that's how she wants to go," I said. "Maybe the flames will talk to her in Hebrew."

"Yiddish," my father said. He took his palm off the receiver and said, "Do we need a lawyer for that?"

"I wish I heard colors," I said loudly. "I bet red sounds like a piano. I bet purple sounds like Joan Baez."

When my mother peered into the closet I tapped the suitcase, three left and three right. But my parents kept getting ready to drive off and kidnap my grandmother. Oleander, when I telephoned, said sure. "Don't you have to ask your mom?" I said.

"Ask what?" said Oly. "Just bring your stuff. You won't believe what's going on here."

The night roof was alive. It ticked and scraped. Tarpaper crackled where no one walked. Ventilation fans flashed in their cages.

"This is where we're gonna do it," said Pansy. She hugged a damp Sloan's grocery bag containing two smuggled towels plus two joints, one for before and one for after, and a rubber stolen from their father's room.

Ten stories below the night roof, the brakes of buses sang. I wondered if I could make myself jump off a parapet. Then I couldn't stop wondering. Fly or die, fly or die. It was like standing in the bathtub and wondering should I touch the switch. Some thoughts I couldn't control when they cycled through my brain. Mrs. Prideau, who was Pansy and Oly's mother, did not have this problem. When we left the apartment she was standing in the kitchen, spooning ice cream out of the Schraft's box and writing on some typed papers in red pencil and ignoring the most amazing things. She ignored the leak under the sink that was wetting the grocery bags, she ignored the paint hanging from the ceiling like notepaper, she ignored that Oly and me threw eggs from the windows sometimes or that Mr. Prideau slept in the second bedroom because it was cheaper than divorce. "Going to howl at the moon?" she said. "Don't fall off." God, I loved Mrs. Prideau.

Standing pipes, tall as people, stuck straight up from the tar. I try to act casual in the face of the enemy so I just said, "I bet those pipes move when we're not looking. I bet they're like the roof police." The pipes tried not to look alive. Meanwhile I was tapping like crazy, fingers jammed in my pockets so no one could see.

Oleander fixed it. She knew what scared me. She touched each pipe, calling PLP—public leaning post. *Fly or die.* Pansy started up the metal ladder to the water tower, which stuck up high above the roof. The water tower had no windows. It had no mercy. I imagined climbing, metal rungs pressing into my arches, and in my mind I spilled over the edge and fell in, gasping in cold water, grasping at walls all slimy below the waterline. I whispered fly or die, fly or die, and prayed God would lift me out, and while I prayed I forgot to breathe, and while I stopped breathing Pansy crammed the Sloan's bag between the ladder and the curving base of the tower wall and came down again, flipping her hair.

"No one's gonna notice *that*," she said, and then I remembered where I was, remembered how Pansy slept on her stomach because she rolled her hair around Minute Maid cans, remembered how Oly neutralized the roof police, and how Mrs. Prideau was downstairs letting ice cream melt in her mouth and reading and maybe smoking at the same time, and that tomorrow night me and Oly would try to sneak back up and watch Pansy do it.

We held the roof door open and waited. Pansy stood at a parapet, looking down at the singing buses. A plane blinked through the black sky toward her ear. It disappeared into her head, then eased out the other side, propelling itself through waves of her Minute Maid hair.

That's when I inhaled—worshipped the night roof, remembered to breathe.

Saturday morning the milk smelled bad, so we got to eat Trix from the box. Then we went stealing. I palmed a Chunky at Manny's Fountain on Broadway just to feel it nest in my hand, silvery and square, like a ring box from a jewelry store. At Ahmed's Candy & Cigarette, Oleander slid a comic down the back of her jeans. I knew how the cover felt against her spine: cool and slippery and stiff. I wanted to read it but she trashed it down the block. No one reads Archie anymore, she said. Oly was almost fourteen so I kept my hands out of the garbage. I liked to look at Veronica's bust, but I knew enough not to say it.

Me and Oly, we were magnetic. Sweet things clung to us. When we stole, we had secrets, and when we had secrets, we shone.

We ducked under the turnstiles on Eighty-sixth and changed subways twice and did Lord & Taylor's, where we tried on five brassieres each. I put back four and Oleander put back three. Then back down the clacky wood escalators to the main floor, where Oly stole the White Shoulders eau de toilette tester without even smelling it, just vacuumed it into her purse.

"You ditz," I said. "My grandmother wears that." Then I browsed at Christian Dior, smiled at the lady and stole the Diorissimo tester. I didn't smell it because I knew it from the heartbeat of my mother's wrist. I almost knew it from the hollow of her neck, but I had never laid my head there.

My mother dispensed strange and dangerous facts. She said department stores had lady guards who pretended to be shoppers. They lingered over gloves or garters, but were actually spies. "They watch your hands, and they look for women who glance around," my mother said. "At night they look in the toilet stalls, so no one sleeps over on those lovely *chaises longues*."

My mother was eating again, eight hundred calories a day, and she worked for a decorator, ordering fabrics and sketching drapes. At night she studied pictures of fancy chairs.

"Don't glance," I told Oly, who had stopped at wallets.

But she couldn't help it. What I did was, I listened with my skin. My skin was electric and it knew when I was invisible, and that's when I made things disappear. Then I tapped on the counter or in my pockets or even on the floor, as if I'd dropped a safety pin. Three left, three right. It made me safe, plus it was something I had to do.

Oleander and I burst out of the same glass slot in the Lord & Taylor's revolving door. We walked fast with our heads down, except Oly kept glancing back.

"Holy Mary mother of God pray for us sinners now and at the hour of our death Amen," she said. Her eyes were like penlights.

"When can I throw up?" I said. Because that's what stealing made me want to do, after.

"In the park," said Oleander fiercely. "Puke in the park."

In Central Park I threw up behind a bush and spit nine times, three times three, to clean my mouth. We bought Creamsicles and walked to Oly's apartment, except on the way we did the Grab Bag on Broadway, where the clothes were all burlap and ribbon and lace—artistic, my mother said, but she lifted the burlap with two fingers like it might be dirty, and she never bought. Under glass, silver earrings lay on black velvet and tarnished in their sleep. On the counter, beaded earrings dangled from a rack; you could strum them with a finger.

"Steal me," they whispered.

Things spoke to me often. I did what they said.

Saturday evening no one said a word about dinner. Mrs. Prideau sat on her bed and turned her manuscript pages and watched Pansy get ready, as if this was what daughters were supposed to do, go out with boys. Sometimes all Mrs. Prideau said about dinner was, "Oh, just forage," and I hoped she would say this soon so we could eat more Trix.

Pansy leaned over the bathroom sink, dabbed blue shadow on each eyelid and stared at herself in the mirror. Then she smiled, or snarled, so her teeth showed. Pansy had a face like a Madame Alexander doll, the expensive kind in glass cabinets at F.A.O. Schwartz—round glass eyes in a creamy round face. Pansy looked like a cross between seven and seventeen. I watched her from the doorway, hoping to learn something. What I learned was how to put on blush. First you grin. Then you rub lipstick on the part of your cheek that sticks out like a cherry tomato.

Oleander opened bureau drawers and slammed them, looking for a bandanna halter top she stole last week. No one at Oly's had private drawers or private shirts or even private beds, because Mrs. Prideau and Oly and Pansy shared two big beds in the one room and didn't have space for private anything. Sometimes this made me so jealous I could die and sometimes it made me want to go home and straighten my desk. The bandanna halter came out with a froth of socks and Oly put it on and went in the bathroom and sprayed a cloud of Right Guard around her armpits.

"Oh, good, deodorize the toothbrushes," said Pansy, fanning at the cloud.

"Any toothbrush of yours it's automatic B.O.," said Oleander, and sat the can on the sink, where I knew it would mark the porcelain with a ring of rust.

"Any toothbrush of yours it's automatic pus," said Pansy.

"Oh, shit, here they go," said Mrs. Prideau, and looked at me like I might actually share some sliver of understanding with her. She lit a clean cigarette with the old one and jabbed the old one out. The butts in her ashtray were all kissed red at one end and bent jagged at the other.

"Your parents go anyplace fun?" she said.

"Massachusetts," I said. "They're kidnapping my grandmother."

Her eyebrows lifted into question marks, thin and elegant. "Are they taking *her* anyplace fun?"

"Old folks' home," I said. "Her mind is deteriorating."

"Really," said Mrs. Prideau. She looked at me like she was trying to figure out where to insert a key. "How can they tell?"

I lifted one shoulder and dropped it. "She sticks plates in the oven and they melt," I said. "They're plastic. She's going to burn the house down."

"She might," said Mrs. Prideau. "That's called dementia. Your parents are probably doing the right thing."

In the bathroom, Pansy sang, "Up on the roof," and Oleander nudged her out of the mirror so she could put blue eye shadow on too.

"Plus," I said, "she sees things. She says nine is green, vowels are white, stuff like that."

I hated the way I sounded, as if she were someone else's crazy grandmother, so I started biting my cuticles.

Mrs. Prideau sat straight up and looked at me. She didn't say stop biting. "Well," she said, "I don't know about the vowels. A is light pink and E is almost scarlet. But nine is definitely green."

Mrs. Prideau was not beautiful like my mother. She had short spiky hair and she wore black turtlenecks and jeans. She had ink on her hands instead of nail polish. But there was some kind of light that went on inside her, and at that moment I thought if I stood very still, the light might shine on something I needed to see.

"Not all vowels," I said carefully. "She said O and I were white like onion. I thought it was because they're in the word onion."

"No, it's because they're white," said Mrs. Prideau. "I also see Q and X as white, but you don't run into those as often."

I didn't move. Tap now, my brain instructed, but for the first time in my life I disobeyed.

"It's called synesthesia," said Mrs. Prideau. "It runs in families, but it missed my daughters. You too?"

I shut my eyes and concentrated on her voice, praying it would have a scent, a shape. I thought it might smell like Diorissimo, or float like a string of pearls.

"It missed me," I said.

Pansy walked out of the bathroom with frosted white lips.

She looked perfect. I wanted to lay her down flat to see if her eyelids would glide shut. "Tell her what her name tastes like, Mom," she said. "Mine tastes like tea biscuits."

"The very thin kind," said Mrs. Prideau. "Leah tastes like cucumber."

"It could be worse," Pansy said. She spotted my new earrings on the bureau, threaded one into her ear. "We had a babysitter once named Reneé whose name tasted like pennies."

"*Syn*, together, *aisthesis*, perception," said Mrs. Prideau, not even flicking her eyes toward Pansy, who was taking one of her cigarettes. "It means the senses work in pairs. It's a gift. Synesthetes are often artists," she said. "Scriabin had it. Kandinsky, though he may have been faking. Nabokov. Is your grandmother creative?"

"No," I said. I had no idea what she was talking about.

"I bet she is," said Mrs. Prideau. "Kandinsky said synesthetes were like fine violins that vibrated in all their parts when the bow touched them."

The door buzzer made its jagged rasp. "Oh my God," said Pansy, and left the cigarette burning on the bureau, a fringe of ash hanging over the edge. Oleander glanced at her mother, whose lap was spread with red-penciled pages, picked the cigarette up and brought it to her lips. I couldn't believe what I was seeing. My parents would have a coronary.

"We are the bows from which our children as living arrows are sent forth," said Mrs. Prideau. She looked at her younger daughter with the cigarette and closed her eyes, as if she were searching for something inside herself.

"Kahlil Gibran," she said, opening her eyes and, as I wondered if I would ever understand her, "Don't be discouraged, Leah. We never know what we inherit."

We watched her.

We hid behind the elevator shed and watched her on the roof.

He did everything exactly in order, first base, second base, third base, home. I liked it, liked the way his hands traveled on her and the way she let her body be a highway for them. He pulled her jeans off. There wasn't any underwear. This was a revelation, that a person could not wear underwear. We saw his hands move where his fly was and then he pushed onto her and Pansy made a sound like she had stepped on a piece of glass, and he stopped and put his hand over her mouth. When he took it away he kissed her. Then he pushed some more. It got boring after awhile but Oleander kept saying "Jesus" under her breath, so I just hung back a few minutes and didn't look and thought about what it was that we might have inherited, me and Oleander and even Pansy, who was fifteen and barely spoke to me. Then we saw the boy peel something off his penis and toss it away like a piece of skin he had shed and pull up his jeans. He lit a joint and gave it to Pansy. The roof police didn't do a damn thing. They just stood there.

They were just pipes.

"Was that *home*?" I said.

"Yeah," said Oleander, "Jesus," and we were breathing words more than talking them. We carried our sandals so we wouldn't scuff and moved toward the stairwell cautiously, as if we were stepping over puddles.

"It hurts," I said, amazed.

"Only when you lose it," said Oleander, and I felt a rose open in my body, all shadow and no color, felt a release as its petals fell open and soft and flew apart, and I wondered what I had lost, and why it did not hurt.

Lisa Teasley
Magda in Rosarito,
Beached

Cheek-lay?" the little girl asks, pushing with a small, thin, dirty brown arm across the table, running her fingers on the greasy Formica, looking up at Magda and Tony with saucer-huge black eyes, her long brown hair falling in messy strands, escaping the green sweat band that holds what's left of a ponytail.

"You like chiclets, Mag?" Tony asks. Magda flips her hand like a fly buzzes her ear, blinks slowly, showing her hangover and a bit of her breasts in the torn Levi jacket she wears with nothing underneath.

"How much, kid?" he asks. The little girl bats her eyes at him, then looks at Magda to see if she has an effect.

"Get a couple, Tone. Maybe Deck wants some. We're out of gum, anyhow."

"Ready?" the waitress asks with a slight Mexican accent and jaded tone of voice. Magda picks up the menu, flips her bleached hair back, and puts a chiclet in her mouth.

"Not yet," Tony says. "How much money you got, Mag?"

Magda glares at him, then sticks her tongue through the gum so he can see it.

"Shit, Tony, are you *forever* the parasite." She motions for the waitress to return. "Get me a beer," Magda says, looking at the menu, "and some eggs, and…that's it."

"Scrambled?" the waitress asks. Magda nods.

"That's *it?*" Tony looks at Magda. "OK. Whatever…I'll have *this,*" Tony says, pointing to it. The waitress nods and walks off. "But no beans!" he calls after her. "Can't handle more beans, man. Shit has me fartin' every night."

"Yeah, yeah, Tony. Always the fuckin' gentleman."

"And ain't you ever the fuckin' lady, my *mag*-got. Heard you two all night, and then fuckin' ice droppin' on the bar floor above our heads. That room is so fuckin' cheap. And it smells like oil. Cold and slimy."

Magda's mouth drops open.

"I can't *believe* you, Tony. Just fuck off. You're such a prick. The *nerve* to talk about last night!" She glares at him long and hard. He blushes, and then as if with a newfound sense of pride and purpose, flushes the shame from his cheeks.

Magda dusts off her beer before the waitress returns with the one she ordered. Then she brushes off her thin, blue Indian skirt, jingling the bells of the drawstring waist.

"Hey, maybe Decker's with those dudes from San Mo."

"Yeah, maybe." Magda looks around, rolls her eyes, really feeling the waste. "Fuck, Tone. I don't feel so hot."

"No fuckin' wonder, Mag. You haven't eaten *shit* all fuckin' week."

Magda flips her hand, then licks her lips.

"I know. I know."

"Doin' toot all night and drinkin' Bs all day—fuck—you party *too* hard, Mag. There *is* such a thing."

"Yeah, yeah."

The waitress brings the eggs and puts the plate down so hard it bucks before settling. She comes back with Tony's.

"Hot plate," she says as she walks off.

Magda takes a cigarette from her breast pocket, lights it, then blows the smoke in Tony's face. Tony smiles his straight-white-teeth-

Pepsodent smile, then pushes back the two straight clumps of black hair from his pink forehead, and leans into the table to look at Magda. He stares into her eyes, then down her long pointed nose to the top of her white-frosted glossed lips, down her tan bronze neck, to the bit of breast peeking out. She opens the jacket up a bit more, the pink-beige skin peeling at her cleavage, and she laughs, blows more smoke in his face.

"I believe someone is *hungry*," she says, still laughing until it sounds bitter and acid. A young boy enters the door with silver bracelets, shoving them in their faces.

"Oooooh," Magda coos. She takes a couple to try on. "Wha' da' ya think, Tone?"

"Hmph," Tony says. He looks away to put the fork in his food. The sun hides out. Tony watches the view down the street, tourists walking around in clusters, toting bags of Kahlua, silver, sarapes, turtle oil, beer, and beads.

Magda puts a five-dollar bill in the boy's hand, then shakes her thin arm with its long blonde peach fuzz, so the bracelets clang in front of Tony's face.

"Pretty?" she teases with a mock stuck-up voice.

"Here comes Deck," Tony says. Magda's smile drops, she doesn't look up. She takes another swig of Corona, plays with the bracelets, then stares at her food.

"What's up?" Tony asks.

"Hey dude, you look cool. Really buffed," Decker says, grabbing a seat next to Magda. She looks up at him from the side of her clear eyes, then she hisses. Decker kisses her on the cheek, and puts his dark brown arm around her bony peeling shoulders. Tony smiles.

"Hey, did you see those dudes from San Mo, this morning?" Decker asks.

"No, I was totally out this morning. Magda lost it in the bathroom too, dude. It reeks in there."

"You OK, Babe?" Decker asks, squeezing her shoulders. She's looking away, playing with the fork of eggs, her cigarette burning, blowing smoke in the faces of people passing by.

"That dude Richie is *hot,* man," Decker says, taking a swig of

Magda's Corona. "He hit the lip with a totally hot slash. Everyone was going whoooah—go baby!"

Magda spits her hack and the gum over the side of the table.

"Hey! You OK, Babe?" Decker asks again. Magda flips her hand. He catches it, kisses her fingers, licks the middle one slowly. Magda bops him lightly on his head with her wet hand, which springs back with the bounce of his nappy orange hair, burned dry from the sun and salt water.

Magda smoothes her skirt down, and then opens her legs to put the fabric between them.

"Where's the truck, Deck?" Magda asks, her eyes looking sleepy, her voice hoarse and cracked.

"Up the street. It's cool," Decker says. He looks at Tony who has his chin in his hand.

"Thinking of pullin' out today?" Tony asks. He puts too much rice in his mouth, some falls out.

"Yeah."

"Where are the keys, Deck?" Magda asks.

"Hey? What-up, Chick? Chill out. You're uptight."

"Dad would kill me if something happened to his fuckin' truck."

"Yeah? Well nothin's gonna happen to his fuckin' truck. The dude has enough fuckin' cars to move an army, no-way."

Magda puts some cold eggs in her mouth, then spits them out. Tony has finished his rice.

"Get the check, already," Magda says to Tony. Tony whistles and the waitress comes out glaring at him harder than Magda does. She puts the bill down so it whips the table.

"*What-Ev*," Tony says to the waitress's back, rolling his top lip up so the gums show. "No one else has been this fuckin' rude. She isn't gettin' *shit* for a tip."

"I'll decide what she gets of *my* fuckin' money, Tone," Magda says. Decker gets up and stretches, then Tony does too. Magda digs in her breast pocket for the cash, sucks her teeth, and pulls out a ten-dollar bill.

"That oughta be enough," Magda says, putting the money

down, then holding out an open hand to Decker. Decker slaps the keys in it.

"Let's go," she says. Magda gets up, smoothes her skirt over her ass, walks in the wrong direction until Decker pulls her arm and turns her toward the right one.

"Got anymore blow?" Decker whispers in her ear, and she cringes. "Woman are you on the rag, or what?"

"I *wish* I was on the rag," Magda hisses, then glares at him. Decker turns from her.

"Dude, you got the toot?" Decker asks.

"Nah, man. Magda dusted the shit this morning. I tell you dude, you better watch your chick, man. She's fucked up," Tony says. He spits on the sidewalk, and an old lady tourist sneers at him.

"Up yours, you old reppy," Tony says. The lady doesn't turn around. "So what's with all the reptiles in Rosarito this week, dude?" Tony asks.

"Who knows, man. This reppy slams on the brakes this morn-ing, for no fuckin' reason other than he can't see shit. I had to swerve into the sidewalk, almost wasted a couple Mexican kids, man."

Magda opens up the truck door and gets in the driver's seat. She wipes her nose with the back of her hand and sniffles when she turns on the ignition.

"So y'all wanna pull outta here now?" Decker asks.

"Yeah. If we make it before noon, checkout time, we don't have to pay for tonight either," Tony says.

"No fuckin' *shit,* Tony, you dumbass. You aren't payin' for shit anyway," Magda says, backing up like a farmer in a tractor.

"Hey, watch the boards, Mag," Decker says with alarm. He starts playing with her hair then stops because he is too squished between her and Tony to maintain the awkward position. Tony reaches across Decker and honks the horn.

"Will you mellow out, Tone! Like, who is the fucked up, uptight thing around here?" Magda says, going the road, looking at both sides of the street at the baskets, ponchos, stone figures.

"You sound like such a fuckin' Val," Tony says, lighting up a cigarette he had rolled over his muscle in his T-shirt sleeve. Magda slams on the brakes and then pulls into the side on the dirt. She reaches across their laps and opens the door on Tony's side. He laughs, blows smoke, but then she looks straight at him.

"What the fuck are you doing, Mag?" Tony asks.

Magda pushes him hard with both hands, so that the cigarette flies out of his mouth as he lands on the ground.

"Close the door, Deck," she snaps. Decker does it. Then she pulls off. Tony gets up and dusts his ass, starts running after the truck but Magda floors it. The dust rises and covers all trace of Tony behind them.

"*Fuck,* Magda. All he did was call you a fuckin' Val, for Chris-sakes. I mean, you are a fuckin' Val. What's the big fuckin' deal?"

"Just shut up," she says. Magda keeps driving, doing eighty. "You closed the door when I told you, didn't you?"

"Well, yeah, but..."

"Then shut up!"

Magda is doing ninety, and Decker puts both hands on the seat, gripping hard.

"MAGDA, slow up, will ya? You don't speed with a brother in your car, especially when it comes to the Mexican police. They could throw us in jail for the least fuckin' thing!"

Magda keeps jamming up the road, almost taking the wrong turnaround to Enseñada, but remembers the motel is just past what seemed to her to be the last of civilization.

"So, where'd you go, Deck?" Magda asks, grinding her teeth. Decker, intimidated by the look on her face, takes his time.

"Told you. Went down to watch those dudes from San Mo."

"At four in the morning?"

"Yeah."

"Expect me to believe that?"

"Yeah."

"What about all the '*babes*' that were hanging with them, camping out in the grass near the motel?"

"What *about* them?"

"I didn't hear them get to sleep all night."

"Just as you mustn't have ever got to sleep all night."

"Look Deck, you had me up 'til four, or don't you remember?"

"Yeah, but who had you up past that?"

Magda pulls into the driveway of the motel with a wild swerve, swinging the truck so the boards crash in back.

"Fuck, Mag, the *boards!*"

"Tony did," Magda says, glaring at him as she pulls into a spot.

"Tony did what?"

She puts the emergency brake on, and turns off the ignition. Magda turns her face slowly to his.

"'Tony had me up past that,'" she mocks with Decker's voice. "He found me in the bathroom pukin' and he helped me back to bed. Then he fucked me."

Magda gets out of the truck. Decker's mouth is wide open, his lip just hanging there, as he sits in the truck. Magda walks on, her ass moving from side to side.

Decker finds her in the room, throwing the few clothes she has into the yellow duffel bag. Decker grabs her by the arm and squeezes, yanking her from her bent position.

"You're lyin'," Decker says, his teeth grit, his eyes red.

"No, I'm not."

Decker slaps her hard enough for her to land on the bed. Then he takes the keys from the broken dresser, and is out of the door. Magda rolls over on the bed, and takes a piece of lint from her tongue. Then she spits on the bed. She sits up, looks around. She can see the cold, ice gray ocean out of the window. She closes her eyes, and rocks a little, but it seems like hours to her.

"What the fuck do you think you were doing back there?" Tony asks, standing in the doorway.

"Didn't Decker catch you on the way in here? How'd you get by him?" Magda asks, opening her eyes, no surprise nor malice in her voice.

Tony enters the room and stands in front of her, his white T-shirt with the "Rip and Tear" on the corner of his chest, a little dirty from his fall. He's red in the face, his narrow eyes piercing.

Magda starts laughing, cackling, then clapping her hands.

"What is so fuckin' funny?"

"You," she says in between breaths. "How'd you get here so fast?"

"I hitched."

"You must have been dropped off the minute Deck was out of the driveway." Magda wipes her nose with the back of her hand.

"I don't think your shit is funny."

"Oh. He doesn't think my shit is funny," she taunts. She laughs again, her clear gray eyes half open in a witchy squint, as she rocks. One of her buttons loosens with her laughter, her pink nipple bouncing out every time she comes up.

"I told Deck you fucked me."

"You *what?*"

"I told him you fucked me this morning after he left."

"You what?"

"You heard me. You're supposed to be my friend, Tone. But you're fucked." Magda gets up and walks over to her small, olive green backpack. She unzips it, then clutches it in front of her crotch.

"Magda, you're fuckin' crazy. Deck is going to…"

"Kill you."

"You mean come back and kill *you*. He doesn't give a shit about your ass, anyway. Not a shit. I was your friend long before you met him."

"My friend," she mocks. "My *friend?* You mean you've been my friend ever since you found out who my father was. You don't give a shit, Tone, about me. You're just star-fuckin'."

Magda digs into the smaller pocket of the backpack, grabs the small, thin black case, keeps it tight in her hand.

"What makes you think Deck isn't just star-fuckin'?"

"Because Deck *is* a star."

"In your dreams, Mag. Decker's no star anymore. You're sick. You're fucked up. With your old black, has-been surf punk, you think you have your shit together. And I've been your friend all this fuckin' time."

Magda jacks the knife out of the case and gets up to hold it to Tony's throat.

"Open your mouth, Tony," she says, digging in her breast pocket for change with the free hand. "Open your mouth, goddamn it, or I swear, I'll ram this in your neck."

Tony's brown eyes bug out at her, his skin a hot pink, his hands clammy as he opens and closes his fists.

"Magda, what the fuck?!" his voice wispy and scared.

"Do it, Tony. Do it! Open your mouth!"

Tony opens his mouth and Magda shoves the coins down his throat.

"Eat it, Tony! It's what you want, you fuck!"

Tony chokes, bent over, coughing the coins out, his eyes stinging from the metal and filth, his mouth running saliva all out on the floor. Magda takes the knife and slices into the back of his neck, as he's bent over, the blood spurts and runs.

He screams and grabs her legs. Magda kicks, knocks his head with her free fist, not letting go of the knife. Tony tries to grab her neck but she slices his hand, and she flees.

Magda runs out of the door, past the courtyard facing the ocean, past the bar, and finally the motel, until she's running on the dirt road, her thin, blue Indian skirt flying, whipping in the wind as she goes. Halfway down the road the spit works up her throat in that nasty way and she knows she has to throw up. She bends over, gets rid of the little nothing she has in her, the taste of stale beer nearly knocking her out.

She gets up again, runs. There aren't many cars that pass her since the motel is so far from town. Once she gets to the first stand, a little bakery, she stops and sits on the road, sees Decker hauling in the truck to get her. She lets herself be pulled in. By this time she's not sure what Decker's saying.

"I'm not even going to stop for your fuckin' things. We're getting the fuck out of here. Leave Tony out on his ass."

In spite of his fury, Decker drives carefully. Magda is slumped down in her seat, her butt almost off the edge.

"You OK, Babe?" Decker asks, softening, turning back and forth from her to the road. Magda barely flips her hand, tries to work the spit for her tongue, but she's too dry.

"I couldn't find Tony. The fuckin' dick disappeared...Hey," Decker takes his eye off the road completely. "Magda-Babe," he says, pulling over. "Magda?" he says turning her face in his hand. White goop in her eyes. "MAGDA!" he yells, shaking her. When she still doesn't stir, he stops, not knowing what to do next.

Lisa Glatt
Ludlow

Jimmy says he loves almost everything about me. Two months before we got married I asked him what about me bugged him. He didn't want to say, I could tell.

"Nothing really," he said. He shifted on the couch, picked up the remote control from the coffee table and turned on the television. I took the remote from his hands and muted the news. He looked at me. "Nothing bugs me all that much, Sugar. Honest," he said.

But Darlene Tate is persistent. "*Please*, Jimmy. Please." I shot up from the couch and went to the kitchen, where I opened a drawer and pulled out a pad of paper and a pen. "Make a list for me," I said, excited, handing him the pad, asking him to write things down so that I could work on them. "I'm all about self-improvement. Darlene wants to better herself," I told him.

The first thing he wrote down: *It bugs me when you talk about yourself in third person.*

"Really?" I said.

Jimmy nodded. He thought for a moment and kept writing. *It bugs me when you take things from my hands, like you just did with the remote. You've done it with other things too—magazines, a can of coke.*

"Interesting," I said.

And once he started he didn't want to stop. *It bugs me when we're in bed and I'm just about to fall asleep and you ask me a question. Like, What do you want for dinner tomorrow or Are you asleep yet? Once one of us says good night in bed, let that be it. It bugs me when I'm reading or watching TV and Annie calls on the phone and instead of going into the other room to talk to her, you stay put and talk really loud.*

I was looking over his shoulder as he wrote. After that last one, I snatched the pad away from him. "Enough," I said.

"See," he said, laughing. "You grab things out of my hands."

"My turn," I said. "Let me make a list for you."

"I don't want a list," he said, pulling me to him and kissing me on the mouth. "I love you so damn much, Darlene. I'll live with all these things and more—that's how much I love you."

Still, I question that love, and am afraid that the only reason Jimmy married me last month is because he thinks I'm going to be the mother of his child, and yes, I'm pregnant now, this very minute, but I bet I won't be by midnight.

Let me explain.

First off, there's that bitch of a psychic who swore I wouldn't make it into my second trimester, who told me in a weirdly high and squeaky voice that I was going to lose the fetus—that's what she called him or her, my baby, my little boy or girl, a *fetus*—I could have knocked her out right there. Then there's my mother's history, and her mother's history, and her mother's mother too. We're women who lose three or four babies first before we're blessed—that's the way my grandmother puts it.

It's Tuesday, the last day of my first trimester, and we've been married exactly twenty-six days and three hours. We got married quickly, downtown at the courthouse on 6th Avenue, with only my friend Annie as a witness, because neither of us believe in abortion, or rather Jimmy doesn't believe in abortions and I didn't want another one.

Ten years ago, long before I'd met him, I'd had one, and then five years ago I'd had another, and then two years ago I had one more. These are three secrets from Darlene's younger days that she's not taking into her thirties. No way.

Now that I'm twenty-nine I'm becoming a new kind of woman, the kind who gets married to the guy who gets her pregnant, not the kind who keeps the pregnancy a secret and ends one when she discovers her boyfriend is cheating, and ends another when the gray-eyed tourist goes back to his home in Mexico, and ends the third when her boyfriend of nine weeks goes on a fishing trip with his buddies.

Okay, there are things I've done that I'm not proud of, and abortions may or may not be at the top of my list, but really, truly, I only remember feeling relief, like I'd had a bad tooth removed or a blister popped—I mean, cramps and all, I felt lighter afterward, and was grateful to the people who helped me out, the doctor who stuttered and spit when he talked, the nurse who held my hand until I lost consciousness—but I'm trying not to think about them today. I'm driving with my husband Jimmy and we're on our way to Laughlin, where Jimmy's dad teaches math at Laughlin Junior College during the day and deals cards at night. Jimmy wants to introduce me to his family before I start showing. He probably shouldn't worry about me showing though because I bet there's blood in my underwear right now. I've got cramps and feel damp down there. I'm moving around, uncomfortable in the seat, but trying to be nonchalant.

The truth is I'm afraid that Jimmy is as uncertain about our love as I am about Ludlow, which is where we're stopping, taking the off-ramp to get some gas. "You sure you want to stop here?" I say, but he's already exiting, pointing out the Texaco station on our right and the coffee shop on our left, which has a sign that's actually visible from the off-ramp itself. It says *EAT* in big, blinking red letters. "We can get some food too," he says. "We'll stop awhile and stretch our legs. Let's eat at EAT," he says, laughing.

"It's not called EAT," I say.

"It's fun to say, though. Try it. *Let's eat at EAT*."

I shake my head.

"Come on."

"Let's eat at EAT," I say, smiling. "It is sort of fun, Jimmy."

"James," he says. "Remember?"

"Oh yeah," I say, "James. James. James."

Jimmy has wanted me to call him James for the last six weeks, since he started his job as a paralegal because he says that a lawyer shouldn't be called Jimmy.

"But you're not a lawyer," I said, which was obviously the wrong thing to say because Jimmy scowled. "Not yet, I mean."

"That's right."

"But you *will* be."

"Damn straight, Dar—once I get into a good law school."

"Don't you have to get some other degree first?"

"I've got a few classes left."

I looked at him.

"Okay," he said. "Maybe five or six."

"You'll buzz through them, Jimmy."

"*James,*" he corrected.

"That's right, James," and the name James felt silly coming out of my mouth like I was talking to someone else.

While Jimmy pumps the gas I go to the bathroom, expecting to mop up a mess. I stand impatiently eyeing the metal tampon box on the wall with my legs together, my dollar poised. I give a smile to the young mother with her little boy at the sink. She's showing him how to wash his hands, helping him. She pushes the silver button and that grainy pink powder falls from the spout into her palm, and then she's putting the powder on his little hands and then cupping them. With both of her hands on top of his, she's rubbing, gently it looks like, but he still says, *ouch,* still winces, but then he's giggling, and what might be a touching sight on any other day is making my stomach hurt, and I'm wishing she'd get the boy cleaned up fast and get the fuck out of here so that I can just buy what I need. I'm smiling at the woman though because I feel like I have to—I give her a tight, insincere smile, thinking, *hurry the fuck up.*

"Come on, Raymond," mommy finally says, "let's go." She looks at me then like I'm the devil and she's got to protect her son from me and my kind. She's hiding little Raymond behind her floral skirt or maybe he's hiding himself, afraid on his own, already aware of the kind of woman I so obviously am.

When I'm finally alone I buy both a tampon *and* a pad. I go into the first stall and am met by one lone turd floating in the water, probably the boy's, I'm thinking, or better yet mommy's, and it gives me a little rush to think of her hiking up her pretty skirt and leaving it. I move to the next stall. I check myself out before I pee. I've really got to pee though, and it takes will and bladder strength to hold it. I'm standing with my legs and knees apart. I pull on the crotch of my white cotton panties and look for signs—the smallest spot of blood. Nothing. Not one red drop. I'm surprised, but the day's anything but over. Darlene's got a feeling and her feeling says that this is the day she's going to lose the baby, and that it serves her right for having all those abortions and for not feeling guilty about having them. That it's just what she deserves for forgetting to take her pill and then forgetting to tell Jimmy she forgot.

I'm washing my own hands now with that cheap soap, and I see what I think is a towel on the floor in the corner, but when I stretch my neck and look closer, I notice it's a diaper, stained yellow with piss. I dry my hands with that awful brown paper gas stations use and stare at myself in the mirror. I look okay, sort of pale maybe, so I get out my blush and put on a little extra.

When I get to the car, Jimmy is sitting in the front seat smoking. He takes a long, last drag, and the cigarette sizzles and shrinks. He tosses it out the window before I get inside. "You hungry, Darlene?"

"No," I say, "but I could get a cup of coffee."

"I want you to eat at Eat," he says, laughing.

It's not so funny to me this time. If I had written a list for Jimmy, it would have started with: *It bugs me when you beat a joke to death.*

"Good girl." He starts the car and pulls out into the street, and I'm thinking that the second thing on my list would have read: *It bugs me when you say, Good girl.*

"It's like nowhere out here," I say. "Who lives here? Everyone is so damn white."

"We're white," Jimmy says.

"Yeah, but everyone's not white where we live."

"Diversity, Darlene—you're a good woman and you like diversity." He's nodding and smiling.

"I guess so."

He drives with one hand on the wheel and rubs his neck with the other.

"You tired?" I ask him.

"No," he says. "I think I just pulled a muscle. Must have slept funny last night." He winks at me.

"Last night?"

"You remember last night, don't you?"

"Yeah, but—"

"But what?"

"You were so..." I begin, and then change my mind.

"What?"

"Nothing."

"Tell me," he says.

I shrug, look out the window.

"So *what*, Dar?"

I turn back and look at him. "You know, gentle."

He laughs then. "Really?"

"Sort of."

"I'll be better tonight. I guess I'm just nervous about the baby," he says.

"Let me drive the next stretch, Jimmy—I mean, James. If your neck hurts."

"I like driving," he says.

Jimmy's not mean and he's not a cheat and he's never given me any reason not to believe him. And if you happen to be in one of the cars we pass along the highway, you would look in and see us, a couple, in Jimmy's red truck, his hand on my thigh, and his puffy, sweet lips pursed because he's whistling, which might mean that he's even happy we're married and about to have a baby, but I can't help thinking that it's the baby he loves, a baby he hopes is a boy, and that I'm the thing housing the boy, and without *him*, Jimmy wouldn't need a house, he'd do just as fine in a one-room apartment.

I've never told him about my mother and my mother's mother, how their first several pregnancies ended in sobs, in bloody cloths and midnight trips to the hospital. I haven't told him about that bitch psychic either. And I haven't uttered a word about the men who came before him—and there were plenty.

I worked the desk in a fancy hotel downtown for most of my twenties, and several of those men were tourists, away from home and only in town for a short while. They moved—with my help and insistence, I'll admit—through my life and body as easily as they moved from city to city. What I'm trying to say is that almost everyone I've ever been with has been on his way somewhere else, and because of who he was, what he was willing or not willing to sacrifice, in addition to the things I did and said, the way I laughed or crossed my legs, the way I talked about big plans of my own that didn't include him, he'd only be stopping through. Like Ludlow—I'm like Ludlow itself—and though Jimmy's enjoying his cheeseburger and fries, licking his fingers, and making those little sighs he makes when he's loving a meal, he'll be happy when we're back in the truck and on our way out of here.

One man who *wasn't* on his way anywhere—actually, he was a boy then, my very *first* boy—was Mickey Hunter, and despite what he said about me, I was not a crazy, jealous, paranoid girl, and I didn't give the worst head in the world—well, okay, perhaps I was a little timid, but I was only nineteen. And even though I wasn't sure I loved Mickey, I did want him to love *me*, if not for forever like he promised, then at least until we graduated from junior college.

I was working at Pretzel Palace in the mall and Mickey worked across the way at The Cheese House. Everything they served there was dipped in this salty orange sauce: apples, hotdogs, mini-loaves of sourdough. Mickey's job was to keep the cheese sauce creamy; he continually stirred the huge vat. Imagine a fondue pot the size of a trashcan and imagine a spoon the size of a small oar and you've got a picture of Mickey at work. He'd stop stirring only to wipe his brow with a cloth or to wave and blow me a kiss.

I'd been at Pretzel Palace for six months, going out with Mickey for five, and the waving and kissing had nearly stopped, and my period was eight days late, when a girl came bouncing into the store to buy a pretzel. Her nametag said *Hi, I'm Candy* and I hated her instantly, and, believe it or not, she worked at the Chocolate Factory two stores down. Candy wore a brown uniform—brown shorts, brown tight T-shirt, brown tennis shoes, and even a silly brown cowboy hat. "It's too bad you have to wear all brown. Kind of drab, huh?" I said.

"It's not brown, it's *coco beige*," she said, all snotty.

"Whatever," I said.

Candy rolled her eyes, which were also *coco beige*, and put a dollar and two quarters on the counter for a Jumbo Plain. "Easy on the salt," she told me.

I watched her walk with her pretzel over to The Cheese House and I knew from the haughty bounce in her step, and from the quick glance back she gave me midway, that she not only liked my Mickey, but knew he was mine, and that this made him all the more alluring to her, which meant that the two of them had discussed me. She stood, cocky, her neck bent to one side so that her cowboy hat hit her shoulder. She adjusted and readjusted that stupid hat and laughed loud enough for me to hear.

Mickey was stirring his cheese sauce and glancing over at me to see if I was looking over at the two of them, which I obviously was. Still, he took the pretzel from her hand and in one grossly gallant, sweeping motion dipped it into the trashcan full of cheese—which was, by the way, breaking store rules. A sign on the wall said: *We Only Dip What You Buy Here.*

He held the now orange pretzel with a tiny tissue and handed it back to Candy, telling me with the gesture that not only did she like him, but that he liked her too, and that the two of them had probably already fucked.

"Hey, traitor," I shouted. "Hey you two," I said. "I know what's happening, you cheese-eating whore."

Neither one of them looked back at me. "I'm going to kick your chocolate ass. Get over here, Candy, so I can kick your ass, you chocolate bitch," I shouted, and then I was trying to make my way to them without, for some reason, using the door. I was crawling up onto the counter, my knees smashing pretzels: cinnamon pretzels, garlic pretzels, and Italian herb pretzels. I didn't make it though, was stopped by my boss' big hand on my shoulder, who up until this point had always been very nice. "You're out of here, Darlene," he said. "No more Pretzel Palace for you," he told me.

Three weeks later I drove myself to my first abortion, lied to the nurse, telling her that my fiancé Michael Hunter, who works in the restaurant business, would be picking me up in the parking lot right after the procedure, so it was okay, fine, to put me out, put me under. "Knock me out," I said.

I remember driving myself home, still fucked up and probably hormonally depressed, thinking, sadly, angrily, that a girl's beginning decides everything that happens next. I doubt now that it would have made a difference in the woman I've become, but sometimes I wonder what I'd be like if Mickey Hunter had been faithful or had broken up with me in a more reasonable way. Like maybe we'd have been sitting side by side on his porch step or my porch step, his hand on my knee and he'd have been lying, sure, but letting me down gently, saying, "I care about you a lot, Darlene, but we're young, really young, and I need some space." And then I would have confessed that my period was late and that it had never been late before, and he would have said, "What, you're pregnant?" and not with a mean voice, but a concerned one. "I'll help you out—it's your body, whatever you want to do, I'm here…"

Our waitress, who introduced herself to us moments ago as the coffee shop's owner, is about sixty. Her name is Darlene too, which embarrasses me for some reason, but she's pleasant with a big smile and friendly manner, and does a good job keeping my coffee cup filled. Jimmy smiles at Darlene when she goes to pour and looks up to make sure that the lip of the pot is green and not orange which means I'm getting decaf. "The little things are important, Dar," he says, "Like getting a good night's sleep and drinking decaf, staying away from cigarette smoke and going for a walk now and then."

I'm nodding and picking at the lettuce leaves, which poke out from underneath my hamburger bun. The burger is half eaten, which is as much as I can take right now, and I haven't touched the fries. They sit in a big, glistening heap on the plate in front of me.

"Come on, eat something. Eat at EAT," Jimmy says, coming in toward me with a couple shoestring potatoes between two fingers. "Come on, Dar," he tries.

"No," I say.

"You still nauseous?"

I nod.

He looks sad a minute and then perks right up, putting the fries in his own mouth. "I was thinking that I'd quit smoking before the baby comes," he says, chewing.

"Good idea."

"In fact, I'm going to make the cigarette I smoke after this burger the last one ever," he says.

"I don't feel so good, Jimmy."

"Let's get you a soda, something with bubbles." He twists in the booth and waves at Darlene, who comes right over. "Can we get a 7-UP?" he asks her.

"Right away," she says.

"You feel really bad, Dar?"

"Yeah."

"Can I eat your burger then?" He's leaning over, reaching for it, before I can even answer.

Darlene sets the soda in front of me. "Anything else?"

"Thanks, no," Jimmy says. "Great burger."

The psychic's name was Brick and this is what she said: "You are worthy of love and happiness but will not find it now, not this time. There's a fetus in you that's about to die."

"What?" I said, thinking maybe I'd heard wrong.

"There's a fetus in you that's about to die," she said again, in a voice so high and squeaky that any news, no matter how serious, would sound like good news.

"About to die?" I said.

"Yes, on Tuesday, this coming Tuesday," she squeaked, "the fetus will quit."

"Quit?" I said. "It's not like he has a job, lady."

She shrugged. "The fetus is going to quit," she repeated.

"What's he doing, selling shoes or serving coffee in my uterus?"

Brick shook her head.

"You don't know what you're talking about. You're crazy."

"I am crazy, yes, but I do know what I'm talking about. I know about babies," she said.

I got really mad then, stood up, and started gathering my things, my sweater and bag, and if there'd been someone to complain to I would have done it. But to whom? I mean, I visited a woman who lives under a bridge, who'd made a house for herself out of boxes. I'd been sitting on a cube of red bricks—hence her name—she'd called a seat.

"He's a she," Brick said then.

"What?"

"*He* is a *she*. You're carrying a girl," she told me.

"Fuck you," I said, walking away from her and her bridge.

Okay, besides being Jimmy's idea of a baby killer, I'm gullible. He should have written on that list: *It bugs me when you're gullible.* I was muttering all the way to my car and even thought about turning around and going back to her, picking up one of those bricks I'd been sitting on, and hitting her over the head with it, but I'm not a killer, no matter what Jimmy would think about my abortions.

We're the only people in Darlene's diner and I'm looking around, wondering how she stays in business. Black and white photographs of cowboys line the wall on my left—men in boots and big hats, like the brown one Candy from the Chocolate Factory wore, one guy spinning a rope in the air, a little girl, with someone I assume is her father, sitting on a dark pig. The mountains outside are brown and gray, rolling into one another so that you can't tell where one ends and another begins. I'm thinking about the way Jimmy made love to me last night, carefully and without confidence, not his style. I didn't like it, him on top of me, completely supporting himself with both arms, so that I couldn't feel his body's weight at all. Him entering me so slowly and gently that I didn't recognize him. *Relax*, I wanted to say. *Let's do it like we did it last month, like lovers. Let's do it like the night we met.*

Jimmy's like his dad, good with numbers and good at cards, especially Black Jack. He's good at games in general, backgammon and darts and pool, which is what he was playing that first night. He was out with his brother Eddie, winning every game. Eddie was cussing and sneering, Jimmy was that good. He hit this ball, which flew to the left and hit that ball which bounced against the edge of the table and hit a third ball, and Jimmy was glowing. In between fine shots like that one he'd look over at me and take a swig of his beer and smile. It was like we were already a team, in that game of pool together, though I was sitting clear across the room on a stool and didn't yet know him. I'd noticed him as soon as I walked into the bar though, even pointed him out to Annie.

I loved watching Jimmy win, his fingers curling around the cue stick, his sparkly dark eyes, his concentration, and all that confidence. It stirred me up, and I was nudging Annie to get us another beer and maybe a couple shots of vodka because that way I'd have enough nerve to approach Jimmy or maybe I'd look at him long and hard enough until he approached me, which is what he finally did.

Darlene isn't just the waitress and owner, but the cashier as well. I wouldn't be surprised if it was she who flipped our burgers and toasted our buns. She stands behind the cash register now, twirling her wedding ring. In an ankle-length pink and white checkered dress and an apron, with her red hair done up in a fat bun, she looks like she's from another world, the way people look out here. She stares hopefully out the front window, across the street at a car that's pulled into the gas station. She's wondering if they're hungry too, I'm certain, hoping that maybe their bodies need fuel in addition to their old car.

A man steps out into the dirt. He stretches and yawns. He kicks a rock at his feet. "I wonder if he's hungry," I say without thinking.

"What? Who?" Jimmy says, turning around in the booth to look at the guy.

"I wonder if EAT gets enough business, I mean."

Jimmy shrugs, then picks up the last of my burger. He puts it in his mouth, then takes a sip of his coke. He leans back against the booth and exhales. He stares at me. "You're so damn pretty, Darlene," he says.

"No," I say. "Not really."

"You are too. And you're also a good woman, which is even more important."

"I'm not a good woman," I say, surprising myself. "There are things I've done, Jimmy. You wouldn't approve of the things I've done." And then I'm almost crying and Jimmy's scooting over in the booth so that his body is right next to mine. "I don't need to know what you've done, Dar."

I'm shaking my head, sniffling.

"I need to know what you're *going to do*," he says. "What we're going to do together."

I pick up the napkin in front of me and blow my nose. "Okay," I say. "Okay, Jimmy—I mean, James."

I went to that psychic because Annie had heard that the woman was the best in town and that she specialized in pregnancy. Annie called her gifted, said she could tell me what my baby's gender was, and if he'd have green eyes, blue eyes or brown, and, if I wanted, for a few extra dollars, on what day of the week he'd be born. She could tell me if the epidural would work or if my labor would still hurt like hell. That was also Brick's specialty—predictions about pain. She had, according to my friend, an uncanny ability to tell you whether you'll breeze through labor or if you'd better brace yourself. "You watch," Annie had said, "one day that woman is going to be on Larry King."

If she's so damn talented, I should have asked Annie, then why does she live under the 405 Freeway?

Jimmy and I are standing together holding hands in front of Darlene's cash register. She's looking down at our check and adding things up in her head. "You've got my wife's name," Jimmy says, smiling.

Darlene nods and smiles back at him. "Where you two headed?"

"Laughlin," Jimmy tells her. "My new wife's going to meet my father."

"Your daddy lives there?"

"He teaches at the J.C."

"J.C.?"

"Junior College," I chime in.

"And he's a dealer. Black Jack," Jimmy says.

"You a dealer too?" Darlene wants to know.

"No," he says. "I'm going to be a lawyer."

"Wow," she says.

"He's real smart," I tell her.

Darlene nods, counts three dollars change into Jimmy's palm.

"I'm feeling lucky," he says. "We're going to strike it rich."

"Be careful," Darlene says. "My third husband lost everything out there. Came home with absolutely nothing. Left in our Dodge Dart and came home on the bus." Darlene shakes her head.

"We're going to have a baby," Jimmy says, letting go of my hand so that he can put his arm around my shoulder. He pulls me to him a little too hard. I wriggle away and leave Jimmy and Darlene to talk about my future while I head to the bathroom.

Then I'm standing in the stall, staring once again at the crotch of my underwear, looking for signs of trouble. Again, nothing—white, clean cotton.

Maybe it'll happen while we're in Laughlin, and Jimmy's making some money at the Black Jack table.

Maybe I'll be huddled up somewhere in the hotel, bleeding.

I stand there a minute, thinking of that first night with Jimmy and all the nights that have come after. I think about how much I love him, and it occurs to me that he might love me too the way he says he does, and that he might continue to love me even if that psychic is right. But she's not right yet so I pull up my underwear and go out to meet Jimmy, who's now standing by the car, smoking his last cigarette.

I thought that if I went to the psychic I'd at least have something to talk about at parties, a story to tell. I did this once, I wanted to say, and she said this and this and that and it all came true. Or, she didn't know a goddamn thing—what a waste of fifty bucks. I'm hoping it's the latter and I'm hoping Jimmy's dad likes me and I'm hoping that if I get to be a mother this time around I'll be a good one.

When Jimmy sees me walking toward him, he drops the cigarette to the dirt and smashes it with his shoe, sending the tiniest dust cloud into the air. He opens the door for me and I climb into the truck. When I go to turn on the radio, Jimmy puts his hand over my hand. "No music," he says, "let's just talk. I want to hear everything you have to say, Dar. You're my wife."

Abby Mims
Me and Mr. Jones

J ones is at least ten years older than me and a few inches shorter. We work together at a small investment firm in Century City that hawks financial advice. Jones is the head of the legal department, I am an assistant in marketing. I was supposed to be a lot of things by now; an actress, an academic, a Vice President of Very Important Things, married. I have, as my mother says, been sidetracked.

Everything I do has to be approved by Jones. Often our conversations go something like this:

"Do you like the color orange?" Jones will say.

"What?" I will say.

"Orange," he will say, shaking a sales presentation in my face, "because that will be the color jumpsuit they will issue you and me and Mr. CEO if anyone who knows what they are talking about sees this. It's fraudulent! We can't promise these kind of returns on investments."

Jones' house is somewhat the way I'd pictured, quaint in a North Hollywood way; peeling paint, concrete steps, front door covered in scratch marks from an anxious dog. His lawn is pretty green though, and a tire swing hangs from a tree that sits at the edge of the yard. He hasn't returned my calls for a week.

I stand on the steps with the groceries I've brought him and watch pregnant clouds fight against the breeze. I want to believe that I am here because I am worried about Jones, but I am really worried about myself, how it is that I didn't see everything with Michael coming, how it is a man who owns a plaid couch seems someone you can trust and is nothing of the sort. That and the fact that I am not that many years from thirty and reading the kind of furniture a man owns like a gypsy would a palm.

Michael is a Jewish kid from Long Island with a thick head of hair and lips that taste of Carmex. He claims to love me, and licks the insides of my thighs like they are slowly melting ice cream. We met at a wedding in Laguna, wandered off from the reception at the Ritz down to Salt Creek Beach. We put our feet in the sand, felt the water on our ankles. The light was tricky that day, the way it made half his body glow and warmed his hands as they pressed against my breasts. It made me not care that he sold flatware for a living, and after an hour of knowing him, I knew he'd bend me over the sink in his hotel room later that afternoon and make me beg for it. I liked the feeling. I wasn't good at being sexy normally, but after meeting Michael, I slept naked and the thought of him kept me awake for weeks. I talked dirty to him on the phone, I bought lingerie with holes in strategic places. He was someone like that for me. He made me brave. Brave enough that day to lift my dress for him behind the latticework of one of the Ritz's gazebos.

I knock on Jones' door and see movement from behind the smoky diamonds of glass that run along its sides, but nothing happens. I ring the doorbell and wait. There is more fuzzy movement and then the door opens to reveal a girl who has curly black hair. Lots of it. I imagine Jones' head might have looked much the same a couple of decades ago.

"Hello," she says, twisting the neck of the stuffed duck she holds. She is wearing a Road Runner T-shirt, and a giant "BEEP-BEEP" streams from the bird's mouth.

"Hello," I say. "Are you Lisa?"

"Maybe," she says, and runs away yelling, "Dad, Dad, someone's here!"

Jones emerges from a room down the hall and squints at the
light coming through the door. He has on the companion shirt to
Lisa's, a purple one with Wiley Coyote on the front pocket. I've
seen him wear it on casual Fridays with a pair of green shorts, white
sneakers and black socks. Jones has fashion issues.

"Hi," I say, holding up the bags. "I have food."

"Oh," he says, looking embarrassed. He has remnants of
toothpaste at the corners of his mouth. Irritated bumps and nicks
pepper his neck like he's shaved in his car for more than a few days
in a row. He tends to do this on the mornings he's running late. He
stares at me like he's forgotten my name, then he smiles. "Well, my
dear Lizzie, do come in for a drink."

"Jones, it's 8:45 in the morning."

"All the more reason, wouldn't you say?"

It was an intern from Operations who found him, some level-headed,
number-oriented financial type, who understands the world via money
markets and things generally adding up, not via Jones looking dead
on the floor of his office, just his calves and shoes visible from the
doorway, the rest of his body hidden behind his impressive Legal
Department desk.

It happened two weeks ago, and until then I was the only one
who knew he was sleeping at the office more nights than not and
that he kept two fifths of Jack Daniels in his bottom left file drawer.
These habits started after his former mistress Cheryl dumped him
and his very recent ex-wife decided he was only allowed one night
a week with his daughter. There wasn't much left to go home to
then, he told me, except the long line of car dealerships on Lank-
ershiem, greeting him at the end of his commute. They made him
feel received somehow, he said, with their strings of silver, red and
sometimes blue flags hanging above the cars like a holiday and the
flashes of sun popping off windshields like flash bulbs. And those
strange balloon figures full of hot air in the middle of it all, jerking
forward and backward at ninety degree angles, cartoon arms flailing.

If he squinted hard enough, he could almost imagine they were real people signaling his arrival, saying welcome home. When he wasn't feeling so optimistic, he curled up on the plush wall-to-wall carpet of his office and tried to forget.

I hand him the bags and follow him inside. His living room shelves are filled with books, haphazard piles of overflow stacked along the walls. The room is otherwise sparse, consisting of a rickety end table, a green La-Z-Boy and a giant giraffe bean bag. On the mantle above the fireplace there is one picture after another of Lisa. Jones has managed to crop her mother out of every photo, except in the cases where cropping was impossible. In those, he's simply cut out her head. So it is Jones and the headless lady on a picnic with Lisa; the headless lady, Jones and Lisa on her first day of school.

He tells me to make myself comfortable and he'll be right out, that if I want to look at some books, I am more than welcome, but it's best to steer clear of the Russians. "Grandpa is always hanging himself in the barn or someone is throwing themselves in front of a train," he says. "Depressing shit." I knew something of that. I had never been able to get more than a few chapters into *Anna Karenina*.

As he disappears into the kitchen, Lisa appears at the edge of the living room holding a snail in her hand. She slides out one foot and then the other until she is in front of me. "Snails are inspiring," she says. The little guy is moving slowly along her palm, leaving a trail of slime behind. I nod and she slides past me to the window, puts him down on the ledge. "He likes it there, especially when there's condensation on the inside. He just climbs right up it."

She is back in front of me almost immediately, pulling a barrette out of her pocket. I don't always know what to do with children. I think she is nine or ten. "Can you put this in my hair? Like twist it back on both sides?" She twirls her fingers around her head to illustrate. "I mean seriously, Dad can't do hair at all."

"My mother can't do hair either," I say. "So don't feel bad."

Jones walks in as I am securing my handiwork, which I am happy to note doesn't look terrible. He stands in front of the fireplace and watches us.

"Thanks," she says and slides back out of the room. I sit down on the giraffe bean bag. Sitting so low to the ground makes me feel like a kid again and I close my eyes and try to recall what it felt like to spend a whole day not thinking about a boy. Before I can remember, I hear Jones clinking glasses together and I open my eyes. He hands one to me. I hear splashing from the back of the house.

"Carp pond," he says. "I converted the tub in the extra bathroom into one."

"You're a good father," I say.

"Could you pass that on to my ex?" He tips his head towards me as he says it, but keeps his eyes on the mantle. "I only have her today because she told the school nurse that she had a stomach-ache and her mother couldn't get off work." He runs his finger around a picture of Lisa in the tire swing. "Fortunately, I no longer have a job."

"They shouldn't have fired you." I take a long drink of what is mostly vodka with a splash of cranberry, then take off my shoes, rub my toes together. "They should have given you another chance."

He starts to laugh like he does when there is something in his mind that is funny but he hasn't shared it with anyone else in the room. "Lizzie, didn't you tell me that your flatware salesman—"

"Silver, Jones. He sells silver. There are frames involved, the occasional crystal bowl."

"Ok, silver salesman, whatever. Didn't he sell something to Daisy Duke once?"

"He's a shit."

He raises an eyebrow and nods. Jones believed from the beginning that Michael is part of the L.A. landscape that he hates. He is from the Midwest and came out here for grad school in Comp. Lit. and met his wife in a class where they were to spend an entire semester on one line of the Odyssey. He dropped out and got married in rapid succession. Now that the wife is an ex, the college loans are still outstanding, and he can't leave because of Lisa, Jones chooses to blame a good portion of the state of his life on this city. When he's drunk sometimes, he'll muse about "the big one," how it could hit and put an end to the misery. He doesn't appear to consider that the big one would take us all.

"Anyway, Daisy Duke was fat," I say. "Like you could barely recognize her, Michael said. No more short shorts. A nightmare to look at. Bloated face, big straw hat, belted dress. Flesh-colored nylons and white pumps. She wanted a hundred and fifty sterling silver cocktail forks."

"Damn," Jones says. "One hundred and fifty cocktail forks? That ruins a lot of my sexual fantasies about her. The Daisy I knew would never have worried about entertaining. I used to imagine she and one of those cousins together. The blond one. I guess that's a little sick, though, given that they were all related. Weren't they?"

"I think so."

"It's fantasy anyway, right? Anything goes in fantasy."

"Right, Jones," I say, finishing my drink. "In fantasy, not reality. That's the whole point." He looks confused. "Which way is the bathroom?" He points and I struggle my way up and out of the beanbag.

I stand at the bathroom door for a long time, watching Lisa. Her back is to me and she is up to her elbows in the bathtub pond. When she manages to hold onto a flash of orange for a second, she squeals with delight. For a few minutes, this makes me forget about the woman who showed up while Michael and I were having dinner last week. He didn't tell me she was coming, and before she got there he was sweet, wanting us to sit next to each other instead of across. He ran one hand up the inside of my thigh and moved my leg so that it crossed over one of his. He put his other hand at the back of my neck, nestled his fingers up into my hair.

She sells custom draperies in the showroom next to his. He'd described her to me several times, in his fantasies about watching me with another woman. What I noticed first was that her skin was unnaturally brown. She smiled as she slid into the black leather of the booth. Her teeth were radiantly white against its darkness. I smiled back and excused myself. I got Michael's keys from the valet and drove to LAX. I left his car in the no parking/no waiting zone, still running. I took a cab home.

I kneel down next to her and the linoleum cools my skin.

"How's my dad?" she says.

"Ok," I say, and take in what Jones has built in there. He's lined the tub with black plastic and scattered colored rocks on the bottom to hold it in place. Sprigs of green tucked into the bigger rock formations at the four corners of the pond sway gently. A downed ship holds mermaids, pirates and deckhands, all frozen in fear or death. There are divers perched above treasure chests overflowing with gold coins and necklaces which are clumped together and painted the same shade of bronze. Half a dozen baby carp flit back and forth. Some come to the surface, mouths open, hoping to be fed.

"Do you want to try?" She motions to me underwater, then claps her hands together, sending out a small series of waves.

"Sure," I say, and we each try and try to get one of them between our palms, pin it there, but they are too fast and slippery for us to hold onto for long.

I am settling into a strange kind of peace when she announces it's time for the Powerpuff girls on TV, and leaves me alone with the carp. I feel silly trying to catch the fish by myself, so I go back into the living room. Jones is in the La-Z-Boy and appears to be asleep. I sit down on the beanbag and listen to him breathing. I notice that the snail has worked its way halfway up one side of the window and appears to be veering towards the center of it. Jones startles awake in the middle of a half-snore, half-snort. He looks sheepish when he notices me. He rubs his eyes and pulls his glasses down from his forehead, tries to focus.

Once he does, he tells me that for the last few weeks he's been sneaking into the ice rink where Cheryl practices. He either stands by the far doors near the janitor's closet or climbs up to the highest seat in the bleachers with his binoculars. Even from that distance he can tell that she doesn't look happy.

"It's her hair," he says. "It looks limp, like she's not washing it enough. There's no bounce to it." She hasn't returned his calls in months and is dating some guy who works in development for Miramax.

She was admittedly the woman he'd dreamed of as an

adolescent—tall, blonde, green-eyed, all curves and dips. He, a self-proclaimed hick with coke bottle glasses, had managed to wrap his hands around her hips and had never wanted to let go. His pupils practically dilated when he told me they'd had sex in an elevator, on a fire escape, and several times, in his car on their lunch hour. It was hard to imagine Jones in any of those positions, but I tried.

When they were together, she would drag Jones to her bi-weekly practices. She'd been semi-pro in her teens and was having a hard time letting the dream die. He said more than once that all that delicate movement made him uncomfortable, made him want to carve his initials into the middle of the ice with the biggest chain saw he could find. I knew he secretly liked watching her touch the tip of the skate to her head and seeing the way her flimsy, flimsy skirt lifted and fell. His gaze lost focus when he talked about her and sometimes that look made me want to put on a tiny skirt and twirl and twirl.

"Do you know what Michael wanted me to do?" I say. "He wanted me to screw this—"

"Don't," he says, wincing and putting his hand over his eyes. He hadn't acted this way when I told him about the latex jumpsuit and the time Michael and I pulled over on the 405 and did it in the emergency lane. Those stories came out in a rush over happy hour drinks one afternoon, after he laughed about his ankle getting caught in the steering wheel while on top of Cheryl, then detailed the marks the iron bars of a fire escape had left on the backs of her thighs. Watching him now, I realize that maybe I don't want to tell him the rest of the story at all, that maybe I don't want to tell Jones anything about Michael ever again.

We sit quietly and he points at the snail, which is now working its way along the top of the window, cutting a trail in the moisture there. I wonder why he didn't take a shortcut through the middle of the glass. I ask Jones to make me another drink.

Jones pulls a book off the shelf on his way back and hands it to me with my drink. "Dorothy Parker," he says. "She reminds me of you. Sad, but funny and sharp."

"I know who she is. I wrote half a master's thesis on her." I didn't like the critical theory part of graduate school so much, I just liked her, which seemed a good enough reason to go at the time. "Such a Pretty Little Picture," I must have read a hundred times, about the man Dorothy loved in real life and his perfect wife and perfect family and how good it looked from the outside to those who didn't know the truth about the inside the way Dorothy did.

Once I called Michael in the middle of the day and he was watching scrambled porn. He worked out of his apartment. All he could see when the picture came in for a second was a nipple here or an ass cheek there, but it still got him hot.

"Do you think I have a problem?" he said. I pictured him, pants halfway down, orders for silver baby rattles and wedding stemware screeching through the fax, his thrusts and moans keeping up with those on the screen. I thought about the magazines he kept separate from the ones by the toilet in the bathroom, the ones with women on all fours in collars and spikes. I thought about the fact that he couldn't say how many women he'd slept with. He'd lost count.

I went back East with Michael a few months ago to meet his family. His mother and sisters reassured me that they'd never seen him so happy, so attentive, and wasn't I beautiful and just consider the big brown eyes our children would have. As his mother was explaining to me how Michael was a little spoiled since he was the only boy, there was a noise from the kitchen; thin, high-pitched screams. I flinched, and kept flinching even after they told me it was the lobsters boiling, just the release of air from inside their shells. I couldn't get the sound out of my head as I watched everyone else dab the meat into the bowls of butter next to their plates and chew. It had faded by the time Michael and I made love in the twin bed he'd had in high school. We were almost finished when he turned me onto my stomach and pulled me to the edge of the mattress, leaving me nothing to look at but a washed out Andover pennant tacked to the wall. He pinned me there, between him and the bed, pushing into me hard enough that it was difficult to breathe. For the rest of the night, the screams were all I could hear.

On the cover of the book, Dorothy is dewy-skinned and

wears a stylish hat and a half smile. I look into her eyes, wanting to understand the things she knew. "I'm not as sad as she was," I say. "I'm just more sad than usual right now."

Jones considers this. "He didn't ask you to sleep with Daisy Duke, did he?"

"No. Thank God, no."

"Well, that's something, I guess."

"Jones, is it ever possible to be enough for anyone?"

"I don't know," he says. "I gave Cheryl everything she wanted. Everything. My life and my marriage and it wasn't enough."

"She's not there for you anymore. If she ever was."

He grimaces in my general direction. I notice that the straight pin holding the side of his glasses together is bent at a dangerous angle. "Have you ever held a gun?"

"I don't think that's funny."

"I'm not being funny, I'm asking you a question. A relevant one."

I think about it. "Yeah, but just once. An old boyfriend took me to a shooting range. It was a .45 and I only lost my balance a few times."

He stares out at the street, puts a finger in his drink and stirs. "I mean really. My job is to stop those idiot guys in sales from presenting false information to newlyweds or little old ladies. To keep them honest about what the reality of the stock market is. It's my job to catch people who are lying so they can't take advantage. Doesn't that make me an honest person, a good person?"

His wife caught him when Cheryl called the house one day. She recognized the voice as one that called her husband too frequently and Cheryl wasn't smart enough to cover convincingly. His wife threw the phone at Jones, then threw him out.

Even though he is sitting above me, he looks compressed, folded in on himself. "You try anyway," I say. "You try to be honest, not to hurt people. That's got to count for something."

He shrugs and points outside, past where the snail sits in the middle of it all, contemplating its next move. "I held Lisa up to that window when she was six months old. 'You see all that?' I said, 'That's what we're up against. It's you and me in here, sweetie, and everyone out there doesn't have a fucking clue.'" He raises his glass to the idea of it all, softening and unfolding himself from the recliner slightly.

I get up from the beanbag and sit on the armrest of the chair, put my forehead on his shoulder. He puts a hand on my thigh. I wish I had found him that day in his office. If I had, I would have taken off his glasses, brought him a cold drink of water and closed the door. I would have put his head in my lap until he woke up.

I stare outside until the street and yard blur and all I can see is our reflection in the window. Lisa appears behind us in the doorway, the stuffed duck back in her hands. I think about what we might look like to someone standing on the sidewalk looking in. Maybe they would see a couple who has been together for years, waiting for the cable guy or the plumber or for the kids to get home from school. Maybe, too, the janitor at the ice rink sees Jones, huddled in the nosebleeds night after night as just a guy who is a big fan of the sport. Maybe when Michael and I barely noticed the waiter come and go that night, when it was only the two of us in the booth, it might have appeared as if we were so in love the rest of the world was of no consequence.

I think maybe it's possible that from the outside we look like two people coming together for one real moment in time, and maybe this is why I let Jones kiss me. Out of the corner of my eye I see Wiley Coyote staring at me from the pocket of Jones' shirt. He stands between us, hands folded behind his back, waiting for the next unattainable bird to race by, the next boulder to fall. For now, though, we are safe.

Michelle Latiolais
Boys

S he is surprised by the amount of affection in the shabby upstairs room of a strip club in Las Vegas. An easy, gleeful warmth, the boys in their loose, pull-away pants—or some already pulled away and so in nylon thongs—their penises half erect and easy beneath the thin fabric, and the women uproarious, happy, probably mostly drunk but somehow unnegotiated nonetheless in their happiness at these beautiful boys in their laps, the gorgeous male loins held within their ringed fingers.

Boys, she thinks, *boys*, but they are men, young to be sure, more than likely gay, male hustlers at later hours perhaps, certainly that insistent retention of the adolescent boy in their grooming which translates to her, rightly or wrongly, as gay. And so not heterosexual, or not *just* heterosexual at any rate, and finally of far more interest is the tremendous amount of sweetness in the room, a suspension of stricture she hasn't ever seen before, and very different from the huge round tables downstairs with their center poles, the calculated variety of female types, the men pushed up to the tables with their wads of one dollar bills, their drinks, their baseball hats reversed so they can bring their faces as close as possible to the naked crotches when they are offered, as close as is allowed without touching. And the men don't touch, don't even raise their arms unless it is to slide a bill across the table, and another, over here! Please over here! Wrap those legs around *my* shoulders—"I'm the one who needs pussy, over here!"

It's tired downstairs, an old contract, so old it might be a covenant. It's all very carefully calculated, welcoming and friendly and the waggling, suggestive finger: "Hey big boy, snatch is over here, just follow me, *And God looked on the earth, and behold, it was corrupt; for all flesh had corrupted their way upon the earth*, and plenty of Leviticus downstairs, too, *When any man has a discharge from his body, his discharge is unclean...And every saddle on which the person with the discharge rides becomes unclean*, but upstairs is frontier unmapped by God.

Upstairs is shabby, though not tawdry, and there is very little money in view, in fact none that she can see, and she hears no talk of money, though there must be plenty about, as several women have boys writhing in their laps and certainly they are being paid for these hilarious displays of bodice-ripper romance which no one that she can see is taking very sexually, and certainly not personally.

Upstairs there is a stage too, but it is long and L-shaped and without poles, more a runway for models, and used that way by the men, a lot of cock-of-the-walk strutting, amused, ironic, and then a retreat and a chair brought on up and then, like dancing with a broom, there is the lap-dance with a chair, and finally, finally, an ecstatic group of young women manage to rustle a bride-to-be up onto the stage where she is sat giddily down and then much moved upon by the dancer, his vigorous legs astride her, the loose silken purse of his genitalia in her lap.

She knows a poem in which a poet writes about the desire to take his infant son's genitals in his mouth, not in any furtive act of fellatio, but rather as an expression—a measure—of overwhelming love and protectiveness.

She admires the bravery of penning the fullest measure of the heart, the bravery of throwing down into shards the tea set of moral convention and saying, "It is my heart that is exquisite, it is my heart!"

She understands the response of the mouth, the desire to take the child back into one's body, the terror that he is his own body now, sovereign—the terror that he is not yet his own body and may never actually be.

When she was eighteen years old, standing in a post office in San Francisco, she had turned to see a line out onto Fillmore Street, a line of boys, uncharacteristically boy-like, subdued, quiet-eyed, and she had finally asked the pudgy, pale-faced one behind her why they were all there and he had said, "registering for Selective Service," in as manly a voice as he could muster. The war was Vietnam and the reports were getting uglier and America was coming around to the idea that it was losing—a truth that just didn't have a thing to wear from the wardrobe of National regalia.

She is not alone upstairs, would not have come here alone; doesn't look for trouble in those ways. He is with her, has ordered drinks, is smoking, his hand holding his cigarette the way his hand always holds his cigarette, snug against the knuckles of his middle fingers, the fingers fanned, his eyes narrowed looking out over his fanned fingers. He is not uncomfortable but he's not all that interested, either, and this compels her. He has gay friends, so there is some other issue at work upstairs, perhaps only that he could be downstairs watching comely young women take their clothes off, something she doesn't blame him for liking—something she isn't particularly threatened by. Wouldn't he be dead if he didn't like that? She'd rather he not be dead.

Nonetheless, a snarly, odd tension insinuates itself between them: "Do you want to leave?" she asks, but not very seriously; they have just arrived. The table is loaded with drinks, a tip tray, her purse, his lighter, his cigarettes. It's like their nightstand in the hotel room; it looks like they've settled in. He is the only fully attired male in the room—or actually, there is a DJ who seems dressed, but he is up a plywood ramp, elevated with the sound system in a wire cage, and so not so much a part of the room as he is a surveillant orchestrator. "We can leave," she says. "It would be all right," she adds.

"When you're ready," he says, but how it has become all about her, her desires, she can't exactly figure. She wouldn't even know about this club if it weren't for him, and she assumes they are here because of curiosity on his part—their part—not something expressly for her. If it is expressly for her, this trek down the strip past the famous casinos, well into the older, more somber blocks, she'd like to be in on the planning next time! Of course, she'd gone along, said sure, let's see what it's all about. She's wearing black, sling-back heels. She hadn't expected the club to be such a hike. It was windy outside, desert windy, that dry mausoleum chill the desert blows and she is still a little unnerved, spooked, the chill weird for June. In her head were the cabbie's words from the airport, "Vegas is the safest town in America."

"Like Little Italy in New York," she joked.

"Yeah," he said, craning up his head to the rearview mirror as though a woman who joked about power politics and human malice deserved a look. "Just like Little Italy."

The dancer is dark-haired, of medium build, and he runs his hand down her back, a tickle really, like a brother coming up behind and saying hello with his fingers. He leans over and whispers in her ear, "whenever you're ready," and the waggish frisson of his hand on her back could make her ready, she muses…but ready for what?

She watches the dancer as he walks off, the saunter and occasional pivot in and around chairs, tables, his hand feathered across a bare, muscled back, perhaps his own lover toiling over a woman. There is something vaguely petulant in the hitch and glide of his walk, something seductive, but not conjured for her, though if she's caught up in his sweep, that's fine by him—it's a show, for God's sake, a show, and so she'll watch, sure she'll watch, amused, protective—she likes this easy affection within the multiplicity of sexualities.

"Whenever you're ready…"

"When you're ready…" and she realizes both her lover and the dancer have said almost precisely the same thing to her, Whenever you're ready to leave, Whenever you're ready to have a lap dance.

Strangely, the idea of motherhood occurs to her, ready for mother-hood.

Tonight, before leaving their room for dinner and the clubs, he had switched on the television. A woman named Andrea Yates was in the news. She had given birth to five children in seven years, five children whom she had drowned earlier in the day one after another in a bathtub in Texas, and later today, not much later, the news showed a sidewalk of Texan women screaming for Andrea Yates to be "fried." These women on the television screen were plump and blonde and fiercely righteous in their insistence. "Fry her!" they screamed in the bright Texas daylight. "Fry her!"

In this dim room upstairs in Las Vegas there are women screaming all around her, boys riding their laps—these women are screaming with laughter, some beast unleashed in their hearts, too. *Whenever you're ready for a lap dance*, the boys are offering, *Whenever you're ready to leave*, her lover says, and above the huge electrical emission of the room she hears the voices of the Texan women, *Fry her,* they scream, *Fry her.*

She thinks about the colloquialism "to fry" for electrocution, the odd disparity between their righteousness and the slang they use to insist upon it. She assumes these women do not know that *fry* also means children, human offspring, *small fry.* "Children her," these women are screaming, "children her! Give her young ones, give her spawn!"

She might be included in this fury, she, a woman sitting in a strip club in Las Vegas watching beautiful young men hustle their bodies. *Fry her,* they might scream, because she feels no need to ask the question so earnestly voiced on the news: How could a mother murder her children? The more she learned about the case, standing in their hotel room, her eyes fixed on the television screen, the icier her clarity became.

There's footage of Russell Yates holding a press conference, his coolness, his righteousness, his religion. She thinks, it took this extreme act on his wife's part to make him listen and yet still he speaks, the mikes all held out to him, the notepads filling up with his words. But there were earlier notepads filled up with Andrea Yates' words, her confession which she gave summarily, simply, which child she had drowned first, Paul, and then which next, Luke, and then John, and how old they were, and how she had laid them under a maroon blanket on the bed, though not the baby, who she left floating face-down in the tub as she drowned the last and oldest son, Noah, *blameless in his time*, but drowned nonetheless. How grisly a detail, the one girl, Mary, a six-month old infant, left to float beside her oldest brother, and why, after the other three had been laid out neatly on the bed?

When her lover leans across to ask her if she'd like a lap dance, no matter how ludicrous the notion is to her, it is, disturbingly, one of those moments in a relationship, one of those beginning-of-the-end moments, if either partner were to allow it to drive its tiny wedge. She can hear the words spoken tearfully to friends: "it seemed like a good idea at the time, or not a good idea, but something different, fun, a lark, for Christ's sake—it was a lark." She can imagine that the image of an essentially naked man moving over her body pushed deeper and deeper into the chair would be an image he couldn't shake, an image his heart had no accommodation for, and she thinks this is true whether he loves her or not. She thinks he doesn't know this about himself. He asks about the lap dance as though he were asking about her desire for another drink, the lap dance and the offerings of the bar unnervingly equal in the register of his voice and she can't think of anything she would find more absurd than this mock display of heated-up love-making happening athwart her legs. She laughs. "I don't think I'm up for that, but more to the point, are you?"

"Yeah," he says. *Yeah*, but it's hardly an affirmative, it's actually a *maybe* or an *I don't know*. She wants to meddle with this confusion, wants to challenge him to understand the treachery of his offer and the menace of what would arise were she to take him up on it.

She looks across at him and he immediately looks down, laughs at himself. "Just being polite," he says.

"Maybe?" she says.

Walking toward her is a new dancer on the floor, tall, slender.

"He's pretty beautiful," she says, and somehow her words are audible within the electronic din, dropping straight onto the dancer's ears. His arms are astride the chair before she can hold her hands up to say, "No, you're like a page in a magazine; I was just admiring the pulchritude." His lips are whispering something near her cheek, a price no doubt, some initial words of instruction. It is not intended that she actually understand his words. She knows why the women around her are laughing hysterically; this is all so ridiculous, this long, tall drink of water doing push-ups, using the chair arms as support, bringing his face down to hers, then pulled back up as his arms straighten—he's been in the military, he's carrying out orders, she's given the orders, fifty push-ups on the double, that sort of scenario, and it's in play before she can even pull it together enough to resist, before she can say, no, really, militaristic domination is not my thing. Jesus, she thinks, not at all, and she starts to be disturbed by how the dancers are reading them. She can't turn her head to signal for help before the dancer's face is once again in hers. The room is smoky, but she can smell him, soap and water and a unisex scent from one of the corporate clothing stores, J. Crew or Banana Republic, not an over-powering men's cologne, and not floral. "I could be your mother," she says to him, and just as quickly realizes the bizarre attempt at shaming him that that comment is, but in his eyes is a look of inter-est, and once again the affection she has been observing ever since they arrived. She wonders what his childhood has been like, this young male beauty. He couldn't have had a particularly happy one if he'd washed up in these shoals, not necessarily her thighs, she doesn't mean that, but this entire shabby enterprise of enticement. Fine by me that you could be my mother, his eyes say, gladdening, all the better, his eyes say, *we're not exactly invested in doing things the usual way here*, and as he raises himself she turns, in time to see a look of unchecked disgust in her partner's eyes, and the dancer, as attuned to a vibe as anyone can possibly be, springs up and away and is as briskly somewhere else as he was initially so briskly doing push-ups on the arms of her chair. "Whenever…" he drones slowly over his shoulder, "you just signal." Lose the ball and chain, his flattened inflection says, lose the breeder.

She laughs and as she's laughing she knows this may be a fatal error, to laugh, and yet, what isn't risible here? She's come by his behest to a strip club in Vegas…of course, she thinks, of course her willingness may be her fatal error, her laughing willingness. The tall dancer turns his face back over his shoulder, fixes her with his flashing eyes, and calls—his voice lilting into the din—words she can't distinguish, isn't—once again—supposed to.

"Anyone else you want to bring down upon yourself?" he asks with good humor, as deft a revision of the earlier disgust in his eyes as he can manage. And he *is* deft, smart, appalled at himself, can't help it, he might be thinking, don't mean it, he might be insisting, I love you, he might be pleading. "That one over there isn't bad," and he nods his chin at a tightly wound blond dancer about to swing up on stage.

"You a small piece of leather but you well put together," a busboy used to say to her, and this dancer is precisely that, as he gazes at the floor, smoothing violet fringe down along the legs of his ultra-suede chaps. His hair has fallen into his eyes, where he leaves it, looks out through it across the stage, a brattiness in his face she couldn't like, couldn't be attracted to. He reaches up and tweaks his nipples viciously, licks the palm of one hand, getting into it, the palm of the other, then slaps his naked buttocks—bare haunches—"Yee haw! Let's ride! It's Showtime—Let the nipples be erect!" And he's up on stage, purple fringe flying, a red imprint of his hand on one cheek, he's leaning over, sassing the audience with his ass, and then he twitches the other cheek at the audience and it too is emblazoned with the angry red imprint of a hand.

Violet Chaps is a different show than the boys before, he's all about himself, and he does his dance churning deeper and deeper into himself—no woman is brought on stage—he is there for viewing and then the chaps go flying and beneath the nylon or Qiana thong his penis is full long, adamantine beneath its thin sheath, and the room begins to change.

Rachel Resnick
Meat-Eaters of Marrakesh

W hen I reach for Frank's hand and that hand is not there, is instead tucked inside one of his hidden Willis & Geiger poplin adventure coat pockets fingering some of his stash, habitually plying for wetness—I can hear the stiff crackling of plastic between notes from the cobra charmer's flute, the crinkle of foil, or coarse paper, the muted come-hither rustle of pill against pill, tablet upon tablet, moist crumbling of dung-style opium, the promise of oblivion and answered need, *not mine, not mine to answer*—when the press of bodies all around us becomes a breath-skinned constrictor that desires to squeeze the very fluids from our viscera, I feel a jerk at my elbow, hear a gargled voice, a hiss, but say nothing, not even when a low cry escapes Frank as he sinks, sinks! glorious defeat of the all-too familiar body which torments as it pleasures, I believe I can even hear the proud steroidal muscles sigh as bunching down they hit the dust of Marrakesh, and Frank's cry is immediately swallowed by more hissing and the distant drumbeats of leprous tribesmen, the stomps and claps of midget acrobats as they form human pyramids to jeer in their own unintelligible clicking language, and "good price" chanted by small women no older than twelve with eyes of dust who weave carpets until their fingers and eyes leak blood, and I, rejoicing, watch all this dissipate in the twisted columns of oily smoke from the food stalls where earlier Frank ate a plate of lamb brain, sopping it up with a torn crust of bread, his mouth transformed into maggotry, into a portal of decay and insatiability; is it any wonder that I now turn and grind my foot into Frank's hand until I hear the concertina of cracking bone before I reach down to help him up with great delicacy of gesture and intention, only to bury my fists in his eye sockets once he is standing, then digging further into the cranial playroom itself, there to cop a feel of his beloved addict's brain, one little affectionate squeeze, knowing nothing except that we are everything and nothing together and I am damned, damned to the bone—my anxious pelvis a shark's gaping jawbone—eternally and with all due disdain, because I cannot erase the vision of two bodies rising, hers and his, his and his, always his and someone's, falling, nor fathom the way I want to think of them in the Kasbah, the way I want to smell each and every smell, from cured goatskin to sewage, from almond soap scum to yeasty orgasmic juices, see each item in the ritual room as it held its fetid breath for the ancient spectacle of the oldest duet, I want to hear the stupid things they whispered, how their bodies slapped and sucked away the two-timed sweat, the way the world's clock cracked its sixty knuckles against their one-two skin and beat mine a shiny purple while I slept in cretinous innocence in the Hotel Amalay around the corner, I confess I am perversely mesmerized by their beasting need, the enormous banality of betrayal, and must play it back again and again until it becomes pornography and me the Fecal Eye that shits in its Sacred Cunt.

It happened in Marrakesh. In the filthy square of Djemaa el-Fna. On a Saturday, the day the Saadians customarily used to display the heads of their enemies by skewering them on iron stakes arranged artfully around the perimeter. The gore would slide down the red walls to form viscous puddles which were boiled away by the sun within the hour, and baked deep into the walls. From anywhere in the square, you knew you were being watched.

Through the corridor of hanging meat they had come into the square of Djemaa el-Fna. Dust boiled, stirred up by stagnant gusts of words, the flatulence of constipated Arabs. Frank stopped at a food stall selling dates. There were dozens of different kinds. Cora calculated they hadn't fucked since Tiznit, ten days ago. And not for two months before that. A date the color of topaz tasted like caramel. Frank preferred the meaty dark ones the color and sheen of New York cockroaches. He bought a dozen roach style, a couple topaz. Even in Tiznit, Cora was sure, Frank had been thinking of someone else when he had fucked her. Like this one. The girl who walked by, giggling with her friend, swaying back to look at Frank as he grinned openly at her, the girl who walked by and stopped at an orange juice stall, to look, her full teenage breasts straining at the cheap shiny fabric of a modern Western-style shirt knotted at her belly so the ample hips and rounded ass could swing free in their tight acetate nightclub black trousers that showed her panty line and the lips of her vagina as she stopped, leaning against her friend, looking, responding to the unspoken language of desire and lust, of need and compliance. Frank had a hard-on. She could tell. Thwarted lust lent Cora mind-reading capabilities, only more; she could actually shrink down, enter Frank's skull, pull the skin over like a snug rubber bathing cap and settle in, like now, for the satyr's ride. The Codeine Maroc was kicking in. She even felt it, her skin being permeable when it came to Frank. She knew he was thinking right now, *Fuck Cora. He liked the girl. She liked him. He figured young whore fronting as virgin. He figured thirty U.S. dollars. Who was it who'd staked the whole trip? Him. Frank. Every red cent. Not fucking Cora. He was bigger than every Moroccan man he'd seen yet. His guns, his abs, his dick, his delts, his brain. Far bigger. He would push the girl to her knees, gather the girl's hair away from her face so Cora could see. He would make Cora watch the girl suck his cock.*

In Ouarzazate, where the world-famous rose water is made, there was a cookie named:
    EAT THIS *&* PRAISE ALLAH.
    Eat this and shit.

The cookie tasted like dust with a few drops of honey.

So many things were wrong.

In the African light, images grew, tubers that would burst from the dark damp soil of your chest, where the rot begins.

Cora sees: the meat is on the hook. Hanging. Skin flayed and stripped to expose magnificent marbling of creamy rat color. And muscular red meat—only in this case, the fat is discolored yellow with orange pustules and the meat is decidedly green—not a uniform green, but pale pistachio at the edges and extending into a sodden green—for the meat, you realize, is rotting before your eyes; the stench is so incomprehensibly vile that at first the brain rebels, proclaiming the putrid scent sweet before the truth assaults the nostrils and one reels backwards.

Poppies. A red minaret. The color of your tongue. You understand now?

Frank stopped at a food stall selling lamb brains. The brains were displayed on thick white ceramic plates. They were putty-colored and looked wet under the single acetylene bulb. The Moroccan boy at the stall grinned at Cora. "My friend!" he called out, addressing Frank. They never addressed Cora. "Big welcome!" One front tooth was gone, the other was decorated with a uvula of brown rot. The Invisible, despised by God the Grand Gynecologist and spurned by the man she craved, loathed by even crawling things, otherwise known as Cora, shifted her gaze from the Moroccan's face to the massive vat barely visible behind him. The water was at a roil and large bubbles were constantly forming. In the queer light of dusk, she thought she saw human heads bobbing to the surface, glaring at her, then sinking again. The bubbles grew and darkened at their crowns. The heads were snorting their indignation. One seemed to bob up more frequently than the others and she thought she recognized something in the baleful cast of the eye. A familiar hunger. But that could have been a trick of the light. The light was tricky in Morocco, casting shadows where there was no reason for a shadow.

"We can wash this filth away, we can erase the dust. I will hold the nozzle over your head," Frank had said in some shit Moroccan hotel, somewhere.

These were the bright ideas born of bellies full of couscous, the stimulation of images that no longer mirrored but did remind one of the libidinal and mutual grooming possibilities before stasis—before damage.

Frank sat abruptly on a wooden bench padded with a few sheets of folded newspaper, pulling Cora down beside him. The Moroccan scraped two lobes off a plate and into a bowl, placed it before Frank along with a disk of Arab bread.

"Have a bite," he said. Cora refused, as Frank had known she would and Cora had known she would. More fucking Puritanism, the great American virus. It was becoming increasingly clear they did not share the same appetites. "Minarets scar the landscape," she thought she said. "They rise like brittle fungus. Bony stems that have lost their bloom." While Frank fell to eating, Cora watched as the Moroccan withdrew a skewer from the sheep's eye socket and hooked another sheep's head from the vat and set it steaming on a board.

"This square is famous," she said flatly, and he conceded nothing with a liquid grunt.

Imagine how the Saadian slave climbs out to the stake holding the head in a golden towel. Imagine him grasping the freshly decapitated head by the temples and plunging it down on the stake until he hears the thud of the skull crown meeting bone, but this time, he pierces the head. What a glorious shattering! A geyser of blood plumes forth, dousing all the lucky ones who have pressed the closest, trampled the many. Where would Cora be in this eager crowd?

Meanwhile the Moroccan, with a sly glance at Cora, drew back the boiled lips of the lamb's head and exposed the teeth. In Cora's discomfort and dimly sensed foreboding, she noted the lamb had an overbite, a clear case of it, and might have benefited from braces, if indeed they masticated the same way as humans. The boy leered at her, running his tongue along the bottom of his upper teeth, causing her to indulge in a fantasy replete with filth and disease and sublime degradation. When that faded, which was rapid, she could no longer deny the stronger vision: there was a spider that had appeared at the lamb's dental gates and stared at her in his radiant magnificence for a full eternal moment, before he retreated to shield her from certain blindness at such a holy vision. What had it meant? Frank was nothing more than a slurping sound; she did not look at him, not daring to look away from lamb or boy.

Before Marrakesh, they had driven all over the south of Morocco. From Agadir, where Frank's wallet was stolen, to Tiznit to Adai to Tafraoute, on to Ouarzazate and Todra Gorge, then Erfoud, through Berber villages. They had even ridden dromedaries through the drifting Saharan dunes of Erg Chebbi at sunrise, on Cora's insistence, but all she could remember was the corpse women. They had passed briefly through one village—she couldn't recall whether it was before or after Erfoud or closer to Tiznit and she couldn't recall the name—where all the women were covered from head to foot in black. Not even their eyes peered out from a medieval slit as she had seen in other villages. Even Frank had been unsettled by the sight, and drove faster; but Cora didn't stop watching until the last silent black-shrouded woman faded into the dusty background.

The boy released his filthy fingers and let the lips slide slowly back into place, at which point he buried the knife in the skull and began to slice. As he did so, the boiled ears flopped, and steam rose in a halo from its head. Cora found herself laughing. She did not respond to Frank's irritable, "What?" A lasciviousness gilded the Moroccan's lips as he continued to carve. She was unsafe, that was what was going on, she had been given a warning, she was in jeopardy. Cora reached out her hand to grab Frank's thickly muscled thigh, but when he turned his face to her his eyes were shining with gastronomic opiated bliss and a bit of brain clung to his upper lip where it glistened like a milky white maggot.

"Last chance," Frank said, pushing the bowl toward her. There was no choice but to watch the boy.

The Moroccan stared at Cora while he cut. She looked at his fingers, saw the black filth gestating beneath his critical nails, the black filth growing in spirals from his knotted knuckles. She thought about how she'd been warned to use only her right hand in public because the Moroccans wiped their asses with the left. It was true, there had been little sign of toilet paper, and what passed for napkins were paper-thin tissues that disintegrated with the least bit of pressure. The skull fell apart. The spell was broken, though Cora continued to watch and shrank away from Frank as much as she could without him noticing. The boy removed the brain and arranged it on another plate, patting it into place as he displayed the plate at the front of the stall. Then he scraped the interior of the head and shook the results into a cone of wax paper. A young Arab couple sat down to their left and spoke rapidly. The woman was wearing a traditional djellabah, but the more modern thin silky kind that actually revealed much of the body, unlike the coarse, shapeless ones favored by the fanatics. Like most women with the sexy djellabahs, she wore cheesy platforms with gold anklets, and Cora could see sleazy red leggings flash beneath the hem. The boy handed them two plates and the cone of wax paper. Still holding hands, the couple both unwrapped the paper and liquefied the face meat with misshapen lust. Frank pushed the empty plate away and stood up.

"Let's blow this pop stand."

The dust was in Cora's ears, funneling. Filth demanded so much. A greasy gray cloud of smoke and cumulus hovered over the square, and she could hear the meat hooks twisting, the damp and sadistic footfalls of desiccated feet and dry-cracked heels storing extra rations of dirt in every crevice. Tearing free of Frank's side she glided down a side alley. Crooked pieces of wood above hung with green plastic, the African sun gilding the filthy walls with false moss, she moved underwater into the medieval, and slowly, the crowds dispersed, and more slowly, the street narrowed until she came to a dead end and above her was one tiny window placed high in the center of a building, and the window was barred, and inside she could hear the keening cry of a woman, perhaps a small woman, she must have worn bracelets or anklets for there was the sound of mad jingling before the keening cry turned to a wail, then cut off. It was then Cora saw the narrow dark entrance to her right, which she took, squeezing her body between the walls, having trouble finding her footing as the ground became more pitted and pooled with foul liquids. At one point, the walls pressed against her ribs and she had to duck, and there was no light anymore. Then the alley gave way into a crude room with a roll of bedding on the floor, a dirty Berber carpet and a pot full of couscous with a boiled lamb's head leering from the center, its teeth like rows of dice. On the wall was a cheap satin Raiders jacket hanging on a nail, and a framed photograph of Johnny Cash. A hand reached out and touched her leg, eyes glittered. It was the boy from the lamb brain stall, but he was younger, much younger. A small man. She shuddered from his touch, and he grew younger still as he groped between her legs; she had not been touched for so long, the filth was warm and damp, then warmer, and damper, until soon he was a wanton child wailing.

Palms. A white wall. The blankness of your face.

Through the corridor of hanging meat they came, into the square of Djemaa el-Fna. Knuckles and hooves and glorious shanks of thigh meat dangling like earrings from iron hooks. Chopped hearts, strangled chickens with bound feet, harpooned bladders, spiny pimply-skinned stomach linings draped over stalls, testicles garlanded over stalls. There were festoons of tripe—Hawaiian leis of tripe—and picture this—the most splendid sight of all, an upside down bouquet, a chandelier of bloody lamb's heads, twisting in the clear African light.

I turn and grind my foot into your outstretched hand until I hear the concertina of cracking bone before I reach down to help you up, knowing nothing more than we are nothing and everything together and I am damned. It is at this point that what connects a man to a woman collapses into the unspeakable filth of a Berber toilet. I stand with splayed legs, each foot firmly planted in the ceramic footholds with the well of filth beneath me, exhale the possibilities in one silvery globuled stream until it disappears in the hole of iniquity. It is a peerless depth that is not even shallow that is woman.

You understand now?

liz gonzález
Destiny

Lu, the famous underground performance artist and palm reader, read my future to me last night. The avant-garde composer who lives in the apartment above me had a party for his artsy friends and Lu came and read palms for five bucks a palm. For most of the night she sat outside on the balcony in a Morticia Addams wicker chair, smoking pink and gold cigarettes, her wild, violet hair springing from her head. One by one, performance artists, experimental writers and musicians, dressed dumpy, thrift-store style or L.A.-trendy, closed the sliding glass door behind them, spread their palm beneath her large, violet contact-tinted eyes, and listened to their destinies.

When it was my turn, I told her to check out my romance line. I've been lonely lately. The last time I met a guy who could keep me listening longer than five minutes was six months ago, and he turned out to be a liar. Lu held my writing hand in her chubby fingers. Her hot-pink nail polish stood out against her white, freckled skin, and the little palm trees painted on her thumbnails waved back and forth as she quickly rubbed her thumbs on my palm. After a minute of rubbing, she lifted my now warm, damp palm under the heat of the yellow bug light in the lamp on the table between us. In her chirpy, almost too happy voice, she went over the usual money line, lifeline stuff, taking a drag on her cigarette every now and then. After she finished telling me I wasn't going to be rich, but I wasn't going to be poor, and I'd live a moderately healthy life until at least eighty, she finally got to my love line. "You're going to meet the love of your life when you're in your forties. You'll have dual careers at that time too." As she scanned my palm with her eyes, the scent of musty sweat wafted from her tight, hot-pink mandarin dress. She leaned close to me and with a serious voice said, "Wait until then to get married, or you'll change the course of your path."

I wanted to ask her more, to find out what the dual careers meant, but there was a crowd in the living room waiting to see her. I stepped back into the party wondering if I had to wait until I got married to have sex again. I'm not going to be in my forties for another ten years.

Two months ago, I went to see a psychic-healer who lives four and a half blocks from my place here in Lincoln Heights. Every day on the way to my teller job on the West Side, I drive by her broken-down Victorian house with the paint peeling off and a warped front porch. A huge white sign leans against the front wall, "psychic-healer" painted on it in dark, purple-red capital letters. No matter if it's raining or super-hot, there are always people standing around on the porch, like they're waiting for the psychic-healer. I asked the avant-garde composer about the house and he told me he'd heard the psychic-healer is a woman who casts spells, and that she specialized in love spells. Well, after hearing that, I wanted to pay her a visit, but I was a little hesitant since I didn't know anyone who had actually seen her.

On one of those unusually blue, smog-free Saturdays in East L.A., I realized that I couldn't face eating another breakfast-in-bed alone and decided to walk up the hills in my neighborhood and find out if the psychic-healer had a love spell for me. I figured I'd tried everything else—online dating, blind dates, sitting for hours at a café pretending to read a heady novel by some famous foreign author—I might as well give the psychic-healer a shot. And I wanted to find out how she cast spells.

The wooden screen door looked like it was ready to fall off and rattled when I knocked on the splintering frame. A tiny blur appeared on the other side of the rusty, sooty screen.

"I'm looking for the psychic-healer," I said.

"I am the psychic-healer," a high-pitched voice replied. A bony, very short girl who resembled a life-sized doll opened the screen door. She looked about sixteen, and I was surprised because the only healers I knew about were curanderas who were middle-aged or older. I wondered if she was for real but still wanted to check her out.

As I stepped inside, I got a glimpse of her right cheek, arm and hand. It looked like her skin had melted in a fire and remolded as it dried. I crossed my arms and squeezed them to keep from cringing. She turned and walked slowly to the back of the house. From behind, she looked like a little old lady. She had her hair woven in a long braid dangling down her back, and she wore a loose-fitting brown cotton dress that hung down to her ankles.

I followed her through the bare entryway, down a hall. The smell of rotted wood and stale air hit my nose, and I started breathing through my mouth. Sunlight snuck through the dirt-coated windows, shining on the yellowed, ripped wallpaper that looked as old as the house. Dust balls and faded confetti floated on the scuffed, dirty hardwood floors as I walked down the hall. The place was completely quiet; I couldn't even hear sounds from the busy street.

She led me into a bedroom that was empty except for an altar that took up an entire wall, ceiling to floor, corner to corner. Lit candles, ceramic saints, rusting coffee cans filled with yellow and pink roses, and crumpled photos of sick or dead loved ones left behind by the people who had visited before me cluttered the altar. The psychic-healer rushed over to one of the shelves and fixed a picture that had fallen face down. A thick smell of burning dust, melting wax, and wilting flowers stifled the air. About a hundred candles flickered from red and blue votives, brass candleholders, and coffee mugs labeled with business logos like Clinica de Mujeres, Wu Chan Funeral Directors,

Chi Massage School, and Barborossa Brokers. Crackling, snapping sounds burst from the altar, like the fire wanted to reach out and catch on something. Instinctively, I pulled my long hair back in a ponytail.

The psychic-healer stood in front of the altar with her head bowed and her hands clasped, praying to a black Virgin Mary the size of a Barbie doll. I hung out in the doorway, away from the fire, thinking about the psychic-healer. I figured she probably identified with the Black Virgin. When I was a kid, my grandpa told me some Catholics believe Black Virgins are more sacred than White Virgins, and sometimes white Virgins turned black from all the smoke in the churches.

I wondered how the psychic-healer could stand so close to the altar of fire. I thought the heat from the flames must hurt her crinkled skin. But as she stood there, the flames seemed to calm down and stop bouncing from the wicks. But as soon as she stood there, the flames seemed to calm down and stop bouncing from the wicks, as though she had somehow stilled the flames. I became lost in my thoughts and mesmerized by the altar. She startled me a little when, without turning to look at me, she called me to her side, the burned side. More curious than leery about what was going to happen next, I joined her.

"Why did you come here today?" she said, without any feeling in her voice, keeping her eyes on the Black Virgin. Now that I was closer to it, I saw that the virgin was made of black stone. She looked cool to the touch, even though fire surrounded her. I figured that maybe the psychic-healer prayed to her to feel cool too.

"I want a spell that will bring me a man." I just told her straight; she's used to people wanting love spells.

"It'll be forty dollars, twenty now and twenty when you come back," she said in a business-is-business manner.

"Okay." I wasn't sure if I wanted to come back yet, but I could afford to give up twenty dollars to find out about her spell. And from the way her house looked, she needed the money. So, I took my wallet out of my back pocket and handed her a twenty.

"You must follow these directions exactly and in the order they are written, or it won't work," she said in the same business-is-business tone. With her crooked hand, she pulled out a broken pencil and a scrap of paper from a pocket in her skirt and rapidly scrawled some words on the paper. Orange light splashed across our faces as the psychic-healer held the paper out to the Black Virgin like an offering and said the directions aloud.

"For seven days, save the water that runs off your breasts when you shower. On the eighth day, at dusk, return here. As night stains the sky, we will light a candle below the saint of love's toes." She pointed her jagged index finger at a chipped and cracked cherub in robes and explained the ritual.

"I'll pour the water you bring into the flower cans and pray, face down on the floor, until sunrise." She lay down, the front of her body flat against the filthy floor, her right cheek pressed to the ground, and spread her arms out like wings in flight, or Jesus on the cross, and continued to describe the procedure. Her voice squeaked even more than before, as though the turn of her neck had twisted her vocal cords.

Within two weeks, a man I could tolerate enough to fall in love with was supposed to come into my life. I didn't know if I was going to go through with it, but I told her I'd be back. As I pulled open the front screen door to leave, she handed me a quart-sized nopales jar and told me I had to use it for the water. The jar didn't have a label and was super-clean, which reminded me of how doctors use sterilized tools on patients. She also instructed me to bring a newly printed twenty-dollar bill when I returned.

I had planned to go to one of my favorite Mexican or Chinese restaurants on the main street after my visit with the psychic-healer, but after all that trippiness, I wanted a treat and headed toward the drug store for a chocolate-chip ice cream cone. While walking to the store, I remembered a story that my mother's friend, Mrs. Mendoza, had told me about an old woman she used to know by the name of Sra. Rosales. When she was real young, Sra. Rosales eloped with an older man who turned out to be a drunk. Every night she walked down to the corner bar to pull him off some woman's neck and drag him out.

After a few years of that mess, she got fed up and went to see a curandera to put a spell on him so he'd stay home. The curandera instructed her to clip off some of his pubic hair, collect his earwax on the tip of her bobby pin, and wrap them up with her wedding band in a pair of his underwear. A few days later, Sra. Rosales returned to the curandera's with the list of items, along with an empty bottle of his favorite brand of beer.

Together, they laid out each item separately in the curandera's cactus garden. The curandera bent down on her knees and chanted the rosary over them. Next, she made an herbal solution with the hair and wax and swirled it inside the beer bottle. The woman had to swallow the brew without taking a breath. When they finished the ritual, the curandera told Sra. Rosales to go home and her husband would be in his easy chair waiting for her.

She found him slouched in the chair, passed out. While she was gone, he had suffered a stroke and sat there for an hour without any help. He ended up like a baby and Sra. Rosales spent the following forty-three and a half years taking care of him.

I hadn't really thought about how badly the spell backfired on Sra. Rosales until I was on my walk to the drug store from the psychic-healer's. The nopales jar started to feel uncomfortable in my hand, like it had a bad vibe or was cursed or something. I got scared that I might have jinxed my future just by going to see the psychic-healer.

When I reached the store, I went around to the back and threw the nopales jar hard in an empty dumpster, wanting it to break. Shattering, tinkling sounds shot out from the bin. I darted inside the drug store and ordered a triple scoop of chocolate chip. I took a big lick of the ice cream to calm down and vowed to never go back to see the psychic-healer.

Now, alone in bed again with real maple syrup and fresh strawberries on my made-from-scratch pancakes, something that happened at the end of the party last night comes to mind. I had gone into the kitchen to get away from two guys that wouldn't stop talking to me about some supposedly happening Italian sound artist who tape records the insides of eggs and seashells. I had the kitchen to myself and was pouring a kiwi-pineapple-cranberry-vodka drink somebody had made in the blender, when Lu, the palm reader, walked in. She came over beside me and poured herself a glass of water. Her skin looked paler, more wrinkled in the glare of the kitchen light. And she acted older, wiser, not so airy. She gulped her water down, and then held out her hand in front of me.

"A year ago, the doctor told me I had to have a liver transplant, or I wouldn't live much longer. My lifeline was cut in half." She poked her long, curled fingernail into a pink root on her palm. "Last month I discovered this." She dragged her fingernail across the crevice. "I went back to the doctor and all my tests came out negative. It's as though I was never sick."

Lu dug through her bag, brought out a small stack of her business cards, placed them on the counter in front of me, and told me that the lines on a palm change every ten months. When she left the room, I picked one up. It had a hand-drawn palm tree in the center. I grabbed two more and stuck them in my back pocket.

As I bite into the last strawberry on my plate, I realize something. Just like I make my ritual breakfasts-in-bed to put energy out in the universe to bring me a boyfriend, there are no spells involved when someone reads my palm. I won't be playing with my future if I see Lu; I'll just be aware of whatever's coming up, so I can be ready. I believe fate happens to those who are open to it. And I have to know that a dual career doesn't mean mother and wife. Besides, I'm burnt out on trying to bring someone to me. Maybe in ten months something much better than a man might show up in my hand.

Anita Santiago
Flying Blind

I rma Magdalena has just placed the last jar of special rose jelly on her stand at the foot of the Guacharo Cave in Caripe, and is breathing in the morning air, when a brown Buick pulls up.

"Ah," she thinks, "the tourists are early today." She expects to see a family, but instead a young American man gets out and nods at her.

"Howdy," he says. Irma Magdalena feels the skin on the front of her neck turn hot, like a salamander changing to red. She is normally shy around Americans, but still she is taken aback by the intensity of her reaction. This is not appropriate for a married woman, but there is something about this man that instantly unsettles her.

"Buenos días, hello," she says, embarrassed at her double greeting, embarrassed that she used both languages. But the man does not notice. He looks up at the huge mouth of the cave and lets out a soft whistle. The cave is majestic, looming high on a hill, the arch of its upper lip blistering with wild purple and white orchids, frilly and intoxicating.

"Whew, it's gorgeous," he says. "Long trip, but it's worth it."

Irma Magdalena wonders why he came alone, and whether he has anyone else in the world. He seems eager to enter the cave, to come into immediate contact with it. As he gathers his hat from the car, he says to her, "Longest cave in the world, you know. No one has ever seen the end."

Irma Magdalena has lived in Caripe all her life, but she did not know that. He has never been here before, and already he knows something about the cave that she does not. He must be an engineer, like so many of the Americans who come to Venezuela for the petroleum. She knows that Americans like facts, and she decides to accept this one as a gift.

She watches him approach the cave, ducking and swaying through buzzing swarms of tiny agitated insects attracted by the orchids. She considers what he said. Where does the cave end? Is it infinite like the universe, or does it suddenly surface again abruptly in the middle of the Amazon jungle, where no one will ever see it? Does the cave swirl around in spirals under her feet, reaching China, where perhaps they also have a cave with no known exit? Or does it come to an end in the deepest recesses of the earth, somewhere near Hell, convoluted like intestines? She imagines the *guacharos*, the millions of blind brown birds that exist only in this cave and nowhere else on earth, flying for kilometers in the dark, exhausting themselves as they search for a way out. No one knows where it ends. Irma Magdalena feels a certain satisfaction in knowing that she and the engineer are joined by their lack of information about this issue.

The engineer disappears into the shadows of the cave. She cranes her neck to see if he has really gone in alone. He has. She is the cave guide, she has a sign on her stand saying so, but he has not asked her for help. There is something different about the engineer compared to other tourists. He seemed too eager to enter the cave. Something in the way he approached it made him seem lost, as if he were looking for salvation inside.

She waits, hoping he will come out again quickly. She distracts herself by noticing the grass glowing with a subdued chlorophyllic green, dense with moisture, the scraggly hills baring a reddish soil on their cheeks and chins. This is her favorite time of day, when the trees look like they've been crying all night and the silence is dotted with the calls of distant roosters.

But soon she begins to worry about him. Men disappear into the cave just like he did, and never come back. Several years ago, three young men, equipped with the foolish will to conquer, went in and were swallowed by the cave. She thinks of them often, wondering if they are living in one of the subterranean chambers, swimming in the icy ponds or sitting at one of the structures shaped like tables and chairs that grow from the ground. She pictures them looking at the rivers and rivulets that crisscross the ground like wet roads where excited coppery centipedes travel. The cave is now their living room, and the lost men wander around sculptures of a woman weeping over a child, a gigantic elephant surprised by rain, a frozen field of lilies bending in one direction. By now, the lost men must know all the secrets of the *guacharos*, who have been put here by fate so that they can lull men to sleep with their moaning.

Irma Magdalena makes a living selling rose jelly to the American tourists who arrive in their big cars, and by guiding them on tours of the cave where she flashes a kerosene lamp around on the structures so they can see them. Local people do not go into the cave beyond the vast expanse of mud that guards the entrance. They've become unnerved by the sounds of grief that come from inside and they do not want the lost men to whisper in their ears.

Americans usually travel together, and Irma Magdalena now hears the soft hum of car engines pushing themselves up the mountain. She feels the cool blue breeze on her face, a breeze tinted with the smell of roses. All of Caripe smells this way, and it is a blessed scent, she knows, because it is the perfume of the Virgin. She straightens out her jars of rose jelly, admiring how beautifully they catch the morning light. She has cleaned them carefully, polishing the jars, because she knows that Americans are concerned about hygiene. The jars are all different sizes because it's difficult to get jars in Caripe. She wishes she could get back the jars she sells to the Americans after they have consumed her rose jelly, so she could refill and sell them again. But she knows that the jars will be going back down the mountain and far away, back to the petroleum camps where the Americans live.

A red Chevrolet arrives and gives a quick honk, piercing the calm. To Irma Magdalena this is very American. A man and woman get out, followed by two boys who scamper like lizards that have suddenly been freed from captivity. Another family arrives and looks expectantly at the cave. They may come here thinking the cave has been conquered by order and rules, by stairways and handrails. But it is just as raw as when it was discovered, a hundred years ago, by a German explorer whose name Irma Magdalena has written down on a paper so she can repeat it to the tourists: Alexander von Humboldt. This natural state makes the Americans pause, gather their children and peer into the cathedral entrance of the cave, trying to decide if they should go in. Because they are American and have seen so much, Irma Magdalena feels privileged to shed light on a world they haven't seen before.

The families come to her table. They seek contact with someone local, anyone, because the cave is too imposing to approach alone. She smiles at them. A woman picks up one of the jars of rose jelly.

"Rosas," Irma Magdalena says to the woman, "De yelly of rosas." Irma Magdalena knows enough English from years of guiding tourists, and she can usually read Americans well. The woman buys the jar and opens it. She dips her fingertip into the jelly and tastes it, exclaiming with delight. Irma Magdalena is pleased by her reaction. The jelly is surprising, offering the gentle but invasive essence of roses, something that is only known to people through smell, and the taste evolves from pink roses to a mild grassiness, to smoked wood, back to pink roses, as if giving the taster an encounter with Caripe itself.

Irma Magdalena points at the sign on her table. She made it with the help of an enterprising American woman who visited many months ago. It says: "See the Guacharo Cave with Irma Magdalena."

"Si de cave?" she says.

The Americans, in turn, cultivate amongst themselves some Spanish words. "Cuanto?" they say, "Cuanto dinero?" They want to know about the money because Americans like to be on firm ground when starting a relationship. She shrugs, to show that it really doesn't matter because it is an honor to guide them, but that being paid would be nice, and then holds up her hand, flicking it twice to indicate ten. Ten bolivares per family. This satisfies the Americans, and she can tell they feel safe together and with her as their guide. They talk to each other in waves of language, growing animated about the prospect of exploring the cave. Irma Magdalena is preparing her kerosene lamp when she notices the engineer stumbling awkwardly from the cave's dark mouth, blinking at the morning light as if awakening. Light glints off his spectacles. He points back at the cave.

"Where do they go? The bats?"

Bats. To Irma Magdalena, this sounds like a strange, harsh word. But she is touched that he thinks the *guacharos* are bats, and she understands that he could be disconcerted by their haunting wails. The word, and his question, make her feel foolish, and she suddenly wishes she knew where the clusters of *guacharos* go at night, and how they know it is nighttime if they are blind. She is a tour guide with no answers, and she feels important and ignorant at the same time.

The engineer clutches his binoculars, waiting for her answer. His hat has fallen back and hangs from a string around his neck; a notepad and a folded map poke out from his pocket. He seems prepared for life. It is true, she thinks, that Americans don't go anywhere without a map. Irma Magdalena pictures the engineer's home papered with maps, to get to the kitchen or the bedroom and back, and thinks how useful a map could be to the blind birds in the cave that spend their lives not finding things.

She shrugs her shoulders, and says, "*No sé.* Nobody knows." Not even the Americans know, she thinks. All she knows is that the *guacharos* are odd birds that leave the cave only at night. At least, that is what she has felt on sleepless nights when Clemencio is away. A dark noisy presence at midnight, outside in the mango trees near her home, disrupting them and making their leaves boil with activity. The *guacharos* return before dawn to the cave, where they spend the day weeping into the wings of their young ones, high up in the folds of the cave. She has never seen one up close, except a dead one she found one morning not long ago. It was large, its eyes were cloudy and there were whiskers around its beak. The ants were already consuming it.

The engineer is odd, too. Although he is American, and his American looks fascinate her, he is not like the others. She would like to stare at him, but does not, out of respect. Instead, she glances at his sandy colored hair. It is a shade that only Americans have, cut short and threatening to go wiry if it grows any longer. It does not shine, like her own hair which is the color of crude petroleum, but instead absorbs the light in a way that reminds her of the innocent greediness of babies putting things in their mouths, a kind of want she can't explain. She notices that his eyes, behind his gold-rimmed glasses, are a muted greenish color like a lawn that has just been watered.

The engineer nods at her, an acknowledgement that when there is no more information, nothing can be done. He walks towards a cluster of American tourists and shakes hands, shifting around on his feet and pointing up at the cave. Irma Magdalena can't hear what he is saying, but he has a dazed look and at times shakes his head. Then he comes back to her table, taking a sudden interest in the rose jelly. He inspects one of the jars, lifting it to the light and moving it from side to side to see how the jelly reacts. It is compact, except for a small shiver. Irma Magdalena has noticed how intently he has been looking at things since he arrived. This must be the way of engineers. This realization comes to her, and it feels right. She is convinced he sees the world in shapes and sizes, in numbers and perspectives and equations, as if measurements could bring him safety.

He buys two jars of rose jelly and puts them in his car. Irma Magdalena is pleased that her work is going home with this man. The pink jars will sit among pencils and papers and books and tools, a feminine respite among his masculine disarray. The money he pays her is still warm from his hand and she reaches into her pocket to touch it.

The tourists are ready to enter the cave. There are wisps of cloud trapped in the highest parts of the cave, near the orchids. It is always a holy moment for Irma Magdalena, entering, and she feels humble, blind except for the ray of light in her hand from the kerosene lamp. The Americans follow her with excited whispers that echo off the walls. She hears the crunching of their shoes on the empty seed casings strewn on the floor by the birds.

She notices that the engineer also follows her, further behind, taking his time. It is interesting that he wants to enter the cave again, perhaps not wanting to miss any information she may have about it. He stands at the entrance, looking up at a dense knot of orchids that drape over the lip of the cave like a bridal veil. Irma Magdalena likes that this time he lets the cave come to him with its sounds and odors. He kneels by a thin stream, watches the busy ambulation of the centipedes, picks up empty shell casings.

She swings her kerosene lamp, shining the light on the cave structures, the crusty pillars, the ragged spikes and salty spears falling like stiff rain from the ceiling. The light tells momentary stories as the shadows grow large and dance and bounce around the cave. She points out the ground structures, thoughtfully arranged like furniture, animals and household items. The children giggle at the dog with big ears, the giant's comb, the coffee pot, the horse with two heads, the ironing board, the king's throne. They hold their mothers' hands tightly, knowing that this is not a place to stray. The engineer, however, moves through the air with a naïve boldness, a compunction to linger in shadows. She worries for him, as he dips in and out of sight, looking out for him as the crowd gathers and shifts.

Irma Magdalena leads the tourists for a kilometer until they reach a fork. This is where she always turns back. On the left, the path immediately gets suffocatingly small and disappears downwards. The middle path leads into a room with many arched doors, and the path on the right rises into a stair-stepped hallway with a pond where water drips from the walls, and every drop is loud. She has never gone any further. It is here that she can sense the Devil, and she feels urgency to seek the light of day again.

Later, when they are outside, blinded by the silvery sunshine that filters through the clouds and grateful to be surrounded by the soft comfort of vegetation again, the engineer muses about the cave with the other men. His comments are technical and numerical. He would like to know how many birds live there, he wonders why they are unique to this cave and what kind of radar they have in order to fly, and what the temperature and density of the cave air is. Irma Magdalena likes that he has so many questions. They go unanswered, because nobody knows the answers, but the questions are pure and they indicate that he cares about the cave. She is moved that he wants to quantify, as if yearning for a new language to worship with, based on what he knows: numbers.

The engineer gets into his car and drives off, waving at her. The families disperse and soon the area is silent again. Irma Magdalena feels like something has shifted inside of her, as when she was a child and a baby tooth fell out, and she could feel the future tooth growing in its place. She blows out her kerosene lamp and goes home to pick up the strands of the day and weave them into chores.

That afternoon, Irma Magdalena goes to the pond of the Drowned Priest to wash her clothes. The jungle hides this pond, although it is quite large and ringed by ferns and minuscule parasitical red flowers, with a modest waterfall that trickles down a rock. Because the pond is so deep, the water is dark blue and has strange currents. The traveling priest who drowned here five years ago was unable to break free from its grip. Nothing was found of him except his undulating habit, floating on the surface with its arms outstretched as if waving. Irma Magdalena is always careful not to slip and fall into the pond. She shudders to think of what would happen if she did: an empty habit embracing her in the cold water. She is afraid of the priest, but always has a kind thought for him, because all he was doing was enjoying the beauty of the pond when it betrayed him.

As she dips her hand in the water, she remembers the sensation that ran through her that morning when she saw the engineer, and she feels she has sinned. It is wrong to feel this way when her own husband Clemencio is sacrificing himself far away from home, working hard for her and the children. She begs silent forgiveness of the priest down below and forces herself to think about Clemencio. It is like thinking about an old rock that has always been part of the landscape, and that one would miss terribly if it weren't there one day. That's how Clemencio is, and he's not very talkative. But she knows he is thinking good thoughts, because his hands do not tremble and he is able to fall asleep quickly at night. When he comes home every six weeks, she makes an effort to cook his favorite meal, *sancocho de gallina*, hen stew, and she makes sure the children are around. Children change so quickly, she is afraid that one day he will come back and not recognize them. She points their features out to him.

"Look at Salvador's eyebrows," she says. "Thick and black like guava caterpillars! Look at the mole on Micaela's chin, and how her second toe is longer than the rest, and it even curves down!" She hopes this will give Clemencio clues if he ever forgets what his children looks like. The Americans have cameras, they can take pictures of their children, carry them around to remember what they look like. But children are like plants, growing, growing. Sprouting hair, their legs getting longer like tendrils. It is difficult for a father who is not watching these changes to keep up.

In the end, they will all be grateful that she has sketched these clues out like a diagram. There is nothing sadder than a father who cannot recognize his own children. Clemencio comes home and hugs them, but she suspects that she could probably substitute other children of similar height and build and he would come home and hug those too.

An engineer would notice these things. The engineer she saw this morning has probably measured the feet of his children and memorized their faces, the angles, shapes and expressions. He understands why moles grow on his children, and he can tell the pitch of their voices in the dark. This is because he is an American or an engineer, or both.

American fathers all know what their children look like, even if they are not close to them all the time. She has seen it in the groups of tourists that come to the cave. American fathers call out "Jimmy!" or "Howie!" or "Cindy!" and the proper child cuts away from the herd and runs to the father, who takes their hand and walks away, claiming what is rightfully his with a confidence that is enviable.

Clemencio has never called his children in public, she realizes. He has not said their names in a long time. He calls everyone by the same indistinguishable word: *mijo*. My child. It is something that people say to each other even if they are not related. The land is scattered with "*mijos*." It is a word as common as a crow.

"Mijo," she says out loud and smiles to herself.

"Excuse me?" She hears a man's voice. Irma Magdalena is startled to see the engineer standing on the other side of the pond.

"Ah, rose jelly," he says, recognizing her. She nods and waves back, turning to her laundry. When she looks at him sideways she sees he's fixed his gaze on the water's edge and not on her as she does her washing. And in this way they fall into an unspoken agreement to share the pond. The red salamander of embarrassment crawls up her neck again, and her heart is beating fast as she busies herself with the blue skirt she is scrubbing. She wonders how he found the pond. Perhaps he has a map, although to her knowledge, no one has ever made any maps of Caripe, not even the German explorer.

She dips the skirt into the water and wrings out the suds, leaving it like a bundle of stiff tobacco leaves in the basket. It will unfurl later, when she hangs it out to dry. At first it will be heavy, its fringes immobile, but as it dries, it will begin to dance, softening up to the breezes, like a saint's gown.

The engineer is barefoot, and he sits at the edge of the pond and puts his feet in the water. The ferns around him dip in the breeze. Though the pond is large, she stops washing, so that the water will be clear for him, but she is concerned that he may not know about the dead priest, or about how deep and deceptive these waters are. Yet he is American, an engineer, he must know. He is long and lean, like Jesus on the cross, coming to bless the priest. Or perhaps coming to bless her.

Irma Magdalena is struck by the thought that perhaps Jesus was an American. How could it be that she had never had this thought before? If the engineer is Jesus, then he is safe from the currents, from the priest in the depths who is said to reach up and pull unaware swimmers down by their feet, taking them to the bottom of the pond with him only because he wants their company.

Irma Magdalena refolds the laundry and arranges it in her basket. She feels the need to be busy, so that she doesn't intrude on him. But at the same time, she wants to watch over him, and does so discreetly. Yes, she was meant to take care of him, because in his head he owns so many facts, so much knowledge, so many ideas that can cause goodness. He is so still that she thinks sadness may have touched him and he is lonely. Maybe he gathers facts to shine light against the darkness and they, like good friends, keep him company.

She will not let him drown or disappear. There have already been too many lost in the world, and tragedy has no nationality. Clemencio told her about an American girl, blonde and no older than four, who drowned in the American swimming pool at the club in the petroleum camp. The pool was meant for strong American swimmers with big backs and muscles, and no one noticed that the little girl had fallen into the deep end until it was too late, in fact, several hours too late. The child lay on the bottom of the pool, against the painted blue of the floor and walls, in her American bathing suit, perhaps with prancing pink and yellow bunnies on it.

Irma Magdalena feels tears welling up in her eyes. She says a prayer for the American girl. The waterfall murmurs back to her and the mist flies up in her face. She never knew the girl, but Clemencio told her the story with his own mouth, so she feels the girl resides on his tongue and among his teeth, and that makes her part of the family. Only a mother can know another mother's pain, regardless of the language they speak in. And the engineer's mother, wherever she is, would be thankful that Irma Magdalena is watching over her son.

A black butterfly with yellow trim lands on a bush near him, and he observes it pumping its wings on the leaf. As if it knows that it is being watched, the butterfly freezes, its wings flattened out against the leaf. The engineer, like a statue from the cave, focuses on the butterfly. They are absolutely immobile, the engineer and the butterfly, absorbed in each other, and there is a sense that neither will break the stillness.

Irma Magdalena knows that this is a good moment to look directly at the engineer, to study his profile, his downcast eyes, his forehead. She lets her eyes race over his face, noticing how the jaw curves to meet the ear, how the lips touch. The more she looks at his face, the more she wants to look. She feels the priest at the bottom of the pond admonishing her for this greedy drinking in of pleasure, yet she remains transfixed on the engineer just as he is on the butterfly. And in this stillness, she becomes unconcerned about her boldness.

It does not bother her that he would see her staring at him, if he were to suddenly lift his eyes.

Carol Muske-Dukes
Contraband

T he pimps got on the bus at the stop just before the end of the line, at the foot of the bridge that connected Riker's Island with the mainland. They left their gleaming Cadillacs in the lot posted with the sign, "New York City Department of Correctional Services"—next to the Hondas and Pintos of the corrections officers.

They lounged in the entry well of the crowded vehicle, tapping the floorboards with their heavy metal-tipped walking sticks, their faces grave under their plumed hats, vibrating slightly, then steadily, as the bus crossed under the flight paths of the jets taking off and landing at La Guardia airport. So close a prisoner could see heat waves shuddering on the taxi-tarmac, a prisoner could smell jet fuel.

The pimps traveled together in a pack but separate from each other. When the bus arrived at the reception center, they eased slowly out through the hissing doors, their walking sticks hooked over their shoulders. The rest of the passengers got off hurriedly, pushing a little, obeying the public address system commands to form lines for the Adolescent Remand Shelter, c-76, the men's prison, or the Women's House of Detention. The pimps did not form lines. Instead they remained outside the reception center, smoking and talking, and when Abby or any other young woman passed them, they would sing out in crooning voices: "Hey mamma…hey mamma." Some would call preemptively: "Come here girl. I wanna talk to you. You hear me, bitch, you hear me?"

The pimps were there because they had both vested and new interests on the Island. Their vested interest was the prostitute who'd served her sentence and was ready to go back to work. The new interest was the releasee who'd never been in the life, never whored before, never knew that a woman fast on her back could make seven hundred dollars a night. She would be dropped on the prison side of the bridge by a corrections van. This woman would be wearing ill-fitting rumpled clothes with five dollars of good luck money from the City of New York in her pocket. Nestled in her other pocket: a hot job tip scribbled on a crumpled piece of paper by a social worker—a position at the phone company, a hundred dollars a week.

When Abby walked by the pimps now she ignored them—although one night after she'd been coming out to Riker's for about three months, she'd turned back to talk to one of them, just to prove she wasn't afraid.

"Yeah?" She had approached the tall, hatted stranger who'd called rudely to her. He was lounging against a Reception Center bench, a cigarette in his mouth. He wore tinted aviator glasses and a gold lightning bolt on a chain around his neck. He watched her coming closer, nudging the pimp next to him, pointing at her with his stick. They trained identical, malevolent stares on her. She felt like someone walking a tightrope, one foot after the other: she kept her own gaze on those armored eye-slits till she looked directly into them.

"You a social worker?"

"I teach a poetry class at the Women's House."

He looked momentarily confused; he seemed to think she was making fun of him. Then when he saw that she was serious, he laughed uproariously, throwing back his head, fanning himself with his stick. The other pimps moved closer. Abby started to back away but the pimp put out a hand, fast as a knife.

"You got a friend of mine in your po-tree class called Dime-a-Time? Old Dime-a-Time, she walk like *this*."

He pushed back his hat, crooked his stick, waggled his hips and shuffled splay-footed in front of her. The other pimps hooted. Abby watched him strut, unblinking.

"Wow," she said, "if *she* makes a dime at a time, how much do *you* make?" She reached into her bag, pulled out her coin purse and flung a dime on the ground near his high-heeled, snakeskin boots. He stopped and looked down at it as it spun, then toppled. She turned and hurried away, blocking out their shouted comments.

That same night, after her encounter with the pimp, as she was pushing through the reception center turnstile, holding up her I.D. card, the guard had stopped her. She'd smiled at him nervously. This was a switch. She hadn't been asked to open her shoulder bag in a while. Most of the guards recognized her now; they'd been nodding and waving her through. Consequently, she'd found it simple to casually smuggle in contraband: *On the Barricade*, a leftist newspaper (*unapproved reading matter*), chocolate candy bars and chewing gum (*impressions of locks could be made*), as well as the forbidden items required to teach her class: spiral-bound notebooks and ballpoint pens (*the wires could be straightened into weapons*). She smiled again at the guard, an exhausted-looking, heavyset man with dark sweat circles under his armpits. He poked through her bag, taking out her wallet and keys and a pair of owl-shaped tortoise-shell barrettes, a clear plastic swizzle stick from the Algonquin Hotel bar, a packet of Beechnut gum. *The Bean Eaters* by Gwendolyn Brooks, *Ariel* by Sylvia Plath, six subway tokens, a tube of grape-flavored lip gloss and a small spiral-bound notebook.

Looking scornful, he plucked out the notebook and chewing gum, glanced at them, then tossed them in a metal drawer behind him. He handed back her bag.

"You went to orientation. Right, sweetheart?"

She nodded, recalling how at Civilian Orientation, the corrections lecturer had smugly held up a thick copy of *Great Expectations* as an example of contraband. The irony of the title, given the setting, made Abby laugh to herself—then out loud, as the lecturer opened

the book with a flourish, revealing its hollow interior filled with a
.45 automatic pistol.

He frowned at her. "Actual recovered contraband," he added
in a reverent voice.

Tonight no one stopped her. She got off the bus, walked past the
pimps through the crowded reception center interior. She flashed her
I.D. card, then jumped aboard the little open-sided corrections van
that took her to the Women's House. She presented her I.D. one last
time at the bulletproof check window, where she read and reread a
sign requesting that she deposit her firearms this side of the gate until
the heavy electric door hummed open.

Inside, it was hot. Even in summer, the thermostat was turned
up—the inmates plodded along, the C.O.'s mopped their brows and
shrugged off their jackets. Into the sealed, unmoving air seeped piped-
in music: great bass shudders and riffs. Down the long corridors,
inmates in pale baggy tunics swayed and gestured in place. "*I Heard
It Through the Grapevine...*" Those on thorazine and methadone
penguin-walked in their midst: stone deaf. Crowds gathered at the
interior gates, where they shot the breeze with the C.O.'s on duty,
many of whom were from the same neighborhoods as the inmates.

Abby phoned the residence floors from the watch commander's
office, then walked down a hallway with a taciturn C.O., La Violette,
who unlocked the door of a small, airless classroom. La Violette stood
singing under her breath outside the door for a while, then wandered
off. Abby sat down at the metal table in the center of the room. Sallie
Chester was the first to arrive. She took what she considered to be the
best seat, directly across from Abby. Sallie had once been pretty, but
now her face was split across the bridge of her nose like an overcooked
hot dog. When Abby had asked, Sallie had told her how one night
she'd walked out on her pimp, intending to leave forever, but he'd
tracked her down. He'd brought her back and tied her up, unbent
a coat hanger, heated it over a stove burner, then drew it again and
again across her face.

"He made damn sure I was no good to no man," Sallie said.
"That's why I had to deal with him."

Sergeant Pike had told Abby that "dealing with him" meant she'd killed him. Neither the sergeant nor Sallie would say how she'd done it. But Pike had laughed over her shoulder grimly, "Honey, she took *care* of him! And let me tell you, for a whore to off her pimp? Uh-ah. His homies'll be waitin' for her *outside*."

"He deserved something," Abby had remarked to Sallie, her voice shaking, "worse than death." Sallie made her nervous. Abby found it hard to look straight into that eager, ravaged face.

Sallie stared at her. "You mean prison?"

Another jet came over low. Sallie's slashed face shook, divided into two expressions. The bottom half smiled, but the upper half above the scar looked cynical.

"I evened *that* score," she said.

Tonight Sallie sat down carefully, adjusted her skirt, licked her index finger and opened her Rainbow tablet.

"I got an excellent image," she said. "I worked on it a long time."

For two weeks, they'd been translating ideas into images. Abby would scrawl abstract words like love, death, justice or friendship across the shiny blackboard with a pebble of bluish chalk, and the women would shout out the first picture that came into their heads. Sallie always came up with the most startling ones. When Abby wrote "Death" and the others yelled out "Coffin" or "Gravestone" Sallie would say something like "Yvette's beehive hairdo" or "The warden's fake finger."

"Here's my image of 'Self'—the one you said was so hard? Once I was looking at my own reflection. I saw my eye and I looked into it. I look in, eye to eye, and then I suddenly seen a baby bird with an open beak." She paused. "*Me.*"

She waited, her strange gaze tight on Abby's face.

"That was *me*, my image."

Carmen Estevez walked in, and Aisha Mahmud and Janella Reedy. They sat down and began to chatter.

"This guy? *Lorca?*" Aisha called to Abby, throwing a book on the table. "He's fucked."

"Listen up," said Fanny Jackson, who'd just walked in behind the other three, with a small pale timid girl, Rabbit Sherman, in tow. She put one foot forward and recited her poem, which was called "Another Zip Code."

> *I am the darker sister.*
> *I live far away*
> *In another Zip Code.*
> *You don't know my number.*
> *One to ten million.*
> *My mamma counted backwards*
> *In the kitchen when I was born.*
> *She saw my number like a shooting star.*

"That's an image," she explained, "there at the end."

"Wait a *minute*." A tall, graceful woman, Sugar Porter, stood in the doorway. "That one line, 'I am the darker sister'—you stole that from Langston Hughes. Didn't she?" She threw the question in Abby's direction, without looking at her.

"I am the darker brother," said Abby. "That's it."

Fanny snorted. "Man said it a whole hell of a lot better than I ever could—why shouldn't I take it?" She slapped palms with Janella Reedy.

"I think it's a terrific poem," said Rabbit timidly and put her head down on her arms.

"An image—" Abby began.

"An image," recited Gene-Jean, who'd just come in, "is a picture in your mind." Gene-Jean was half man and half woman. Her voice was deep and she had facial hair. She sat down, as Sallie Chester had, pulling her skirt down primly over her knees. Then she patted her beard and waved two fingers at everyone.

"Listen here," said Sallie Chester. She looked at Abby. "I got pictures all the time in my mind. I see a charm bracelet but with living charms: I see a little twirling ballerina dancer, and a shark made of green lightning bolts, and a little baby fetus charm with its umbilical cord connected to the head of a dreaming person, whose eyes open and close—"

"Girl, you crazy!" said Aisha. "How you get all that trash in your head?"

"I'm not crazy, I'm a poet." She looked at Abby again. "I'm a poet, isn't that right?"

A plane went over, very loud and low, and Abby noticed a change in their faces. She glanced over her shoulder at the doorway.

Lily Sheldon stood there—a young woman who'd only come to class once, the night before. Last night she'd been silent. Tonight, waving a paper, she strode back and forth in the doorway.

"I got a poem," Lily said.

Her eyes were red from crying. "They won't let me go to my baby's funeral." She glared at the others accusingly. "All I want is to go see my baby laid to rest."

She stepped forward, brandishing the paper. "They say no. My little girl's going in the ground in three days and they say no, her mamma can't go."

Like Fanny, she put one foot forward and began to read from the paper:

> *My baby girl lyin' in a cold steel drawer, dead.*
> *She fell down through a rotted hole in a rotted house.*
> *Slumlord wouldn't fix it,*
> *Cause I'm a whore.*
> *Two years old, little like her mamma.*
> *She had the gift of song.*
> *I'm a whore, he said,*
> *But my baby girl could sing.*
> *She could sing, Lil Bit.*
> *Now I can't touch her, but I still hear her call.*
> *They lock me up—and why?*
> *I'm a whore!*
> *I'm a whore, but my baby could sing.*

I hear her voice,
I hear her singin' to me
Under the ground, singin'
How'm I gonna shoot my way to her?
One for the warden, two for the dep.
I'm gonna shoot my way to her, over the dead bodies,
Over the screw blood that oppresses our people.
—But I'll be kneelin' at your grave,
Lil Bit. They can't stop your sweet voice singin' to me.

There was a silence. Then Fanny said softly, "Lemme see that poem."

Lily began to talk, standing on one foot and then the other, her face contorted, her voice calm. She said she wanted to put her poem on the drum, which meant passing it along hand to hand throughout the prison.

"Well, it's a very good poem," said Abby, shaking her head. "It's really very strong."

"No," Sallie Chester said suddenly. "No. It isn't very good. I don't think the images are good at all."

Lily Sheldon stopped pacing and turned toward her. Then she looked slowly up at the ceiling. She smiled slowly.

"Shut up that talking slash, bull-dagger."

"Then slide on over here, flatback," Sallie said. "Can't quite hear you."

Lily put her poem on the table, then stepped forward. The other women perked up, eager. Gene-Jean covered her eyes. "Oh my God!" she cried. Abby stood up and positioned herself between the two women.

"Stop it!" Abby said. She faced Sallie. "Come *on*, Sallie."

"Why? That poem don't show nor tell, it hasn't got any pictures for the mind…"

"It's got something else." Abby felt shy, aware suddenly that the other women were listening.

"It has feeling," she said. "That's what all the images and words are for—don't you see?—to let us feel what the poet is feeling." She paused. "Come on, Sallie."

Sallie had bowed her head. Abby found herself telling the top of Sallie's head that this was the point, this was why she smuggled in Neruda and Ishmael Reed and Mandelstam and Gloria Fuentes and Margaret Walker. So that Sallie, all of them, could write as these poets had written: their feelings, the truth of their lives.

"Sallie gettin' a little *bald*," Janella murmured behind her.

When she had first started teaching the class, Abby had found that despite her efforts to block the images, she had seen the women's convictions printed out, superimposed over their faces like a list of rolling movie credits. Janella Reedy was a "mule" who carried drugs back and forth between Kennedy and Bogota; Sallie Chester had killed her pimp; Fanny Jackson was a prostitute who picked pockets; Rabbit Sherman was a strange, wan girl who'd held her baby out a seventeenth floor window in the projects and then let her go, convinced the baby would fly; Carmen Estevez forged welfare checks; Gene-Jean Bondy was halfway through a sex-change operation when she'd propositioned a cop; Sugar Porter shot up; Aisha jostled.

As she talked, legal descriptions and numbers unscrolled again in front of their listening faces. She knew what she knew about their records only because the C.O.'s had filled her in—Gene-Jean or Aisha or Rabbit would never talk about what was written under their mug shots in criminal court. Pictures in the mind. Here they were not supposed to be jostlers or forgers—she had told them that the first day: they were poets.

She saw Sallie before her again, glanced down at the wrinkled Rainbow tablet clutched in her hand: a lined page covered with elaborate cursive handwriting in neon purple ink. At the top of the page in huge purple capital letters were printed the words: SALLIE CHESTER, A.K.A. THE GREAT POET!!!

At last Sallie raised her head. There was an unreadable expression on her split face.

"You said there was supposed to be images." She stepped

back, flicking her tablet closed, holding Abby in her gaze. Then she shrugged, shot Lily Sheldon a long fathomless look, pocketed her tablet and walked out.

Abby started after her, but Lily put a hand on her arm. Her eyes were huge. She was tiny, barely up to Abby's shoulder, like a child herself in her ribboned cornrows.

Without introduction, she broke the taboo: she began to talk about the crime she was accused of committing. At first, her account followed a sad, patented kind of girlfriend/moll plot, the inevitable Woman's Story: *aid and abet.* The Woman did not fire the gun or break through the second story window or pull on a ski mask and kick in the door of the Seven-Eleven. But The Woman approached the mark sitting at the bar, smiled at him, The Woman put the drugs or money or bullets in her bag—The Woman slid to the floor when the gunshots started, she crawled out the back entrance on her hands and knees, with the bag clutched in her hand.

Lily paused suddenly, her face determined, her eyes on Abby, as her story abruptly shifted gears into an experience she owned.

"What do you think?" she cried. "What do you think happened? I get back to the apartment and the old woman I left Lil Bit with is out cold. I check her bedroom and she isn't in her bed. I go back to the living room—maybe she's sleeping on the floor in front of the TV with old Mrs. Johnson? No, she's not there. I start to cry, 'cause I know the police gonna be here any minute and I can't find my baby. I was gonna get away with her, run. I go into the kitchen and I hear this sound—at first I think it's water drippin', then I listen and it's her. A tiny, tiny voice so faraway sounding, crying and calling Mamma, Mamma. And then I know where she is. I tear into the bedroom and sure enough, the boards of my closet floor has given through. And then the po-lice is there, breakin' through the door. And I'm on my hands and knees, tearin' at the broken boards—just below me her *voice…*"

Lily stopped. She put her hand on Abby's arm, then pulled it away. "You got kids?"

Abby shook her head.

Lily laughed bitterly. "I don't think anyone but a mamma can get this thing."

"I can."

Lily came close to her again, vibrating. "You not a mamma."

"Your poem told me all I need to know."

Lily smiled her slow, menacing smile. "The po-lice took me out the door of my house when my baby was still under that floor callin' for me." Her mouth widened again, turned up at the edges and Abby saw at last that it was not a smile, but an expression of disbelief. "Do you see why I have to be there? I'm her mamma. She can't die. How can she be dead, when I'm her mamma?"

Before she left that night, Abby left a note in the warden's mailbox which began:

> *Dear Superintendent Ross,*
>   *I don't know if you remember exactly who I am. I am the Columbia student whom you hired as a part-time aftercare worker. Since then, Dep Warner gave me permission to teach an evening poetry class. A student in my class, Lily Sheldon, needs to attend her daughter's funeral.*

Abby wrote for quite a while. She mentioned Lily's "psychological well-being" and a prisoner's traditional right to funeral and deathbed furlough, anything she could think of that might persuade the warden to let Lily go.

"You can't just leave a little note for the warden," said Amy Malechech. She set her empty Pepsi can on the coffee table and prodded it with her sneaker. It nearly tipped, then righted itself again. "You have to go back out there right away. You have to do something to help this woman."

Another young woman named Connie Owens looked up from a pile of *On the Barricades* and Women's Bail Fund flyers that she was collating on the table, lifted her fist and brought it down, smashing the Pepsi can. Abby jumped.

"Abby's been going out there for almost two years. She *knows*."

On the wall above Connie was a poster-size photograph of a group of men with shaved heads, wrapped in thin grey blankets, seated around a makeshift bonfire. Across the top of the poster a single word dripped in blood: *Attica*.

Abby sat with her head down, listening as the discussion soared into argument. She felt comfortable at these meetings. The voices rose around her, heated, passionate—a flowering wall of righteousness. Everyone in this room cared about Lily Sheldon, just like that.

A heavyset young woman in a gray Columbia University sweatshirt with "SLUMLORD" scrawled across the school logo in huge orange letters stood up, waiting for silence. She quoted from the Little Red Book. "Who are our enemies? Who are our friends?" then sat down emphatically, as if she and Mao had settled the argument.

Abby looked up. "What is *that* supposed to tell me?" Somehow, it had ended up that she was the only one who actually went out to Riker's Island. Everyone else gave advice, which she often had trouble interpreting.

The sweatshirted woman put her hand to her forehead and closed her eyes. She kept her hand over her eyes as she spoke, not looking at Abby.

"I'm saying we have to ask ourselves what good it is, finally, having Abby teach poetry at the Women's House? She's supposed to be a conduit for the *Barricade*, yes—and she gets us the names of women with low bail, yes…but it seems to me that she's more into the poems these women write than her real reason for being there."

Connie Owens stood up, accidentally bumping a faceted glass lamp hung low and lopsided on a chain from the ceiling. As it swayed, cubes of light multiplied across her face and hair. She frowned, her eyebrows knit, one lit and jumping.

"Deanna," she said, "Don't be so *literalistic*."

She opened her hands. "*Let a hundred flowers blossom,*" she misquoted, "*Let a hundred schools of thought contend…*"

Abby sighed. "Mao could have used a writing workshop." She grinned at the others' shocked faces.

Someone began lecturing her, ending with Mao's most famous quote, the one about revolution not being a dinner party.

Later that evening, Abby was at a dinner party given by one of her Columbia professors—seated next to a famous man, a poet. Abby had read his work for years and admired it. She knew some of his poetry by heart.

Dessert had been served and the guests were lingering over coffee. Abby had drunk some wine and was telling the famous poet about what had happened at the Bail Fund meeting earlier that evening. In front of her was a fluted glass dish containing a fleshy white pear in a pool of amber liquid. She set her wine glass down, accidentally pinging the dish.

"I'm sure of my own political commitment. I found that I could do it. I could smuggle newspapers and messages and things in."

The famous poet nodded. Every so often he looked down at his wine glass, smiling, swirling the dregs and shaking his large head.

"But you see, the women don't really take to the political articles in the *Barricade*—they read the Personals—you know, like: 'Well-hung sensitive Scorpio desires to write to firm-bodied Libra vixen. No Geminis, please.'"

The famous poet laughed heartily. Abby looked around the table. "Everybody there wants to write *love* poems. The women at the Bail Fund find that unbelievable. But there it is. Now, finally, one of my students writes a poem that's *real*. I mean, tragically real, but the poet's not a victim. She's breaking down the walls with this poem—its truth is its power." She glanced at the poet. "Although it's certainly not a work of genius."

"But that's the question one has to ask oneself, isn't it?" His voice was amused. Abby looked up. "How *good* are these poems?"

"Well, as I was trying to say, they're not good the way you might define good..."

"Recite one." He lit a cigarette and leaned back in his chair.

She pulled Lily's poem from her pocket and heard it on her lips as if from a distance, her voice not doing it justice, the words turning flat—she finished up and looked at the poet. He blew smoke through his nostrils, then winked at her, waving away smoke, shaking with laughter. "Terrible," he gasped. "Just awful."

Inside the Women's House, there was a long line of inmates snaking past the lawyer's cubicles, round the corner and into the auditorium. It was Sunday. Movie night. Abby had made a special trip to the prison to talk to the warden about Lily Sheldon. Lily's daughter wouldn't be buried till tomorrow. It wasn't too late.

Abby heard someone calling her from the movie line. Aisha Mahmud and Rabbit Sherman. They waved and hooted.

"Listen," said Aisha. "You know that poem Lily Sheldon wrote? It went on the drum and C.O. Carter got a copy of it and showed it to the dep."

"Where's Lily now?"

"That's what I'm *tellin'* you. She's in the Bing."

"For *what?*"

"For the poem she wrote for our class."

Abby flushed, embarrassed. She'd caught it: a flash of something like *pride* running through her, before the shock of the words set in. *Locked up for writing a poem? It was true then, what she'd told them: words had power. Poetry did make something happen.*

"How long has she been in?"

"Since the night of our class, Friday night. They gave her another Disciplinary Board hearing this morning and she told them to take a *bite*. So they threw her back in."

Abby nodded, sighing. She said it was a good thing that no one could be held in lock longer than three days. It was a prison rule, maybe even an international human rights ruling.

Aisha dropped her jaw at Abby, put on her "Is she for real?" look. Rabbit smiled and turned her head away.

The line lurched suddenly toward the auditorium. Abby leaned toward the two women, a finger over her lips.

"I'm going to see the warden about this," she whispered.

Rabbit smiled vaguely at her. "We're going to see The Sound of Music."

Superintendent Ross looked up as Abby entered her office. She seemed about to speak, but Abby cut in.

"Where is Lily Sheldon?"

The warden smiled. She was a slim woman in her fifties, military-pretty with light skin and straightened copper-colored hair. Nothing about her suggested a medium-security keeper; she looked more like a flight attendant in her trim navy uniform.

"Lily Sheldon is in punitive segregation."

"I demand to see her."

Superintendent Ross sat back in her chair. She looked bored. To Abby's amazement, she touched the intercom button on her desk.

"Josie," she said, "could you please find out if Captain Santos is in the tour commander's office? Ask her if she would please accompany Abby Lyman to the Bing to see Lily Sheldon, the inmate from Two Upper who's locked."

Abby felt a smooth dropping sensation in her stomach—maybe they were going to lock her up too.

"After I visit Lily, I'd like to talk to you."

The warden nodded once, then turned her face away.

The Bing was an architectural migraine: a long straight corridor, white-lit, with heavy metal doors on either side. Each door had an eye-level opening the size and shape of a mail slot. As Abby and the captain passed, doors on either side shook with resounding blows and kicks, there were garbled shouts and accusations.

Captain Santos stopped at a door midway down the corridor, shook out the waterfall of keys hung next to the nightstick on his belt, and opened the door.

The cell was so small there was barely room to enter. A bald overhead light in its claw-socket burned mercilessly. Lily lay on her back on a thin mattress, her arms and legs thrown out casually, her face lifted to the light like a client in a tanning salon. She pulled herself up to a sitting position. Her hair was wild, the cornrows half-unraveled and sticking straight up. She did not appear to recognize Abby.

"Sheldon," said Captain Santos, "your teacher is here to see you."

Lily looked idly at the guard and spit. Captain Santos looked down at the saliva which hung on her skirt, then fell. Abby watched the Captain's face grow very calm. She moved to the door and stood there. "I got my eye on you, Sheldon."

Abby sat down tentatively on the edge of the mattress and touched Lily's hand.

"What the hell *was* the matter with that poem you wrote?"

"No images!" Lily croaked and they collapsed against each other.

"Are you sick?"

Lily rubbed her forehead and laughed sadly. "My body's okay but my head's *dyin'*."

"What do you need?"

"I need a furlough by tomorrow to hold my baby one last time. I ain't gonna get it! Am I?" She slumped into Abby. "Look what's *happened* to me." She lifted her head and put it on Abby's shoulder, like an ill, exhausted child. Abby followed Lily's gaze to the wall. There was graffiti scratched on the cement—how? Hairpins, a bent spoon, bones? There were names of former residents: Sweet Duchess and Cola, Death Mamba, La Reina de Dolorosa, Cruise Top, Shudder Honey: a cobweb of names. Fresh scratches beneath: Lil Bit, Lil Bit.

Lily drew an audible breath. "I need something to write with. I need a pen. I need paper. I'm *bleedin'* poems."

"Captain Santos." Abby cleared her throat. "Could you please see that Lily has some pens and paper?"

"You just go on ahead and bring that matter up with Superintendent Ross, Miss Lyman."

"Come on, Captain, what are you afraid of?"

"Time's way up."

"The truth?" said Abby. She pulled gently away from Lily and faced the woman.

Captain Santos gave her the same "are you for real?" look Aisha used. She moved a fraction of an inch closer to Abby.

"I'm not afraid of anything in *this* room," she said. She cocked one hip and waited.

Abby turned back to Lily. "I'm on my way to Ross. I'm going to *make* them let you go."

Lily's smile pulled apart into a grimace. She grasped Abby's hand as she stood up and Abby bowed awkwardly to her, her arm pulled out in a kind of downward salute.

"I'm gonna write a book, Abby. I'm gonna write this down for the whole world to know."

Superintendent Ross looked up as Abby walked boldly in and sat down.

"I just want to ask you the reason for Lily Sheldon's confinement in the Bing and then I want to know what I have to do to get her released. In the meantime, I'm requesting that she be given writing materials."

"For more 'poems' perhaps?"

"Perhaps."

The warden laughed. "You must be kidding."

Abby stood up, then sat back down again. She took a breath to steady herself.

"What was wrong with that poem? Why did you lock her up for writing it?"

"You know," said the warden, smiling, "you really are an ideas girl. When you first came up with this notion of a poetry workshop, I wasn't inclined to approve." She leaned toward Abby, emphasizing each word. "A *crea-tive wri-ting class?*"

She winged at Abby, then leaned her hand protectively on a framed desktop photograph as a jet roared over. Abby started to speak, but the warden continued.

"Then they brought to class all those things they'd written, whatever you want to call them: poems, little sob stories, diaries. And here's this do-gooder college girl sorting them all out…" She chuckled to herself.

Abby opened her mouth again, but Ross held up her hand.

"I'm aware how you think poetry's so important. I also know you think the ladies are victims of an unfair system. Isn't that how you might put it? 'Victims of an unfair system?'"

Abby straightened up in her chair. She could hear a series of muffled announcements over the public address system.

"I know for example, that you bring in that newsletter, *On the Barricade*, and Hershey bars, cookies…and you bring in other contraband: spiral notebooks, pens. Unauthorized books. You seem to think our security regulations don't apply to you."

Abby sat very still.

"I suppose, on one level, you're right. A little bit of irregularity, a little sugar allowed now and then, and they think they're getting away with something. It amounts to nothing. But you see…" Another smile. "That's not the way it is."

She lifted a little glass bell shaped like an angel from her desktop and rattled it twice. There was a barely audible *clink*. She set it down, smiling to herself. "Christmas here at the Women's House—can you imagine what *that's* like? Ladies ready to break out, ladies ready to stick their heads in the toilet after one visit from their children who can't remember then anymore—it's a free-for-all. Plus all the big companies send us holiday guilt donations: clothes, teddy bears, fruit, candies, games. One year some cosmetics company decided to send a little care package: a black satin pouch stuffed with cologne and powder and lipstick and deodorant. We checked for possible contraband uses: took out all the metal nail files and the non-shatter-proof bottles and the plastic bags. We worked overtime Christmas Eve and then, finally, Santa Claus was sent off to all the floors to deliver the gifts. We waited: all was calm and then…" She shook the glass bell again. "Clink, crack, clink! All over the institution we heard the sound of glass breaking." Abby cocked her head, interested in spite of herself.

"The cosmetics company had tucked a deodorant with a little glass roller ball into the lip of the pouch and we hadn't caught it. Within five minutes of distribution, they were *armed* with glass, had cut their wrists with glass or swallowed glass." She snapped her fingers. "*That* fast."

She shook her head at Abby and laughed. "Still, your contraband's a little different. Nobody in their right mind would ever take *On the Barricade* seriously. We pick it up all the time on raids. The inmates throw it away—we read it at coffee breaks for laughs."

She laughed again, as if to capture the mood of these high-spirited coffee breaks. Another plane shook the building. "Do you think" she asked, "that I don't know what's going on? I found out finally that you *were* teaching them something about the subject. About how to write. I have my eyes and ears in that class—or didn't you know?"

Abby, stung, was already unrolling the list in her mind: Fanny, Gene-Jean, Sugar, Janella, Rabbit, Carmen...

The warden smiled at her expression. A C.O. knocked softly and entered, carrying a stainless-steel coffeepot and a white china mug on a tray. She set the tray down in front of the warden and exited, with a quick sidewise look at Abby.

"Coffee?" The warden poured and drank.

"No," said Abby. "No thanks." She was still running through names and faces.

"When things get confused, I step in. Some things went wrong in your class. Let's say you betrayed a certain trust." She looked up mildly from her coffee, blotting her lips on a paper napkin.

"Excuse me. Did you think we had some sort of unspoken agreement about subject matter?"

Another laugh. "Miss Lyman, here we have an inmate who writes down on paper that she intends to murder the superintendent and the deputy warden in order to break out of prison. She received praise for this from a teacher in an institution classroom. The teacher further encouraged class members to copy these threats of violence and spread them throughout the facility—"

"I didn't do that. I simply said—"

"What you've done is tantamount to inciting a riot. In many ways you're guiltier than she is, since you were in the position of responsibility."

Abby started to say, "No, I wasn't," but stopped herself.

"They were *dancing* in the halls to it. Finger-popping, 'One for the warden, two for the dep,' like that."

Abby pictured the inmates, jiving up and down the L-shaped corridors, snapping their fingers. She coughed into her hand.

The warden sat back in her chair and pulled open a desk drawer, fished something out, then slammed it shut.

"You feel sorry for Lily, don't you? I mean, seeing her up there in the Bing crying?"

She slid a manila folder across the desk to Abby and flipped it open. Abby glimpsed her second finger, left hand: a stiff, too-tan prosthetic digit and bright-painted nail. There was a story that circulated about this finger—that years earlier a very young C.O. Ross, on duty in the kitchen, had tried to show an inmate how to chop marrow bones for stew—she'd gone so far as to graciously offer her own finger as an example. Seeing the finger made Abby think of Sallie Chester: her image for death.

Then she looked at the contents of the folder: an 8 × 10 black-and-white photograph of a dead two-year-old girl. The tiny naked body was a storm of bruises and welts, from the great blood rip of scalp sheared away from her small, corn-rowed skull to her battered legs, bird-thin. At the top of the photo was stamped in red indelible ink "Manhattan County Coroner's Office." Abby located the child's expression, a miniature of Lily's, the lips upturned in a smile that was really a grimace of disbelief. Abby turned her head away.

"Why are you showing me this? I know how Lily's daughter died."

"Like you, I'm aware of Sheldon's testimony. Look at *this*."

She pulled a second photograph from beneath the first, this one taken of the child's body on its face. Tiny bruised buttocks and spine, the arms and legs, like Lily's in the Bing, thrown out to the sides.

"See this large discolored area? The coroner told the D.A. who tells *me* that this is a contusion caused by a blow, or a series of blows, to the head and neck. I asked for these at the time of Lily's request for a furlough. The coroner, you see, examined this discoloration and the others here at the child's autopsy. He maintains that they could not have been caused by a fall, even through a floor—he thinks that they are the result of blows from a blunt instrument, a heavy boot heel, or a...walking stick." She made her hand into a battering wedge and struck a rounded glass paperweight. "Crunch," she said. "Crunch-crunch!" Abby looked up, shocked, but the warden was not laughing.

"Are you telling me that the old woman Lily left her baby with did this?"

The warden shook her head. "The D.A. feels this evidence indicates the child received this treatment from an adult—an adult with some *strength*."

Abby placed the photos on top of the folder.

"Look." A magnifying glass blazed in the warden's hand. It slid across the first photograph and the frail arms and legs leaped wildly at the lens' touch, then a patch of skin stood out, proffered, like the enlarged surface of a jewel. Abby could see the faintest brushing of hairs on the forearm, then three circular puckered wounds.

"Blisters? Or cigarette burns? What do you think?"

Abby pushed the lens violently aside—it slid upward, magnifying the child's open left eye, which stared back at them, huge and expectant.

After a moment she spoke. "Someone 'else' who lived in the house. You mean Lily's husband?"

The warden put her head down, then looked up and shook it to and fro. "*Pimp,*" she said. "Lily's *pimp*. He went out the back door that night. Do you think he'd be eager to be caught inside with a dying kid, and child molestation already on his record? Lily is refusing to turn state's evidence against him, though the D.A.'s office has been leaning on her. These whores are very loyal to their pimps, did you know that? You've seen those roosters waiting out there on the bridge?"

Abby hears, far away, another plane. It seems to hover overhead, drowning out the sound of the warden's words, though another part of her mind still hears her talking.

"The D.A.'s office feels it would have been hard for someone of Lily's baby's size to...break through the floor. *Somebody* jammed her down through the boards to make it look accidental."

At last the plane disappeared and another sound took its place: water dripping, then barely-distinguishable speech.

"Then why would Lily want to go to her daughter's funeral?"

"What funeral? Tomorrow the Baptist church in her neighborhood will bury this little girl...a few words repeated over her coffin and quickly into the ground she goes. People want to *forget* these things. As for Lily, I'd say she had in mind to *walk*."

The warden pulled the folder back towards her, she seemed relaxed suddenly. She held the false finger daintily aside, a teacup effect, the thumb and third finger held pincer-like. A bass female voice thundered over the P.A. "Count unverified. C.O.'s check your populations."

The warden nodded at Abby over her coffee cup. "The count's off. We know what that means, don't we? You and I are prisoners now too. Can't go home till they find out who's missing."

Abby nodded back.

"Who do you believe *now* Miss Lyman?"

Years later Abby would recollect that look: grave, keen, but somehow invested—as if she thought Abby might cry, as if she thought she'd break down before her—and this would be a victory.

Abby said nothing. There were no words for what she was feeling, no image. There would be no way for her to talk about it, though now it was her—her, like a thumbprint, a mugshot.

There was a loud blast of static, followed by an announcement: "Report 104 sentenced, 256 detention, 23 adolescent. Count verified."

The warden was still staring at her, but her look had hardened. Her desk intercom buzzed. She sighed and stood up. The shift was changing, she was expected to hold inspection of the officers who'd just come on duty for the graveyard shift.

Abby stood up too. She gripped the desk in front of her. "I'd like to say this. Lily is locked up there because of me…"

"Lily Sheldon will be released from the lock when the board determines that she is no longer a threat to internal security." A pause. "Soon. And now I'm going to give *you* a punishment. I'm going to let you keep teaching here at the Women's House."

She glanced ruefully at Abby, shook her head and turned to go.

Abby moved in front of the warden at the door: she touched her arm.

"Sallie Chester."

The warden stared at her.

"She was your 'eyes and ears' in my class, wasn't she?"

The warden started to brush past Abby, then turned almost coquettishly, touching her false finger to her lips.

"Eyes and ears wouldn't hurt a poet, would they, Idea Girl?"

Abby waited a long time for the bus back to Manhattan. She sat on a bench outside the reception center and counted the planes: fifteen went over while she sat. She thought about the passengers seated in the airborne cylinders, the stewardesses already moving up and down the carpeted aisles, the jingling drinks cart rolling out high above her. Then later, a movie screen enlarging with light, a roaring lion's head, a spot-lit colossus.

There was one pimp left, standing in a shadowy corner of the building, chain-smoking, though there were no more whores left to pick up. He was like the last sentinel of an occupying army, Abby thought. He was here to stay, he'd be back, they'd all be back, standing watch on the bridge, the next day, and the next.

She and the pimp boarded the empty bus together and sat far apart. He got off across the causeway and she rode back alone through Queens into Manhattan—no one else got on, no one else witnessed it: the huge lit-up famous skyline that she loved unfurling like a banner as the bus crossed the Fifty-Ninth Street Bridge.

At that moment, she felt the need to write something down. She reached into her pocket for the pen she'd put there earlier. It was gone. Then she remembered Lily holding her close. She thought about it—a writing instrument and a weapon in one. It had been a ballpoint, and contraband.

Rochelle Low
Where Angels Tread

M

y daughter Kira sleeps peacefully, her flesh warm and relaxed as she leans into me. I could kill her.

The morning light, harsh, nearly blinds; traffic below, noisy, buses churning up the hill, horns blaring, cars pushing their way in. I didn't hear her come in and I know by looking at her that she won't wake soon. You can't drive me crazy like this anymore. Your Aunt Cyn has won. She's right to have no faith in you. I've been humiliated. How can I defend you?

Kira stirs, turns away from me. Shh, her father would say, "You're getting a little shaky, ease up. She's here. Doesn't that make everything all right?"

So maybe Cyn hasn't won after all. Isn't that what matters?

I push Kira over to the other side of the bed, slide down, move the blanket up over my shoulders and close my eyes. Soon the sun will arch its way westward, heat draining down through the windowpanes into my pores. For now, I won't fight sleep, even though, when I wake, she might be gone again.

"Why are you staring at me, Mom?"

"It's twelve o'clock."

"So?"

"Get up."

"You're in a bitchy mood." She lies back down on her pillow. "I'm not getting up."

Strangely she seems perfectly sober.

"What are you thinking about? You look scary."

"At least you haven't tried to phone anyone yet for your usual drug run. But then you could've gotten today's stash last night."

"Aunt Cyn crawling in your ear?" she smirks, then turns sullen, glances out the bedroom window. "Guilty? Not the perfect parent?"

"You were supposed to call your father. You're not exactly on the right track to get back in his corner."

"I'll call him later. He doesn't care anyway."

"Don't start."

"I'm here."

"You and Cyn win all the arguments."

"Well, you don't have an answer, do you?"

"I'm tired of visiting you in the hospital."

"You think I like being an addict?"

"Sometimes."

She gets up, her body nude, skinny and white. All bones and teeth and long black dip of hair that stays shiny no matter what she does to herself. She grabs a towel from the dresser.

"Well I hate it," she says, and slams the bathroom door.

Kira and I are mesmerized as we walk up the steep steps to the stained glass door with its intricately colored pattern of angels hovering in flight.

"It's beautiful," she whispers. "The garden. Roses as nice as ours." Still, she's terrified.

We wait on a bench on the back terrace. "Look," I say, trying to ease the strain of the moment, "They have cherry blossom trees. It must be wonderful here in spring, when everything's in bloom."

Jerking her head away from my shoulder, she gives me a dark look. "Spring is a long time from now. I'm not going to be here forever."

I put my arms around her. "I didn't mean it that way."

"You'd like me to be, wouldn't you?"

I think about what a relief it would be to always know she is safe. "Long enough to get well."

Doors open and close. She doesn't appear. She's been in the interview more than an hour. I don't know what to do if it's 'no.' Where do we turn? A long interview could mean anything. I hate that holier-than-thou attitude that makes me want to smack her. Perhaps there's something undefined about her that makes them unsure, something they can't quite put their finger on. I should be old hat at this, but I'm going to throw up on the velvet settee if someone doesn't do something soon.

I'll call Cyn; interrupt her literature class. I have a question for you: Is this how Holden Caulfield's mother felt at the intake interview at the psychiatric hospital?

Our first rehab three years ago, Serenity House. We must have looked like death to the psychologist, who wore her Twelve-Step ten-year pendant around her neck. In a waiting room much like this one, Lin slouched beneath his newspaper at a table facing a window. After all, we might run into someone we knew. What would they think? We were the perfect family. Just a slight problem of drug addiction. We were so naïve then. Puff, puff, a few months and everything back to normal, we thought. We could say she was doing a year abroad.

Two years and several aborted attempts at sobriety later, I sit by the window, staring at the sign above the door, "Don't leave before the Miracle happens." What does that mean? This isn't Lourdes. I twist my Kleenex into knots. Damn allergies, my right hand broken into a streaky rash.

She was upbeat this morning on the way over. "I've heard a lot of good things," she said. "Remember my friend Perry? He really did good there."

"The one who worked at Trader Joe's? I thought you said he didn't have a drug problem?"

Kira shrugged, turned to look out the window with an embarrassed grin.

Perry, the tall rugged blond surfer from home. "I seem to remember, and I quote, 'You're suspicious of everyone. He's up here to go to school.'"

Kira is over me, shaking my arm.

"Mom, you're dozing. Come on, we're taking a tour," introduces me to Raoul, a fair-skinned Hispanic man in his early thirties. He shakes my hand.

"I think she'll like it here," he says.

I feel my mouth form a silly, gratuitous smile. "I'm so relieved. We've heard wonderful things."

He smiles broadly, his teeth aged and yellowed for someone so young. I can't recall the last time Kira had her teeth cleaned.

"She needs dental work," flies out of my mouth. A puzzled look rearranges his face.

"We can take her over to UC in an emergency," he responds.

Kira pinches my elbow. "Shh," she whispers. We follow Raoul. Then in my ear, "Your hair is messy."

"Let's start our tour." Raoul begins walking ahead of us, looks back at me. "I want to show you how our dining room is set up. Our tables are for not more than six. Nice and intimate."

Each table has a bright yellow cloth and a small bouquet of daisies in the center. There is an aroma of fresh bread baking in the oven. "It's really lovely, isn't it?" I nudge Kira.

Raoul continues, "We make our own breads and pastries. We can stop by later for a sample if our cook's around. Gym's in the basement. We'll skip that, go up to the second floor now. She'll be sleeping in a dorm. All new residents do." He tells us how those who are completing the program have only one roommate. "But there's a meditation room on each floor, somewhere to go for quiet time. It can get pretty hectic here." He opens the door to a room with a couch and table. Stained-glass panels hang on the windows, the walls are painted a Mediterranean blue. Everywhere we turn, work parties of residents gather. "Everyone has a job here," he explains, "Those here longest get the one they want. Now," he says, as we walk up the stairs from the bedrooms, "My favorite, our main meeting room and party room."

I run my hand over the banister as we climb to the third level. Every inch of wood is polished to a satin sheen and scented delicately with lemon oil.

Raoul opens a large double door at the top of the stairs leading onto an enormous space with floor-to-ceiling windows on both sides. At the front, a podium and stage that once must have been an altar. "This was the chapel," he says, winking at us. "Reminds me of my days as an altar boy."

On the frescoed domed ceiling float round-figured angels in sheer white Grecian gowns. In awe of the beauty of this, I go over to the window, sit down in a high-backed carved mahogany chair. "How wonderful for the sisters to come into this space of meditation. They must have felt such joy." I turn my head back up to the ceiling. No, there must have been darkness sheltering them from the world. Heavy velvet to protect their reverence. They never experienced these cherubs in all their erotic brilliance.

"What do you suppose the old nuns would think about this now?"

A bewildered look crosses Raoul's face. Kira gives me a signal with peevish eyes.

"I think they must be very happy," I say, ignoring her. "To know their work is being continued. I somehow feel their spirit here."

"Maybe," he says thoughtfully, "But this isn't a school for children."

Even though Kira looks at me triumphantly as we walk back downstairs in silence, the beauty and serenity of the angel's room calms. I feel suddenly peaceful. Unafraid. "I could be very happy here," I murmur to her.

"God, Mom, shut up," she whispers, punches my arm lightly.

Raoul brings us back to the entrance of the main reception room. "She can come Monday. I'll give her a list of things that she'll need. And then to Kira, "I'm sure you two won't mind a little shopping trip," giving her a gentle hug, "Hey, welcome," then turns to me. "Mrs. Prescott, if you could wait here, I'll take Kira to her counselor."

Once again I'm in a chair by the window overlooking the street, watching the grand ballet of people come and go. Quite freely. I never thought of that. It would be easy for her to leave, to buy anything. Maybe this is a mistake. Maybe we should send her somewhere isolated, like that ranch in Montana close to the Canadian border. No possibility of contact with anything or anyone capable of polluting her for at least a year.

"Excuse me, is someone sitting here?"

I look up, startled. A pasty-faced woman, long gray hair, velvet beaded dress and crystal earrings to her shoulder in a very fashionable seventies style, stands in front of me. Her lips are a brazen blush pink, thickly applied.

I shake my head no.

"Can I have this chair? My daughter is coming to visit me."

"Sure," I say, moving my purse and book off the chair. I move closer to the window, letting her have a private space.

A tall blonde girl, perhaps a little older than Kira, with a boy of about two in her arms, comes in. "Here, Jamie," she coaxes him, "Kiss Grandma." Tips her head toward the woman, "You look good, Mom," kisses her on the forehead, "how are you feeling?"

"Better. Getting all that shit out of my system. Can't take it anymore."

The daughter runs her hand over the mother's cheek. "I hope you can give this a chance."

"It's going to work this time, honey. It's just losing the job, and Harry leaving."

The daughter frowns and her voice becomes harsh. "I'm glad he left. He treated you like crap. I don't know why you never see it."

The mother stiffens, moves her hand from her daughter's lap, reaches into her pocket for another cigarette. "Why do you always start? Can't we have a nice visit?"

"Sorry, Mom," lifts her child up from her mother's arms. "Jamie's missed you."

An intruder, I turn away, noticing a small boned, curly- haired woman in a long denim skirt, bright red cotton blouse, walking toward me with two mugs in her hand.

"Mrs. Prescott? I'm Alexandra, Kira's counselor. She'll be down in a minute. I thought you might like some coffee."

"I feel like it's my first day at kindergarten."

She sits down next to me, pats my hand. "She's lucky to have a mother so supportive."

"I don't know what else to do."

"My mother never gave up on me. I know it's one of the reasons I'm still in recovery today."

"She must be very proud of you."

"She was. She died of breast cancer last year. Thank God I was clean. She was happy."

I smile a silly bland sort of grin; nod my head affirmatively. I have nothing profound to say. Simply, "I'm happy she's coming here." Yes, that feels right. I am happy she's here. Which is different than saying, I'm happy. "I feel that she's safe." Yes, I do feel a relief, as if I've completed a long journey.

"It's beautiful," I say, squeezing Kira's hand as we walk down the steps to the car.

She's irritated. "'The spirit of the sisters is still here.' Raoul must think you're a whacko. How do you know what they were like? I heard they used to lock children in the basement."

"Rotten rumors."

"Anyway, I thought you were Buddhist?"

I ignore her. "There's a very special spirit there. One day you'll appreciate it. You're just upset now."

Kira leans against the car door, disgusted with me. "Whatever. I'm hungry. Let's go to Chinatown. I need good luck things for my new room. We can go shopping after we eat."

We drive in silence, the sun beginning to set over Pacific Heights, its glow reflected on the Golden Gate Bridge.

That woman with her daughter and grandchild; close to my age and still searching for her salvation. Who would be with Kira in the waiting room? Her brother? Her own grown children and grandchildren? I have her in law school after this brief detour, on the road to middle class morality. I smile to myself, look over at Kira, still pouting. The sign above the reception room door, "Don't leave before the miracle happens."

I won't God, I promise. Just let it happen soon.

Jody Hauber
Between the Dog
and the Wolf

Adele's hair lies stiff on her neck after the long plane ride from Paris. She stands in the middle of the elevator car, which is cavernous, big enough to accommodate wheelchairs and walkers. She holds a black leather purse in one hand, flowers in the other. In an early memory of her father, a Fourth of July sparkler is shooting stars from his seersucker pants. The sparklers are in his pocket. He's handing them out when one suddenly explodes. Adele watches him do many things at once: jump back, grab the sparkler and throw it on the grass, warn her back with his hands. Where is the occasion now in which danger can be averted, she wonders. Where is that sparkler to keep hissing and spitting stars onto the warm lawn? Where is the verbena and honeysuckle to mingle with the reek of scorched fabric? She looks straight ahead at the seamed doors. She closes her eyes, gives herself over to verticality. Then the elevator shimmies to a stop. The doors open. She steps out into the familiar shit and talc smell of the third floor of the Garnet Hill nursing pavilion.

The night supervisors, Mary Ada and Jen, are behind the desk working on patient charts. When they see Adele, the calla lilies she has been carrying for hours curling brown at the edges now, limp inside their nest of green wax paper tied with straw-colored raffia, they set their pencils down.

—I said you wouldn't get here fast enough, Mary Ada says. I predicted it. I was right. She wipes her eyes with tan freckled fists.

Jen stands up. Her air of forbearance has always reassured Adele, the scooped cheeks, dust brown hair and ropy neck straight out of Dorothea Lange. She keeps Adele's father's beer stash in the nurses' refrigerator. Now she leans on the desk until all her weight is in front of her. Her fingertips are pink with dead white behind them.

—It was peaceful, she says. He woke up, asked if his shoes were polished, and left us.

—Arpie said six o'clock.

—Three minutes to. Mary Ada's small, black-bead eyes focus over rather than on Adele. Adele doesn't know if it's sadness she sees in them or anger at the distance she's had to travel to get here, distance Mary Ada interprets as willful separation, something Adele has imposed that others have had to worry about, that has made them timekeepers as well as caretakers, timekeepers even for the local sister, who once again has shown herself to be inexact about details.

—Five fifty-seven, then, Adele says. She's grateful for the particulars. Even if grounded in hostile inferences, they define the present and place her in it.

Tuesday. October first. Shortly after eleven P.M. Cincinnati; not the city per se, Greater Cincinnati, Garnet Hill Senior and ElderCare Village, seventeen-plus miles north of the Ohio River, on the same sylvan grounds and bearing the same name as the home for unwed mothers that stood here throughout Adele's girlhood, beacon of shame and admonition, dingy brick reminder of the consequences of bad behavior.

Adele takes a deep breath, tucks the hair that has fallen over one eye behind her ear, hands the callas to Mary Ada the way she might proffer a broken vase for gluing.

—Add ice. Cold might revive them, she says.

—In Ohio, lilies are only for Easter.

Mary Ada goes into the kitchen on the other side of the nurses' station. The minute Adele and Jen are alone, Jen's shoulders collapse inward, exposing the bony arc of her collarbone. Her purple blouse shakes under her white lab coat.

—He called me Good Looking, she says, weeping silently. Hey, Good Looking. Me.

Her sadness is so immediate and acute it reminds Adele some part of her is still missing from this scene.

—Jen, she confesses, it doesn't feel real yet.

—It never does until you see the body. Still crying, Jen sits down again, picks up her pencil and twirls it.

Adele turns the corner, glad his room is at the end of the hall because she needs the path between here and there, the visiting area littered with newspapers, the half-open bedroom doors behind which people lie in charcoal shadows, sleeping and dreaming and breathing normally. She needs the Garnet Hill decor, the cheery falseness of mauve and aqua bouquets in the carpet, strewn in happy profusion about the upholstery, the wallpaper border around the ceiling. The kinetic swirls assault her eye, draw her into their intricate distraction as if to persuade her that what has happened hasn't happened: Her father hasn't died. He's not the fourth Weems to depart this world, leaving Adele and her younger sister the last two survivors of a family which has not reproduced, which will, with their deaths, come to the end of itself after only one generation, like a failed experiment. A failed experiment tunneling back, back…always to October, their Achilles-heel month, mortal, void of protection…five years ago. In 1993, their mother Margo succumbs to respiratory failure; 1962, their eldest sister Janet takes her life; 1947, another sister, Grace, falls—or did Janet push her? It has never been determined—into a fishpond and drowns, a death that perhaps occasions the subsequent births of Adele and Arpie but perhaps not. Who can say?

The multiple deaths have not lent insight or familiarity. Quite the opposite. If there's one thing Adele is certain of, it's that each person's mortality exists in a crystal mystery. It isn't until the crystal cracks open with the final breath that the mystery is released, and then it's more like fog than perfume, it settles like murk around those who are left, turning them strange and surprising to one another, recast as they are in the raw light of absence.

This is why she arrived with offering in hand, a bridge between worlds, beneficent act held up as a garlic clove against loss. She'd tended religiously to the lilies' hydration during the long flight, wrapped them in wet towels, periodically trimmed the stems with her dinner knife, filled a drinking glass with bottled water, added sugar, placed the lilies inside, and sat with the arrangement wedged between her feet.

All to what good? she wonders. She can't keep anything alive.

His door is closed. She straightens her shoulders, is very aware of the bones in her neck and shoulders, intersection of vertical and horizontal. *Cross of my body*, she thinks, *help me.*

He is smiling. Close-lipped and closed eyes. His wrinkles are gone. His skin is tight, fine-pored. He looks like an earlier version of himself, the tennis player in the framed photograph over the bed, the one where he's springing for the ball with everything pulled, straining into a forehand smash. The cavities that made his cheeks sink have filled out. His fingers clutch the lip of the cotton blanket as if he'd been trying to pull it up over himself when he died.

Where did she read that at death, all the emotion unused over a lifetime turns a countenance young again?

The room smells like vanilla. Arpie's idea.

—I'm spraying as we speak, she'd said. Vanilla is the universal scent of home, it reminds everybody of their mother.

So pleased with herself, coming up with *the* aromatherapeutic link while Adele sat trapped, the plane a blinking green arrow halfway between Glasgow and Halifax on the map charting the flight's progress on the screen at the front of the cabin.

Adele takes his lime aftershave from the nightstand, pats it on him, pats it on herself. She inhales until the citrus tang wipes out the milksweet drench.

—You never liked women who smelled like kitchens, she says.

She puts her cheek to her father's. He feels dense, coagulated. The opposite of his final years, when he seemed to be made of onion-skin. She runs the back of her hand across his five o'clock shadow. Compares their hands, which have the same shape, small but square, hands that can do a job.

The minutes stretch out and all she is doing is touching. The top of her father's head. His eyelids like petals. The hollows under his eyes. A small sore on his right ear. An old bruise, magenta and healing, at his throat. She holds his head. Skin and bone finely honed as river rock. Soft indentation at the temples. She rests her palm on his heart, thinks what an ardent part of him it was and how, for as long as she can remember, she has been fascinated and awed by the pumping and paths of men's blood. Coolness now, all the way down through his layers.

—We're nearing the end. Arpie had been almost inaudible over the drone of the plane.
—How can you tell?
—His breathing. Jen says it's withering.
—Withering is visual.
—To you, Arpie had said. Because you're not here.
Adele had tried to imagine the sound of breath shrinking into itself. Guttering candle flame? Crunch of dried leaves?
—What's he dying of exactly?
—They can't say for sure without disturbing him. EKG. Temperature. An agitated buzz in Arpie's voice. She'd sounded worried Adele might try to drag it out.
—He says he has friends and a taxi waiting, she added. He made me promise not to mention anything to mother. He keeps asking, Where do I go?
Where do I go? The pale image of Adele's face twisted in the window's reflection. Clouds sucked up the light. Leaving Paris at six o'clock meant she'd been flying west into evening for hours, a never-ending transition of day into night, point of crossing, cinnamon rose and violet-streaked, as though something had laid into the sky, raising welts. She didn't completely trust Arpie's accounting of events. She

had no basis for contradicting her sister, but she felt her own eyes and ears would inhabit the situation differently. She would not be so distressed by their father's disoriented questions. She would have a context for comprehending his state of body and mind that was lost on Arpie, who took what she saw and heard as literal measures, lucid or off-kilter, of the external world. Adele, on the other hand, thought it possible the co-mingling of past and present, fantasy and fact, did not indicate disintegrating consciousness but, rather, a consciousness becoming whole, freeing itself from the obstacle of coherence.

—Don't move him, she'd said. Don't change anything. Even a light. Don't open the drapes.

Arpie's sigh was so long, so tired, Adele could feel it like a shudder, it came out of the cloud reef to enter her own tired body, knotted calf muscles, aching lumbar, the place where her back didn't quite meet the seat.

—Adele—the way Arpie bit down on the name, trying to be patient—I'm playing Schubert *Lieder* so he can go out hearing German. Jessye Norman. Listen.

Where do living people store death? Does it grow in us, like cancer, or on us, like a beard? Does it crawl, pant, stretch, shatter? Where does death end and the memory of death begin? Do we really believe laying a coin over a dead person's eyes will keep them from seeing? Do we really believe burying someone and marking the place with stone will keep them in the ground?

A young boy sitting across the aisle from Adele spied something through the airplane window.

—I just saw Buddy, he told his mother excitedly.

—Where? she asked, startled. Dead cat, she mouthed silently to Adele.

—There—the boy pointed to a cloud—he just went by.

Later, he picked up the phone mounted on the seat-back in front of them and demanded to speak to someone named Honey.

—We can't call Honey on the phone anymore, his mother said. Dead grandmother, she whispered to Adele, again over her son's head.

—Yes, we can, the boy insisted. You pick up the receiver but you don't push the buttons. When the wing people answer, you ask if she's all white yet. You ask when her heart is going to come back as a bird.

Adele's father saw her dead mother. Just months ago, on the occasion of his eighty-fourth birthday. Adele had been driving him to Arpie's and he kept turning sideways, straining against the seat belt to peer worriedly into the back seat.

—Where's Mammy? Did we forget her?

Adele had taken a long breath. Mother's no longer with us, she'd reminded him. She had expected an abject gesture, slumping shoulders, a drooping chin, but her father had continued to stare blank-faced into the rear well of the car.

—I know that, he said reasonably. She's gone, but she keeps turning up.

He died the moment the sky turned. The plane came out of the cloud folds into a blue so spectral and unearthly Adele could walk through, be there. It was not a color of water or garden: delphinium, cornflower, spruce, indigo spires salvia. Not laser, or the hot gas blue of a Bunsen burner, or chilled cerulean, like a freshly stripped vein. Not cobalt, azure, sapphire, aquamarine. Drugged blue. Or Giotto, saturated and euphoric, cathedral blue, the blue of an aquarium, soft and benedictive, offering asylum.

Because it had no equivalent in the natural world, this blue did not comfort her. She could not see her father in it, hear his rustle. Her only sense was of his swimming upward, kicking free of gravity. Meanwhile, the arc of the plane had changed. The arrow on the map at the front of the cabin was a downward trajectory. They were over Nova Scotia, banking south now, into the depression of the Ohio Valley, the blinking red eye of Cincinnati.

She collects his sweaters, the thick white cotton sock full of quarters for the vending machines downstairs, the postcards she sent, photographs of street scenes that conjured his old life: two young women in scarves and cloches at an outdoor café; Bernard Berensen at ninety, impeccable in a linen suit and straw fedora, browsing a Rome museum, infatuated with the marble breasts of Pauline Borghese.

The silence is not the room holding its breath. The sense of compression is the actuality of death bearing down (as Jen predicted) on the flowered drapes and wingback chair, the walker in the corner, the low bed with its side rails, the tubed fluorescent lights ringing the ceiling, the clock radio with the neon red digits, the large numerals on the telephone push buttons and the remote control, the panic button connecting him to the nurses' station.

Adele wonders if, at the end, the buttons and numbers reassured him, satisfied his engineer's craving for order and fixed sequences. Towards the last, boundaries had seemed so necessary. She'd wanted him to fight, be haughty or righteous. Instead, he faded, retreated bit by bit behind the artifice of mauve and teal. He detached himself from color.

—How about the pale-blue checked shirt?

—Whatever you like. He would stare. He kept the drapes closed day and night.

—Let me open these, she'd say. Bring the outdoors in so you can see green.

—Green interferes with the television picture.

—Something yellow to cheer you up?

—Don't be ridiculous. Yellow is the color of insanity.

But he always knew what time it was. He wore his watch in the shower, stole discreet glances at it while eating or watching television. It was the last thing he took off before sleep, and when it had been placed on the nightstand he would rest his hand on it and then, when his head was on the pillow, look back to make sure it hadn't moved. Adele had thought it no more than a debilitated person's obsession with time. Now she wonders if he was counting the minutes and hours to make his life go by.

Where *is* his watch? She scours the room, is on the verge of storming out and hunting down Mary Ada to accuse someone of stealing it when she remembers that Arpie removed it for safekeeping, but not until after he was gone.

—If I'd done it before, he would have known.

—Oh, yes.

—And it would have upset him.

—Definitely.

—Even though he was unconscious.

—Unconscious. Adele had spat the word. What does that mean besides does not respond to pain?

She wonders what the last thing he saw was, his last sound. If it's true about hearing being the last sense to fade and if so, why was Arpie so intent on Jessye Norman, why didn't she just turn on a Reds game, let him enter and be lifted up, whipped mitt to mitt, Tinkers to Evers to Chance?

Knocking.

—Yes?

—I did what you asked, put ice in the water but it didn't do any good.

Before Adele can respond, she feels air strike her neck. Light from the hallway falls on the dimness of the room. Mary Ada tiptoes. She's a short, doughy woman without physical definition. Every part of her appears to melt into the flesh around it except her glittering eyes and her mouth, which is a slit, tan like the rest of her, so she looks as if she has no lips and is perpetually indignant. She's put the lilies in a large wine carafe, which she sets on the dresser.

—They're still drooping, she announces in a nursely manner, the manner of someone whose personal and professional mission is to eradicate droop, sag, slouch—anything less than ramrod.

In the past, Adele has confronted her: *Why Tylenol six times a day? Does it always take fourteen minutes to answer his buzzer? There are buttons missing from his blue dress shirt. He's concerned about his elimination.* Mary Ada, in turn, has brandished things in Adele's face: patient charts, gallon jars of pills, one time a corked vial of freshly drawn blood. Now she looks haggard. Her white lab coat is stained and smudged. There are shiny trails on her cheeks where tears have dried. Much as Adele would love to continue to loathe her, she feels kindly. She can't help it. Mary Ada's face is impassive, but her hands, those keen, apprehending parts of her, are clasped tight over her abdomen. Her two thumbs worry one another. She could be palpating an organ or saying a rosary.

Adele rests her hand lightly on her father's chest. Mary Ada, she asks, have you slept?

Mary Ada looks from Adele to the body on the bed to the small pile of belongings on the floor to the memorabilia on the walls—photographs of tennis tournaments and award acceptances, an oil painting of the house Arpie and Adele had grown up in, a rambling blue-gray Victorian with forsythia growing up over the living room's bay windows. Above the living room are tangerine dabs in two upstairs windows: Arpie's room, July '68, she'd spent a month camping in the Yucatan and had returned to Cincinnati demanding gold curtains, Aztec red walls.

Mary Ada nods at the house. I used to imagine him there, she says. If he was happy. Was he happy?

—Yes. Adele presses her father's sternum.

Mary Ada nods again, pleased that something she intuited has been confirmed. I thought so, she says.

Adele tells Mary Ada how there used to be lilac bushes in the side yard until a neighbor's son chopped them down with an axe he got for his birthday. She tells her the forsythia grew from bare root plants given out at school each Arbor Day. Their mother would stick them in the ground, christen them with bourbon, and warn Arpie and Adele not to count on anything. She points out Arpie's bedroom, and hers, over on the east side.

—Before it was mine, it was my older sister's.

—Janet...

—You know her name? Adele's surprised.

—The one who.... Mary Ada is flushed, animated. Adele realizes her knowledge of the family in this house is specific.

—killed herself, Adele says, matter-of-fact.

—Your father told me he used to have four daughters and now he had two. The first time he said it, I thought he had pneumonia again, that he was delirious. Then he told me about Grace and Janet.

Adele is taken aback that her father would have confided this to Mary Ada. She's not close, like Jen. She doesn't even like them. Plus her father was a bon vivant. He charmed people with lightness and wit. He avoided discussion of what he called the problem side of life. People had enough tragedies of their own, he said, there was no need to burden them with yours. Adele had always thought he was afraid of sadness, its boundlessness. Whereas that was the precise aspect that had attracted her mother, that made suffering the last way she could love her lost girls. What had possessed him to open up to Mary Ada, of all people?

—Before Janet's suicide, there was Seconal and vodka, Adele says. She jumped from the window of our parents' bedroom. It's next to Arpie's, around the corner, on that side. You can't see it from this perspective. It was Christmas Eve. We found her in the snow on our way back from church. She hopes Mary Ada will see from this how separate Janet was from the rest of the family. Doomed, her death could not have been prevented. The loss of her was regrettable but not personally overwhelming, as is the death in front of them, the one Adele literally has her pulse on.

—I suppose you and your sister were reined in. It would be natural, after losing two children. Mary Ada seems to be speaking not to Adele but to the extremities of the room, the walls, the shroud of drapes.

—Oh, yes. Arpie and I were watched over.

They ran wild, but Adele would rather expire here and now than admit further failure, the family's inability to learn from its mistakes and watch over itself.

—Still, our mother never stopped worrying, she adds.

Mary Ada comes over, pats Adele's shoulder. Do me a favor, she says. When you're ready to leave, throw me a signal. I'll be passing out meds. You don't have to say anything, just nod or wag, and I'll know to call the funeral home to pick him up.

As she closes the door, she takes the light with her.

Adele knows she should go find Arpie, who is waiting outside. She should comfort her sister, be comforted by her. They should cry on one another, lean. But she can't do that. She feels love for her sister, tenderness towards her, but also suspicion, wariness, the distrust of someone who knows upheaval is all around but can't yet gauge the meaning of it. She and Arpie are at a crossroads. They've run out of parents and spare siblings. That frame is no more.

How to confront this without illusion, the nicety of illusion?

—What then? She asks the question aloud, draws her black jacket around her, looks on her father for almost the last time, bends over and takes hold of his arms, which are soft and wrinkled, gathered like the sleeve of a woman's garment.

—What? She is both imploring and castigating him.

See this? Under the mattress? Mother's deboning knife? Play my Johnny Mathis one more time without permission and you'll never be cute again. Scarves? Let me show you how Isadora Duncan died. My hair looks terrible. I'm not leaving the dormitory until the ends go under. Did mother remember to send my pink curlers? I can't live without them. If they're not in Roanoke by Friday, I'm going to slit my wrists.

Adele winces, shakes off Janet's nasal singsong as she would a nasty dog. She shakes off the memory of the sharp watery smell that clung to Janet from her daily soaking baths. She's not surprised her sister has insinuated herself into Garnet Hill. The girl always did have a knack for attaching herself to bad situations for the purpose of making them worse. What pleasure invading their father's spirit must give her.

Adele clearly sees the boning knife, not in Janet's hands but her mother's, she watches Margo peel whole vertebrae from the flesh of trout or Dover sole, hold the white needled spine aloft, murmuring, in appreciative wonder, Doesn't this remind you of a leaf skeleton? She sees Calamine-colored sponge rubber curlers resting in a box that was returned from Janet's Virginia college stamped NO LONGER AT THIS ADDRESS. The box stayed for months, maybe years, in the hall closet, the curlers webbed with Janet's long brown hair and smelling slightly of home permanent solution until someone, Adele never knew who, mercifully disposed of it.

In one brisk movement, she pulls down the sheet and coverlet. Her father's rib cage is exposed, the gaunt, slack, crosshatched musculature of his once-sinewy torso. He is cold to the touch, even in the room's faint glimmer Adele can see his blood has settled, he's blue-tinged like the edge of a flame. The red band of a diaper seals his waist.

Harshness. Numbers and dead flowers, everything in opposition to something else. Slightly at war. Yes. And limbo, the room's limbo. That, too. *L'heure entre le chien et le loup*, the hour between the dog and the wolf, what the French call dusk. Yes, yes, that's what she wants, to sink back into the twilight of the plane, the lovely oblivion when some part of her was still unconvinced.

When she was still waiting for something.

What is the sense of trying to hold him to this room, its reek of rubber and emollients, its jars of Vaseline and boxes of disposable gloves, its dim half-light that leaches pink from skin?

Adele gets up from the bed, turns off the fluorescent tube. Her father is now bathed in the neon of lit numerals. His faint halitosis surrounds her: ammoniated citrus, overripe bananas. Her mouth fills with the metallic taste of iron and nails. She crosses to the room's two large picture windows, opens the flowered drapes and peers out. Arpie's station wagon is parked just beyond the ellipse of the porte cochere below, but her sister is nowhere to be seen. The car sits deserted at the curb. Another body abandoned. Adele feels a pervasive sense of longing but has no idea what the longing is attached to or what would satisfy it. Only that it resides in a cavity, an open pit, and the pit is her.

The feathers in her chest become part of a greater movement, time stretching through the walls to the stands of pin oaks and sugar maples and hundred-year-old elms, the duck pond, the latticed gazebo, the path studded with exercise equipment. The course, her father called it. Do you want to walk the course?

Beyond the course, fields pool black. Moonlight vanishes in them, becomes lost until the ground opens back up at the periphery of Garnet Hill and releases what it has held. At that point, lights from Highway 4 flash between the trees, the places where the plump trees open into passage.

His face is hers. The hands. The part inside that travels.

Where are you now, Daddy?

I'm not sure. A park, maybe. The trees have scalloped leaves and pods.

I imagine you living, but on the other side of your bones.

You mean I'm coral reef? He laughs. That's the only organism I know that lives outside its skeleton.

I would say or do anything to keep your life from being over.

In its end stages, Parkinson's locks you in. For all intents and purposes, you're frozen.

Didn't you once say you had two regrets? Not voting for Adlai Stevenson and not knowing Shakespeare better?

Not voting for Stevenson twice, but don't jinx me with regrets. I'm too grateful for the Vicodin, the emperin-codeine. My neuro-transmitters are resuscitating.

I guess I'd better dump the lilies.

The gardener in you will never give up.

I can't help myself. The catalogues. The glossy photographs. (Sketches of root balls unfurling deep in the earth, tunneling, sending out tendrils. Vivid descriptions promising extravagant growth, growth as never before.)

That's you, kiddo: Bulbs and bare roots. The thrill of spring in the dead of winter.

II.

Meanwhile:

Arpie lies like a prostrate cross in the adjacent pasture of horsetails and dried wheat grass and hollyhocks. She's a tall, solidly built woman, with freckles, a snub nose, and a fan of corkscrewed, flame-red hair that gives the impression of pre-Raphaelite delicacy or bohemian abandon or witchy will, none of which apply. She's waiting for Adele just as earlier she had been waiting for her father. She spent the entire day waiting. She has spent years. Why is she here? In the field? On the ground? To be solitary. To get as far away from Garnet Hill as possible without actually driving off and leaving Adele. It was either here or the A-frame Church of the Nazarene across the street. Arpie is aware this might appear the stranger choice, but sometimes strange is better, the skewed perspective. Besides, once, on her way to visit her father, she spied people milling outside the church holding snakes.

Garnet Hill spreads out behind her on three sides. Excepting the four-story nursing pavilion, the complex rises low and benign, clapboard cottages and town-house-style apartments set on curving streets named for semi-precious stones: Topaz Way. Jade Circle. Via Aqua Marine. Three words. In the Miami Valley, where no thoroughfare is remotely a via, or remotely turquoise, or within hundreds of miles of salted water.

The turn-of-the-century relic that housed pregnant girls had been razed in the Seventies, but Arpie has never forgotten its dismal, punitive ambience. The dry, uncut yellow grass. The massive bird and insect nests furring the eaves. The brown bricks and dirty white gingerbread trim. When Arpie drove by, in spring or summer, girls would be sitting on the steps. Garnet Hill was set back from the road, on a slight rise that drew attention to the architecture while keeping the inhabitants undefined. There was no driveway, just an asphalt walk leading to the front stairs and porch. Arpie's mother and her friends donated their daughters' old clothes to Garnet Hill. To Arpie, it was like seeing herself and her friends in different bodies, Ginny Morrissey's paisley skirt on a tall girl with oily hair, Arpie's own powder blue mohair sweater from sixth grade riding above the waist of a girl whose round belly protruded under it.

Arpie worried she might be sent there. At ten, twelve, maybe up through junior high, she thought there was a possibility of getting pregnant without a preceding act. And not in the manner of Mary, the virgin birth. What bothered Arpie was the idea of mutation. Patty Duke. The bad seed theory. Scientists could talk about genus and class and order all they wanted, but there was always—and Arpie knew this, she spent hours cataloguing evidence of malformations in people and nature—the rogue molecule, something spinning off wildly, catastrophically on its own. Furthermore, rogue also meant capricious, instantaneous. Something that could cripple you out of nowhere, in the middle of the street, the crosswalk for God's sake, in the safe zone. While she slept. Arpie feared that more than anything, feared going innocently to bed and next thing, wham, she was blind, wham, her skin had been leached of its melanin and she'd turned albino, or she had polio, her spine was jellyfish. Or: she got knocked up. Something she couldn't get rid of was inside her and when they pointed a finger, all she could say is, I didn't do anything, I woke up and—

Stricken. That was the word. Eleven year old Barbara (Arpie) Weems was suddenly stricken with—

The reincarnated Garnet Hill retained the old name. *Because of the fields of amaranth that once grew here,* the brochure said. *Amaranth: commonly called bleeding heart or love-lies-bleeding. It is not hard to imagine how beautiful and untouched the land must have looked then. After the city's urban sprawl, fields carpeted in purple soothed the eyes and the spirit.*

In homage to its past, the Garnet Hill administration building contains in its lobby a plaster of Paris statue of a young woman cradling a newborn. To Arpie's eye, it has that looking back quality, all curves and idealization, the mother's tender smile, the baby's hand reaching for her face like a tiny, unfurling claw. *Dedicated to the brave women who gave birth here*, the inscription says.

Brave as opposed to what? she asks herself every time. There's not a straight line in the statue, a definitive angle or edge. Light pours in, and she remembers how the shades at the first Garnet Hill were always drawn. Summer and winter. She wondered how the girls could stand it. Never seeing out.

Her legs feel like lead pipes protruding from her cotton skirt. Her arms splay out like a child playing angel in the snow, a posture comprised of equal parts of martyrdom and trust. From one of the houses beyond the field, she hears Willie Nelson singing. His plaintive twang and unique phrasing mix with the rustle of stalks and the tickle of straw like a final musical judgment on the day, an elegy for the slow suicide of hours.

Her father's death was proper. That pleases Arpie, the word itself, its clean borders, its essence of order and civility, quiet echo and timeliness. He died in his bed. Without undue pain or physical suffering or discernible human struggle. Of natural causes, or, rather, causes not unnatural to those with a degenerative disease like Parkinson's. This event had occurred six months, three days, and several hours after the celebration of his eighty-fourth birthday.

In other words, this isn't a death anyone can complain about. It's proper in the decorous sense, right and gentle with its lack of blood or brutality. It didn't involve trauma, murder or a car crash. What it was was a measured dissolve of life, nothing abrupt or hammering, rather, a slow body fade, not just over the last twenty-four hours but back through the last blurry years.

And weren't they resigned? Hadn't they all accepted that one way or another, life would arrive at this juncture? Hadn't they registered each and every new physical diminishment with a sharp, secular eye, again, all of them? Hadn't they, frankly speaking, already begun behaving in cautious, veiled ways toward one another, not inhabiting the present so much as enameling it with the distance and sheen of memory? Hadn't the *pater familias* himself, when pressed by Arpie to reveal what he had wished for on his birthday candles, said, *To not break apart at the end.*

Well, that aspect didn't stick to plan. He did break apart. One minute he was happily eating lemon meringue pie and the next he had begun sweating profusely, waving his fork angrily about his left ear, as if, reported Jen, he was furious at some voice he was hearing.

But still, up until that point, wasn't he…

—Alzheimer's? Do you worry about that? Arpie had once overheard another resident ask him.

—Not at all, her father had answered, proud. Forgetting doesn't run in our genes. We Weems die remembering every detail.

Hadn't he lived up to that and didn't Arpie love it? Love it when he had corrected a Trivia Hour quiz that listed the chemical symbol for Potassium as P?

—The answer is K, Oak had informed Mary Ada.

—That's not what my crib sheet says.

—Your crib sheet is mistaken.

Loved it when, the few times an aide had asked him, in Arpie's presence, who the current Chief of State was, Oak had rolled his eyes before answering, in an uncharacteristically Puckish tone that made him sound like Truman Capote, *Coolidge? Grover P. Cleveland?*

No. Nothing about this passing could be called unseemly or unfitting, tragic, unanticipated, or, for that matter, even inconvenient. Actually, it was a fine death, a beautiful death, benign, ordinary, simple, graceful.

Willie sings of pennies in a stream, falling leaves, a sycamore. The words make Arpie yearn for cooler weather, true autumn, but beyond that, nothing. No twilight for her, trying to coax life back into ruined lilies. The realm she shares with her father—shared, she has to keep reminding herself that all tenses are now past—is—was—the world of The One Within Reach. She took possession of the parlor grand piano, the toolkit with its dazzling array of electric drill bits. She was also the recipient of the telephoned alarms in the middle of the night: We found him in the dining room. We found him in the utility closet. He thought it was Grand Central Station, he kept asking which way to the Oyster Bar.

Arpie loved her father. But long before the warning call from Jen woke her this morning, she had taken to loving him the way—as the urban expert in the Development Department who has won the informal Wrecking Balls of Steel award so often she has pretty much retired the title—she loved a venerable building marked for demolition, that is to say, as a respected icon whose usefulness and function have been effaced from her imagination and passed into history some time before the dynamite is actually strapped into place. When Arpie visited Garnet Hill, she kept her coat on. She touched her father as little as possible so as not to take into her dreams the tactile sense of his softening and shrinking. She did not sit for long spells. Her purse stayed on her shoulder, car keys at the ready, poised for the get-away.

Now that the event has actually transpired, she can't immediately retrace her steps. The full emotional impact of the loss she's been living well in advance of is, for the moment, beyond her. She can't go there yet, can't get past the pallor of her father's calm face expiring colorlessly, the people filing in and out to say goodbye.

Thank you, thank you for coming, Arpie had murmured over and over. At the same time some unknown person residing in a deeply buried part of her had held an invisible knife to his throat, had muttered—not hostile, more like a cartoon character mouthing words voicelessly, harmlessly into a balloon—Murder would have been easier. Or if you'd just wandered off like an Eskimo.

Actually, Arpie is not an unadorned prostrate cross, but one sporting a Marlboro Light at the extreme right of its horizontal crossbeam. She's nearly forgotten it. Upon lighting up, she had brought it to her mouth. Now, it sits wedged between her fingers, the weightless plume of it a ghostly exhalation. She looks up. The crescent moon sky brims with stars but the night is stagnant and hot. The wind, fierce until a few minutes ago, has momentarily retreated. Even the shadows are still. They have no flicker, skeletons reaching for one another's hands. The only moving things are gnats and motes. The heat makes Arpie feel swollen, cobwebbed. Sucked down, her whole body, as if into quicksand. She thinks she smells blackened weeds, but it is parched air, fatigue, darkness swarming the flatlands stretching towards Hamilton, it's the acrid sting of Indian summer, the rancid frying grease of the fast-food restaurants that line Route 4 past Garnet Hill. The odor of the long day sticks to her, the number of times she's broken out in perspiration and it has dried, layer on layer.

She sits up, circles her knees with her arms. Willie is still crooning:

> *telephone cables how they sing*
> *down the highway and travel each bend*
> *in the road, people who meet*
> *in these romantic settings*

are so hypnotized by the

Arpie turns, picks out her father's corner room. It's the only non-dark window on the third floor, the single one, paradoxically, showing signs of life. Pencils of pearl-colored light seep through the center of the drawn drapes, around the edges. Usually, she avoids this window, doesn't let herself glance up at its anchors, the Kleenex box within reach of the wingback chair, the books stacked on the radiator, partially visible beneath the curtain hem. This is the window seen from the Garnet Hill parking lot. Where she always feels late. Rushing to catch up. Even when she arrives early, with sufficient time to park in the visitors' section, she pulls into one of the Reserved for Physician spaces closer to the entrance.

The books are still there, but the Kleenex has been moved. To the nightstand. To accommodate the tears and running noses of those paying their respects. *From all over,* she had whispered to Adele, who was still mid-flight. *Even the people we can't stand.* She'd held up the phone so her sister could listen, had wondered what the fluted, rheumy voices sounded like to someone flying above clouds.

—Is the door to the room open? Adele had asked.

—Yes. Why are you asking?

—I'm just trying to picture it.

Wrong. Adele was mentally arranging the scene, wiping his brow, tucking the sheet just so around his form. Adele, making it pretty, and not, Arpie knew, for cosmetic reasons. To Adele, beauty had intention, was a way of claiming space. Beee-uuu-teee-ful. She blew soft air into the word, made it a caress, a beatification, an application of natural law that knit disparate elements into a profuse, compensatory whole. Arpie understood all this but nonetheless considered it idolatrous. To her, the flesh-and-blood father was sacred, not the appearance of shapes and textures and colors surrounding him.

—The door's open for practical reasons, so people can come and go freely, she had informed her sister.

—I see, Adele had murmured.

—What do you see?

—Nothing. I'm just glad it's not closed. Being an extrovert, I think it would bother him. Even now. I think he would know and not appreciate being shut off.

—He's on a sedative drip.

—Know on a molecular level.

—Let's not talk about it.

As Arpie watches, the light in the room changes to red. The drapes are thrown open. Adele stands framed in the aperture, slender as a ruby ghost. Her dark hair falls in a sheaf over one side of her face. She peers out quizzically, as though trying to locate Arpie in the darkness, then raises her hand in a slight wave. It is a beckoning gesture, one based on faith since Arpie's presence cannot be seen, verified. Even in pain, Arpie thinks, her sister can have faith and beckon.

Arpie waves back. The titters and brittle clicks of dark heat rise around her: night birds, cicadas, the swooshing grasses and crumbling leaves. Rather than ground out her cigarette, she licks her thumb and index finger and lightly presses the glowing butt until no embers remain. She gets up, brushes off her skirt, and heads back toward the porte cochere and the entrance where her car is parked.

To the immediate right of the overhang, the door to Security is open. A rectangle of light falls on the pavement outside. Herman and Cale, the night-shift guards, are playing cards at one of two identical Formica-topped desks. Two metal lunchboxes sit side by side on the floor. Classic Coke and Dr. Pepper cans and pretzels and Fritos and Cheese-Its litter the area immediately in front of them. In front of that, a bank of television monitors surveils Garnet Hill in an ever-changing collage of grainy half tones. Rooms, doorways and corridors come into view and then fade, replaced by other rooms and doorways and corridors, all murky, as if seen through mist or drizzle.

Herman, the older of the two guards, turns, spies Arpie. He is a big smiling German, a retired butcher, paunched and spider-veined. He tips his Cincinnati Bengals cap. Praise Gott, Mr. Weems enjoyed long life, he says.

—Long, yes, Arpie replies.

—What can I say? Herman shakes his head, sympathetic. At least it's over. Both parents. Nobody else for you and your sister to lose. He reaches behind him, grabs a pink pastry box and proffers it. *Zwetschgenkuchen*? he asks.

—Plum cake, Cale explains.

Herman's wife Oma works at a bakery that for decades was called Little Prussia. Due to a recent change of ownership, it's now Zeitgeist. Every day, Oma packs Herman's lunchbox with day-old desserts offered gratis to the employees: fruit *streusel*, *linzer*—or *kirschtorte*, *pommern*, or some other German confection.

Though born in America, Herman and Oma possess detailed knowledge of regional German cuisine, which Herman shares with Arpie, letting her know, for example, that the *badishen zwiebelkuchen* or onion cake she's so fond of comes from the Baden area, just as *biersuppe* (beer soup) originated in Bavaria, where beer is an official food product that by law must be available at all times, even in the event of war. Arpie in turn relates to him anecdotes about her paternal grandmother, also of German descent and also a baker. Arpie made donuts with her. When she visited they would rise with the sun and tiptoe down into the kitchen, which was soon redolent of flour and butter and frying grease. By the time the rest of the household was awake there would be a platter of warm irregular rounds drenched in powdered sugar. But no centers. They had already been devoured. Arpie's grandmother would punch them out with her red plastic cutter, fry them until they were golden brown and so filled with air they would bob and bounce like ping-pong balls on the surface of the sizzling oil. Then she would remove them with her slotted spoon, drain them, roll them in sugar, and pop them in Arpie's mouth, telling her that the center was the prized part of a doughnut, like a chicken's wishbone or calf brains.

—Eat, please, no argument, sugar is aspirin for tears, Herman says now.

—I'm not crying.

—Ah, but you will be. Herman cuts a generous slice of the plum tart with a spade-shaped server, hands it to Arpie in a paper napkin. She waves away his offer of a plastic fork, preferring to eat with her fingers. The texture is between a tart and a cake. Flaky crust, baked fruit, lemon peel and autumn spices—nutmeg, cinnamon, mace—crumble in her mouth to a sweet-tangy mash. Arpie leans against the doorjamb. This is the second time today (the first was when Adele alighted from the plane) she has felt unalone, grounded in her body, accompanied. She always feels that way around Herman and Cale. The homey disarray of their lair makes Garnet Hill seem less alien and lonely. Here, in this room, watching the monitors, her father's decline and the amorphous world he was inhabiting seemed more manageable and contained, heavy with portent and shadowy meaning yet controlled, less ominous. Arpie still knew the experience was true, yet it seemed to be happening at a gray remove. The monitors provided a visual filter. Herman and Cale provided the filter of pinochle or gin rummy, bakery smells and forgiving conversation. At Garnet Hill, Arpie usually felt numb. She walked with her gaze down. She gave the impression of being preoccupied, not wishing to be spoken to, yet she gravitated towards Herman and Cale as she would a confessional.

—I don't know what I'll miss more, you two or Oma's cooking, she says.

—Will you and your sister need help moving? Cale asks. He's a prim, blond, fortyish man with a stem of a neck and pale, smooth-knuckled hands, which he clasps prayer-like to his chest.

—I'll let you know, Arpie says. Adele's husband Lewis would orchestrate the heavy moving when he arrived. Arpie's own mental inventory of what should be saved from the room is meager. The transition to Garnet Hill had represented a true winnowing. Her father had brought few personal effects with him; his wingback chair, a few treasured books: Bruce Catton's Civil War trilogy, *Death Comes for the Archbishop*, the T.E. Lawrence biography *Seven Pillars of Wisdom*—Oak had hoped the brilliant strategies and tactics of the Arabs' guerilla warfare against the Turks might adapt to his own battle with Parkinson's—an Oxford Unabridged dictionary, and, finally, a dog-eared, brown-tinged vintage edition of *Canterbury Tales*. In high school in Cleveland, Oak had had to memorize long passages, which he still proudly recited in Middle English.

—If it were up to me, I'd burn it all, Arpie adds. She's still leaning against the doorjamb, facing in, away from her car and the porte cochere and her father's room. Once again, the unseasonable heat settles on her cheeks and neck, making her feel flushed, feverish. She folds her arms, exhales in a sigh.

—It's very quiet, she says.

—It always is, Herman replies.

—And hot.

—False summer. It will end.

—Yes. Arpie sighs again. It went by so fast, she says.

—His final hours?

—No, the four years he was here.

—It's better that way, Herman says.

—I think it is better, Arpie agrees. It's just that at the time everything seemed slowed down, dragged out, but that was wrong. Actually, everything was zooming.

—Will the services be here, at the Garnet Hill chapel? Cale asks.

—I don't know yet.

—Will there be a casket or are you having him cremated?

—I don't know that either. (Both traditions apply. Her mother was cremated, Grace and Janet, no.) We're not one of those families who plan funerals in advance, she adds. We let people die and then decide what to do with them.

—Look. Your sister. Cale indicates one of the middle screens. Adele can be seen walking down a corridor. Her hair is mussed and her traveling clothes—black jacket over a black blouse and black jeans—are in disarray. She looks confused, as if she's coming to after a deep sleep. Both hands are full, but Arpie can't make out what she's carrying. Her image is clouded, her head and extremities wavy like the sheen of a fish. The picture switches. Adele is now coming upon Mary Ada in an adjacent corridor, next to a tiered cart stacked with bucket-sized containers of pills. After consulting a chart, Mary Ada measures out a dosage into a miniature Dixie cup that looks like a thimble. The two women speak, lean solicitously toward one another.

Mary Ada puts a hand on Adele's back. Adele doesn't pull away, which startles Arpie. She's used to gestures of objection between the two. Adele moves on. She shifts whatever she is carrying and wraps her jacket around her as if she is chilled. Her hands, clearly seen now, are balled into fists. As she exits the picture, a skin of light surrounds her. The camera angle pulls her bones longer, attenuating and distorting her thin frame.

Minutes later, she comes out the double doors. Spying Arpie, she walks toward Security. Her purse hangs from one shoulder. She holds out the postcards and sweaters and the coin-filled sock.

—I got rid of your vanilla, she tells Arpie.

Arpie takes the sweaters. Despite the heat, and the lateness of the hour, and their exhaustion, the sisters are loath to leave Garnet Hill. This is their last opportunity to live in the unexpectedness of their father's death. Tomorrow, each will wake with reality solidified around her. Each will begin to consider what it means to have the other her closest blood relation. Each will evaluate where that sister can be counted on to be loyal and where she has a history of lies, deceit, cruelty, betrayal. Overnight, the tasks and rituals of burial will have begun to impose themselves on the anarchy of fresh death. Time will be dictated, activities. Tonight's sky, with its silvered moon and amber Venus and the filigreed arch of trees filling with wind, this will dissolve when day resurrects its bright, shiny surfaces. The social, public aspects of death will supplant the private. Fantasies of survival will supplant fantasies of death, and who knows what that will bring?

So they linger, make small talk with Herman and Cale in the cramped Security office that opens to the grounds on one side and, on the other, connects to Garnet Hill through a narrow umbilical of corridor. Cale asks if Adele will be needing the key to the yellow guest room where she customarily stays. No, she replies, the soft mattresses at Garnet Hill hurt her husband's back. She and Lewis are staying downtown. She'll miss the yellow room's bamboo wallpaper with the violet ceiling border, though she welcomes the view of the river.

—You don't like water, Arpie reminds her.

I do, but at a distance, Adele thinks, but doesn't say anything. Giving Arpie the last word lets her be right. Arpie needs to be right.

And when's her husband arriving? Soon, Adele says, then, immediately after, Later.

Herman offers Adele a slice of *Zwetschgenkuchen.* She declines, but suggests that Arpie never turns down dessert, which Arpie doesn't. Arpie no longer leans against the doorjamb. She's next to Adele. The sisters' bodies brush and press. This seems good, reassuring. Their father's death has made them more acutely aware of one another. Each feels on her skin the notice of the other like a pressing of earth. A bonging clock echoes from one of the Garnet Hill living rooms. The wind inflates, sending branches ticking against plate glass. A weeping willow by the entrance pitches and shakes. Shrubs and bedding plants bend so flat to the ground their spines appear in danger of snapping. Arpie lifts Adele's hair off her neck. Adele massages the small of Arpie's back, the exact spot where, earlier, Arpie had witnessed Mary Ada touching Adele. It reminds her to ask Adele about that once they are alone. Arpie wants to know exactly what went on up there.

A buzzer sounds. A light blinks on one of the monitors. A dark, boxy hearse can be seen idling before the wrought-iron gates that enter Garnet Hill from Route 4.

—They've come for your father…. Cale looks at them, uneasy. A meaty, tattooed forearm with a bandage at the wrist crooks out from the driver's side to impatiently push the buzzer again. Behind the hearse, trucks and cars hurtle along the highway. The Dutch elms that line the driveway writhe and swoop in the wind.

Herman frowns. They're in a hurry, he says disapprovingly. The monitors on either side of that in which the hearse looms portray empty corridors.

—We're not delicate, we can watch anything, Adele declares.

Arpie can't witness this anymore than she could the contraption they rigged to fit over his penis to catch urine at night when he was no longer able to lift himself out of bed and get to the bathroom in time. *Not physical incontinence, functional,* Mary Ada had informed her. *It's the Parkinson's. Do you want to see how the device works?*

Certainly not. In every incarnation and no matter who it housed, the pregnant or the infirm, Garnet Hill made people give up their bodies. Arpie couldn't stand that. Hated the imposition of this unwell, exposed father onto his earlier wholesome selves in which much had remained hidden from them, in the respectful distance between parent and child Arpie found not only apt but comforting.

—I have to get out of here, she says. She wrenches Adele away, which is not hard to do. Her sister is so thin.

—We're leaving him alone, Adele protests. She begins to cry.

—He's not alone. He's with Fish Brothers Mortuary.

—Something could happen to him.

Arpie freezes. She drops Adele's hand, stares at her weeping sister, flabbergasted. What? she demands to know. What more could happen in this place?

an excerpt from a novel

Mary Rakow
The Memory Room

38.

I pour a cup of coffee. Unfold the concert program from my evening
purse. Yo-Yo Ma played the First Bach Suite, then a new work by
David Wilde, "The Cellist of Sarajevo."

Composed to honor the cellist who played at the site of the
bombed bakery. Every afternoon at four o'clock, in full concert dress,
mortar and machine-gun fire, his folded chair, silk tails falling to the
dusty road. A requiem for the dead.

I saved the clipping from that bombing. Years ago, when I
still read the papers.

I find it, frayed and yellowed, in my box. Bakery, bombed.
The flustered birds.

It was the girl on the left-hand side of the photograph that
made me keep it. A teenager, perhaps fourteen, her jutting jaw, the
downward crescent of her fastened mouth. Pulling back her hair.
Fingering, with her other hand, the coins she'd tied to the corner of
her scarf.

I set her picture on the table next to the program of Ma's
playing.

I want her to know that in Los Angeles, halfway around the globe, no one stirred in the hall when Ma played Wilde's "Lament in Rondo Form." We were startled in unison. Like strangers, immigrants, carried in a boat. Newly landed in a harbor, I was exhausted. Rags over my knuckles, my wool coat wet with fog.

I want to say, This is how notes travel. Like a key sewn in the lining of a coat.

We emptied our pockets, our small treasures, a locket, a letter, a key. Leaning against gunny sacks on a different shore. Waiting for our new names to be penned in ink.

I bring the photo and the program closer, so their edges touch.

Perhaps.

The young girl went to buy a loaf of bread. A simple errand. After hearing the blast, her mother finds her. Twenty-two others in the bakery, dead. She thinks, My daughter, not even wounded! And weeping, draws her down onto her shoulder. Thick arms, her wrinkled neck.

Already, handkerchiefs on the faces of the dead, a fluttering of white.

But the girl does not see this. She is saving herself. Making herself blind. And it is not the tilting racks, rye breads rolling on the floor, the wedding cake behind shattered glass, not someone else's blood splashed across her checked skirt like paint that made her do it. It is the woman to her left, propped against the wall, who rocks her child, not seeing that the baby has no head.

The girl falls into the texture on her mother's arm. Caught in the sweater's weave, garlic, onion, marjoram. The fragrances of home.

Perhaps,

For three days the young girl doesn't eat. When touch and appetite return, and speech, and sleep, she still does not see. Her father snaps his fingers before her face, talks too loud. On the tenth day, hits the table, calls the priest.

No one asks if she wants to see.

On the fourteenth day, the girl smells paraffin and beeswax in the night. Her mother whispering prayers. Matches struck, one by one. She counts them. Twenty-two in all.

Candles set on small tables and chairs around her bed.

When the candles burn their way and there are no more in the drawer, her mother does not buy new ones. The girl wakes to find something cold and wet on her eyes. "It's just a compress," her mother says, but the girl smells sour earth, cow dung mixed in. She feels bits of eucalyptus leaf shard against her lids, the bits of straw. Her mother pats it down. "It's just a compress," she repeats, an urgency in her voice like a tangle, and the young girl thinks, Now even my body does not belong to me.

A young American doctor with instruments in his backpack finds nothing in her eyes. She feels his fingers on her cheekbones and wants to stay in that warmth of skin on skin. She holds his hands there, considering how touch is better this way, without sight interfering. She wonders if he knows this.

She would like to tell him what she preserves in the darkness she's created:

The memory of a hair ribbon her boyfriend returned. Apricot satin against the mat, when she opened the door and he was not there.

The autumn mist shrouding the Mary window of St. Margaret's Church, fringed blue gray like a shawl.

Her father's back, looking out from the balcony, coffee in hand, waiting for an answer from the sun. Copper sunlight on the telephone wires, the train station, the domed roof of the mosque.

Her grandmother's cramped hands, pickling cucumbers lowered into a vinegar bath, one by one. Marking the arrival of summer.

Grains of sugar suspended in the clear flesh of a just-peeled pear. Sweet taste of fall.

Aspen trees in winter.

The gilding of chocolate on cherries in a tin hinged box.

A lipstick kiss she put on the bathroom mirror, the heart she drew around it, the initials of his name.

❦

39.

With thin needle and a fine thread I sit in my now-black room and bind the edges of the frail photograph. Then the pages of the program. I sew the two together like leaves, sheaves, the bakery girl and Ma's playing. It takes the afternoon.

I want to tell her, I haven't experienced the explosion of breads. But I know how a melody, a lament, can be heard inside one's head. Bearing down with its own necessity.

This chain of laments can link us across oceans. Notes lifting up the wreckage.

an excerpt from a novel

Contributors

AIMEE BENDER's short fiction has been published in *Granta*, GQ, *Harper's*, *The Paris Review*, *McSweeney's* and *Fence*, among others. She is the author of *The Girl in the Flammable Skirt*, a New York Times Notable Book of 1998, and *An Invisible Sign of My Own* (Doubleday), a Los Angeles pick of 2000. She teaches creative writing at the University of Southern California.

Aimee Bender

SAMANTHA DUNN is the author of *Failing Paris* (The Toby Press), a finalist for the PEN West Fiction Award in 2000, and the memoir, *Not by Accident: Reconstructing a Careless Life* (Henry Holt & Co.). Her work has appeared in numerous national publications including the *Los Angeles Times*, *O Magazine*, and *Ms*. Her most recent memoir, *Faith in Carlos Gomez*, is published by Henry Holt & Co.

Samantha Dunn

LINDSAY FITZGERALD grew up in the Adirondacks of New York. She holds a B.A. in literary journalism and an MFA in creative writing from the University of California. She currently teaches English and writing at colleges in southern California. Her stories have been published in

Lindsay Fitzgerald

Santa Monica Review and *Alaska Quarterly Review*; she is twenty-six and lives with two cats and a shark fish.

Lisa Glatt

LISA GLATT's first novel *A Girl Becomes a Comma Like That* was published in June 2004 and her short story collection *The Body Shop* is forthcoming in April 2005, both from Simon & Schuster. Her poetry collections include *Shelter* and *Monsters & Other Lovers*. She currently teaches at California State University, Long Beach and in private workshops. Glatt is married to poet and visual artist David Hernandez.

liz gonzález

LIZ GONZÁLEZ's poetry, memoirs and fiction have been published in numerous publications. *Beneath Bone*, a volume of her poetry, was published by Manifest Press in 2000. She teaches writing at the Long Beach City College Pacific Coast Campus Writing and Reading Center and creative writing at the UCLA Extension Writers' Program.

Jody Hauber

JODY HAUBER recently completed her latest novel, *Wild Chickens*. Her short story "The Hole Where A Glow Should Be" was selected for the anthology *Long Baptisms: Writings by Daughters of Alcoholic Mothers*. She has been a feature prize winner in the Writers' Digest Personal Essay Contest and has published two other novels.

KAREN HORN is a fiction writer and essayist. She has published in the *Pacific Review*, *Two Moons* and the *Topanga Messenger*. Formerly she worked as a film editor in Los Angeles and New York. A member of the Hard Words writing group in Los Angeles since 1997, she would like to thank the Djerassi Rerident Artists Program for the space and time to write this story.

Karen Horn

DYLAN LANDIS is writing two interlocking books: a novel, *Floorwork*, and a collection of linked stories. Her fiction has appeared in *Tin House*, *Bomb*, the *Santa Monica Review*, and the anthologies *Bestial Noise: The Tin House Fiction Reader* and *Best American Nonrequired Reading 2003*. In a past life she wrote six books on interior design.

Dylan Landis

MICHELLE LATIOLAIS is the author of *Even Now*, winner of the Gold Medal for Fiction from the Commonwealth Club of California. She is an Associate Professor of English at the University of California, Irvine.

Michelle Latiolais

Rochelle Low

ROCHELLE LOW holds a degree in English Literature from UCLA. She began her literary life as a poet publishing in small local journals while still a student. After a twenty-year hiatus from writing to concentrate on motherhood, she has been a member of the Los Angeles women's writing collective, Hard Words, for the past nine years.

Erin Julia McGuire

ERIN JULIA MCGUIRE's "Crowfeathers" won Chicago Public Radio's Stories on Stage fiction competition and was performed and recorded at the Museum of Contemporary Arts in Chicago. For her fiction and plays she has received fellowships from the Ragdale Foundation, The Playwrights' Center, and the Minnesota State Arts Board. Originally from Minneapolis, she now makes Los Angeles her home.

Abby Mims

ABBY MIMS resides in Los Angeles. She has an MFA from UC Irvine and her stories have been published or are forthcoming in *Pearl*, the *Santa Monica Review*, *Other Voices* and *Swink*. She is currently finishing a collection of short stories and is at work on a novel.

CAROL MUSKE-DUKES is the author of seven books of poems (the most recent, *Sparrow*, Random House, 2003, was a finalist for the National Book Award), three novels and two collections of essays. She is professor of English/Creative Writing at the University of Southern California and founding director of the Ph.D. program in CW/Lit there. She reviews for the *New York Times* and writes a monthly poetry column for the *LA Times Book Review*, "Poets' Corner."

Carol Muske-Dukes

JULIANNE ORTALE has an MFA from UC Irvine and her stories have appeared in *Alaska Quarterly, Salmagundi, The Malahat Review, Stand, Paris Boulevard*, and *Gobshite Quarterly*, among others. She is currently finishing a collection of short stories and is at work on a novel. In her secret life, she's a *tanguera* and a *salsera*.

Julianne Ortale

ANITA SANTIAGO grew up in an American petroleum camp in the middle of the Venezuelan jungle. In 1980, she moved to the United States, where she now owns a successful advertising agency in Santa Monica, California. Her fiction, which has been published in anthologies and journals, focuses on issues relating to women caught between cultures.

Anita Santiago

Contributors

Mary Rakow

Rachel Resnick

Lisa Teasley

MARY RAKOW, Ph.D. has degrees in theology from Harvard University Divinity School and Boston College. She was awarded a Lannan Literary Fellowship for her debut novel *The Memory Room*, which was a Finalist in Fiction with PEN/West. Rakow conducts private workshops and edits poems, novels, memoir and non-fiction.

RACHEL RESNICK is the author of *Go West Young F*cked-Up Chick: A Novel of Separation* (St. Martin's Press). Her work has appeared in the *Los Angeles Times*, *Tin House*, *The Best American Erotica 2004*, *Dictionary of Failed Relationships, Swink*, and *Black Clock*, among others.

LISA TEASLEY's first book, *Glow In The Dark* (Cune Press), was the winner of the 2002 Gold Pen Award for Best Short Story Collection, and the Pacificus Foundation Award for Outstanding Achievement in Short Fiction. Her many past awards include the National Society of Arts & Letters Short Story Award. Teasley's 2004 novel *Dive* (Bloomsbury) has been critically acclaimed in publications such as the *New York Times Book Review* and her second novel, *Heat Signature*, (also Bloomsbury) is forthcoming in 2006.

JANET FITCH is a novelist, essayist and short story writer based in her native Los Angeles. She is best known as the author of the novel *White Oleander*, which has been translated into twenty-eight languages to date.

Janet Fitch
Introduction

Acknowledgments

"Milk" by Julianne Ortale first appeared in *The Malahat Review*, Spring 2002.

"Debbieland" by Aimee Bender first appeared in the premier issue of *Black Clock*, March 2004.

"Going Green" is copyright 1996 by Samantha Dunn. First published in *Voices West*.

"Hunger" by Lindsay Fitzgerald appeared in the *Alaska Review*, Spring 2005.

"Rose," copyright 2002 by Dylan Landis. First published in the *Santa Monica Review*.

"Magda in Rosarito, Beached" is from Lisa Teasley's collection *Glow In The Dark* (Cune Press, 2002).

"Ludlow" is from Lisa Glatt's collection, *The Body Shop*, Simon & Schuster, April 2005.

Acknowledgments

"The Meat-Eaters of Marrakesh" is copyright 2000 by Rachel Resnick. First published in *Chelsea*. Also appeared in *The Barcelona Review*.

"Destiny" is copyright 2003 by liz gonzález. First published in different versions in *Caffeine*, 1995, and in *ArtLife*, 2003.

"Contraband" by Carol Miuske-Dukes first appeared in the *TriQuterly* review.

"Where Angels Tread," is excerpted from Rochelle Low's completed novel, *A Borrowing of Bones*.

"38" and "39" are excerpted from Mary Rakow's novel *The Memory Room*, (Counterpoint Press, 2002).

The fonts used in this book are from the Garamond family

The Toby Press publishes fine writing,
available at leading bookstores everywhere. For more
information, please visit www.tobypress.com